SPACEPORT
HMALAYA

IFTIHKAR AZAM

Printed in the United Kingdom

First Printing, 2019

ISBN: 978-1-9162683-0-2 (Paperback)
ISBN: 978-1-9162683-1-9 (eBook)

TRAILBLAZING PUBLISHING
244, Fifth Avenue, Suite 1276
New York, N.Y. 10001

www.spaceporthimalaya.com

Contents

Preface

Introduction

"Spaceport Himalaya" by Iftihkar Azam.

This book aims to offer a perspective into the future of space colonization, by investigating the challenges potentially encountered at each stage of the process.

There would be geopolitical issues, tensions and conflict.

With earth resources at an all-time low, conflict and war over certain precious elements are no surprise.

This book considers real-life nations, and their interests, and creates a fictional scenario – but who's to say it couldn't become a reality...

I believe it could, and I believe anyone with similar knowledge who subscribes to a scientific approach would agree.

Given the laws of physics when it comes to gravity, air pressure and atmosphere, and altitude, and how these affect a space launch, my aim is to demonstrate how science shows this could happen – while at the same time entertaining you.

I hope you enjoy reading this book just as much as I did writing it.

Chapter 1
Acquaintance

The dustbin rattled as screwed up pieces of papers were thrown into it.... except it was more than a bit of scrunched up paper; instead, it was a whole bunch of drawings. It was what Jared Neal had just flung in.

There were twelve in the room. They were in a brainstorming session to come up with possible future designs which could be put forward for testing a development, and all twelve had suggested identical ideas.

These twelve were NASA's finest minds, headed by Chief Engineer Jared Neal, and had realized that their efforts were futile.

Just as they were all giving up, Elouise Brewer from The Goddard Space Flight Center spoke up.

"Slush."

They all looked at her in confusion.

"If we keep pumping seawater onto the South Pole, it freezes. We need to keep up this process until we have a mountain of ice so high that we are above the atmosphere from which we launch our spaceship in pieces, from there propelling them into orbit. We will use nuclear power to pump the water from the sea up to the tops," said Elouise.

'Err," muttered Alan Morris from the Ames Research Center. "Salty water doesn't freeze very well. What you see there frozen is as a result of years of snow."

"Yes, yes," Adrian Moody from the Kennedy Space Center interjected. "The water might need desalination. Fresh water is produced from brackish or seawater – very energy intensive."

"We are on the wrong side of the world when it comes to the capability of a large space mission into deep space," said Jared. The Chinese have an advantage, even the Indians. It's the great peaks in the Himalayas that we require."

He got up and walked across the room.

"However, this is as yet all speculation, and next week we are embarking on our biggest ever experiment into electromagnet propulsion. We shall conduct experiments into how the air pressure and atmosphere affect the shuttle fired and the depth and distance it will need to reach the speed required to leave Earth's gravitational pull, to put it into orbit effectively."

All eyebrows raised at this.

"Jared," Gail Burke looked apologetic – "I might need to turn down this invitation, got a little one. But be sure to keep me posted on any findings."

"Wait, wait hold on, we're building our very own Tibetan plateau out of candy, and you're not showing up? Such a let-down! Women need to prove we're equal to the men!" said Lillian Turner.

The general response to Gail's reaction, with two of the others giving a thumbs-down gesture, suggested this wasn't the first time she had given the group reason to feel she wasn't pulling her weight.

Gail's expression was unreadable.

Outside, rain could be heard spraying down the window.

"Everyone's attention, please. We have produced a report outlining a timeline. Copies are in this box; please help yourself on your way out." Jared pointed to a plastic box.

They all began to leave the room.

Jared approached Gail.

"Hey, is everything okay?" he asked.

She was busy tidying the table of her few possessions.

"Just fine, everything's fine, it's just not easy being a single mum. It's been very hard for us ever since Guillermo passed away," she replied.

Guillermo was a technician at NASA; he had a fatal accident at the launch pad. While carrying out an inspection he fell and was pronounced dead at the scene. Jared put his hand on Gail's shoulder and squeezed it. It remained there for a few seconds.

"If there is anything that I can do to help, just ask. I'm only a phone call away. The agency owes it to you, after all," he said. "Let's go and get some lunch."

He smiled at her. He had a rather pleasant smile. Gail smiled back. They headed off to the campus canteen, which meant a ten-minute walk, much of which was canopied to shield against the elements – handy considering the rain today.

The leaves were piling up against the road, and covering the walkway in a golden-brown blanket. It was Autumn in Virginia USA, and there were now more leaves on the ground than on the trees.

They reached the canteen. Jared opened the door for Gail and she entered amid a gust of leaves with him stepping through the doorway close behind her.

"Gail, why don't you find us a table and I'll go and get us some lunch. What would you like?"

"Just a light salad for me. A Caesar salad, please. Oh, and a bottle of still water."

She looked round for an empty table, just as they both heard their names called amongst a ruckus just behind them. Jared turned to find the 'Oak table' they usually ate at – the canteen had a multitude of tables all named after trees – had been occupied by chief scientist Dr William Cannon and chief technologist Dr Fred Cohen.

"Here you are; may we?" Jared said in a rather loud manner.

"Sure, feel free to join us." Dr William offered hesitantly.

Gail took a seat while Jared walked over to the coat stand which stood by the door, and today was unsurprisingly draped with coats and umbrellas, hung his raincoat on the one remaining peg, and briefly rejoined the group before heading off to buy Gail and himself lunch.

"I hope the agency is taking good care of you, Gail. We're a family here; your loss is our loss too," said Dr William.

"Sure, that was a huge loss. Guillermo was obviously an amazing husband who made you... well, we always saw you happy," said Dr Fred.

"Well, as long as there is a thorough investigation and no stone left unturned, just as I'd expect, then I'm as happy as I can be," replied Gail. She began rummaging in her bag. "I'd hate to see the same thing ever happen again." She pulled out her cell phone to check her messages.

There's a brief lull in the conversation. The two doctors turned their attention to their meals while Gail put away her phone. A cleaner passed by, glancing at the table just as Jared returned with a tray full of food.

"Hot dog for me today. Gail, they had two salads left – here's one Caesar salad, and one bottled water, still." He sat down next to her, and dived into the side of his hotdog and began to munch away at it.

"I suppose all the talk is on the upcoming experiment, on the revolutionary rail gun theory of delivering spacecraft." Dr Fred muttered.

"Well, I'd certainly think so... it's pretty much the talk of the day .... being able to send shuttles into orbit using electricity generated from renewable sources. Just imagine what outcome that could have on the world... firing shuttles into space using magnetic levitation," Dr William said excitedly.

"I'm also guessing this development might well become contentious, such is the magnitude of air travel supremacy," commented Jared.

"These developments are sure to spark controversy, just as rockets that could be used to carry a weapon across the world did," Dr William answered while trying to chew on his food.

"Yeah," muttered Dr Fred, somewhat grudgingly affirming Dr William's response.

Jared lit a cigarette as he waited outside the canteen for Gail to return from the bathroom.

He took a long draw and inhaled deeply, and checked the time on his watch, just as Gail appeared.

"I'm going to Communications tomorrow... just want to make sure Media is well informed of our research on the magnetic levitation and upcoming experiment next week," said Gail. The rain was blowing on her face; she tried turning her face to one side. As if that was going to help at all.

"I'm sure the public will want to be able to sit at home on the couch and marvel at the spectacle." Jared smiled. Gail nodded in agreement, while still shielding half her face.

"I'll be seeing you soon. Bye..." she waved with one hand while the other held her belongings, and she was still trying to keep the weather off her face as she briskly walked off.

Jared began to walk the other way.

The following morning, Gail had a coffee cup in one hand and a bunch of papers in the other. She stood in front of a sign saying "Communications". It was a big bright shiny metallic sign above an array of evergreen shrubs, as green as they are in the middle of the summer.

She was facing the building. Just as she was about to step forward, she felt a tap on her shoulder.

"Good morning," said Janet Dennis from CNN.

Janet was a reporter who generally covered topics associated with science and technology. Today was the right day for her to bump into Gail.

Janet also had a coffee cup in her hand – not surprising given it was just before 8am.

"It certainly is a lovely crisp, clear one," said Gail.

It was a very clear blue sky; quite a contrast to yesterday. Gail spotted Janet's CNN badge: the bright red lettering on the badge's white background contrasting with Janet's gray and white colored attire.

Gail extended her right hand while trying to juggle her coffee and paperwork, so as to shake Janet's proffered hand.

"You arrived on the right day. I was about to brief and update the Directorate of Communication on new exciting research," said Gail.

"Oh cool, that's awesome... I've been on the chase for something to get my teeth into. That's what I need to get my career moving," Janet said. She swept her hair back off her face as they entered the building, their heeled shoes clickety-clacking on the ceramic floor tiles of the reception.

Gail handed her ID badge to the security guard who proceeded to swipe it through the terminal, his expression blank as he stared at the terminal screen. Janet handed over something which looked more like a sheet of paper than an ID badge. Again, no expression from the security guard, until he said in a clear, calm voice, "Excuse me, Ma'am, your clearance level has dropped: you will need to be escorted during your visit at the premises."

Janet looked up, a fixed smile on her face which could not have more clearly said 'What?!! Unacceptable!!' She turned towards The Stennis Space Center representative who had materialized beside her, and was clearly about to speak when Gail said,

"You can stay with me. In fact, I have a few things I need to share with you."

Janet smiled at her. Her reply of "Thank you" was effusive in its simplicity.

"In which case, Ma'am, I need you to sign here," the guard said to Gail, gesturing to a register.

Gail did so, placing the pen back in the register's centerfold.

"Ma'am, I need to request that you stay with Ms. Burke at all times while you're here today," said the guard.

He then pushed a switch which opened a glass door allowing both ladies to pass through into the lobby area.

Gail pointed to the bathroom sign while beginning to walk towards it.

"Let's get the bathroom first."

The bathroom was right beside the lobby. Janet was washing her hands when Gail joined her in front of the mirror to do the same. She noticed a ring on Janet's wedding finger: a band. The spotlights above the mirror caught it and made it shine and shimmer.

"You're married I see; what does your man do?" Gail asked.

"Oh, my other half supposedly died in action during a tour to Afghanistan," Janet replied.

"Supposedly?" Gail said, frowning.

"Yes, his body has never been found, and to this day I've always worn this ring. It's been twelve months or so," replied Janet. She twisted the ring with the thumb and forefinger of her right hand, looking at it in the mirror.

"Elijah Moses, he was with the marines... I was told he never returned to his vehicle with the others in his company. The DOD have given me the full honors and a pension, but I just needed to see him, to get closure. Surely that's what anyone would want, right?" She lowered her eyes briefly and then looked back in the mirror at her hands.

Gail turned her head to look straight at Janet. She was almost stuck for words.

"How bizarre... that's the two of us with almost identical circumstances. I lost my husband in a freak accident almost a year ago too. His body was beyond recognizable. It was an accident while fueling a rocket before launch. The explosion engulfed everything in the building," she said.

Janet stared at Gail, now even more shocked than she was previously.

"So, you've not had his funeral, and you've received the advantages offered to those widows who have lost their partners in active duty, while never in effect having ever seen him?"

"Exactly," Gail nodded her head.

Chapter 2
Intel

The two ladies left the bathroom.

"Let's visit the third floor, and the director," said Gail.

She walked over to the elevator and glanced up at the screen to see which floor it was currently on, while her left hand pressed the button to summon it. She looked across at the stairs, doubtless wondering whether the stairs might have been a quicker option.

There's a gentle ping from the elevator, suggesting its imminent arrival.

Then almost immediately afterwards the doors opened with a much louder ping, and there's the sound of a woman's voice saying 'ground floor'. Gail stepped into the elevator with Janet close behind. She didn't press anything as the button for the third floor was already illuminated: clearly already pressed. The doors closed and it began to travel up to the third level. 'Third floor', the woman's voice confirmed as the doors opened. Both ladies stepped out onto a shiny floor, blue in color with patterns of stars all over it, quite appropriate given the nature of the building. The glitter effect dazzled under the intense lights. It was our Milky Way, or at least a part of it.

The click-clack of heels continued until the pair reached a door that had a sign reading 'Director of Communications'.

Gail paused for a moment. She heard the sound of the Director talking to someone on the phone. It sounded heated and personal, and ended abruptly as she heard the phone handset slam down onto its housing. Gail knocked on the door and then opened it, stepping inside the room, leaving the door open for Janet.

"Hi Dad."

The Director of Communications was Gail's father.

"Was that Mom?" she asked.

Gail's parents had broken up, and it had got rather ugly recently.

The room was very dark as blinds were still covering the windows. The only light was coming from a lamp on the desk which, to its credit, was doing its best, beaming like a small star.

"Yes," replied her father. Derek.

Clearly uncomfortable, he looked at the floor, and then walked over to his desk and opened one of its drawers, making a show of apparently looking for something.

Gail walked across the room to the window and pulled on the blinds' cords to raise them, daylight pouring into the room.

Derek pointed both forefingers at Janet.

"Can I help you?" he asked.

"Hi, I'm from CNN," Janet said.

"Another damn reporter. I hope you're not here expecting to report on my divorce!" Derek growled.

"No, I'm not, I have been newly assigned as the Correspondent for Science and Technology at CNN and am really keen to take on a new topic," replied Janet.

"Oh yeah," Derek semi-sneered.

"Science and Technology correspondent who wants to make a name," she said.

Derek suddenly smiled. "Well, it's good to put a face to a name. I received an email from you... just hadn't had time to reply." He walked towards her, extending his arm as he did so.

Janet dug into her handbag and pulled out a notebook before she saw Derek's proffered hand, which she then shook, smiling.

Gail put down her laptop bag and pulled out her laptop.

"Dad, I have something important to share with you. Remember when I mentioned electromagnetic propulsion?"

She plugged cables into a projector and continued.

"Well, you two know we are conducting our first ever experiment in this field. It's groundbreaking!"

She switched on the projector, and the wall behind Janet and Derek was lit up with highly detailed visuals depicting a delivery craft, or shuttle, accelerating through hoops within a larger cylinder.

"Imagine, if you will..." Gail smiled "...a gel cap of medication traveling through a series of polo mints, inside the polo mint tubing. This is our concept, taking forward the railgun technology that was developed by DARPA twenty years ago. It's simple and self-explanatory. The rings you see traveling through the cylinder are magnets, which discharge an electromagnetic force repelling the ones attached to the shuttle. Elevate the shuttle up one notch, and it becomes able to be influenced by the magnet above, and be repelled by the higher magnet. Lasers are used to track the progress of the shuttle, which in turn control power to the magnets. With multiple magnets, the shuttle gets ever faster – its acceleration dependent upon the amount of energy fed to the magnets... that determines the speed at which the shuttle will travel up the shaft, through the cylindrical tunnel."

Derek placed his hand on Gail's shoulder and smiled.

"So, as I see it, this will be a completely clean, renewable source of energy, not dependent on fossil fuels, for launching and delivering the spacecraft of the future," he said.

Gail's facial expression altered slightly, to a somewhat skeptical one.

"Except the challenge is to see if we can deliver a shuttle up through our dense, thick atmosphere –" she gestured at the visual on the wall – "and to test a multitude ... of types of vehicle. After all, the shuttle is required to maintain a perfectly straight line: any slight deviation will significantly reduce its velocity, which would amount to a poor design creating unnecessary drag." Gail turned to look at Derek.

"Carry on, I'm following you," he said.

"Dad, I need you to organize a press conference, on the day we deliver, please. It's Monday 11th September 2000," said Gail.

Derek walked to his desk, dropping onto it a pen he'd held in his hand up until now. Looking out of the window, he frowned slightly. Then he shrugged his shoulders.

"Gail, I think we'd be best to wait for the outcome of the tests before we get the press involved. Any failure would be a huge embarrassment, not to mention answering all the questions I'd be left to deal with."

Gail raised her hand and rubbed her forehead, then looked at her display on the wall.

"I think I'm going to need to take that Paracetamol capsule," she said, pointing at the shuttle.

Meanwhile, Janet had pulled out her cell phone and discreetly taken a photo of the projected display.

Gail turned and walked over to her laptop, and began to disconnect and pack it away. While doing so, she asked her father;

"Has Mom been and got the stuff she left behind when she moved out in such a hurry? I've wanted to go and pay her a visit at her new house.... "

Derek nodded.

"It's all been taken care of. I arranged a courier service to drop off all her property. Initially, I had U-Drive in mind except I hadn't time to drive all the way to the other side of the state."

Gail smiled.

"Then I will visit her tonight to help her unpack. It'll be a pleasant surprise for her, to see me," she said.

She placed her notebook into her bag, then walked over to her father and gently kissed him on the cheek.

"The simulations will happen at the Armstrong Flight Research Center on Monday 11th, Dad. I'll keep you posted."

"Thank you Gail, I wouldn't be anywhere else. In fact, there was an internal memorandum on the matter, although it was a little uninformative and vague," Derek replied.

Janet had already reached the door, somewhat eager to leave as she had complete dynamite information to help with her investigative journalism. She opened the door, waving farewell to Derek and waiting for Gail to catch up before leaving the room.

Gail held on to the door handle, and before leaving said:

"Dad, I'll be seeing you soon, love you."

She waved with one hand while the other clasped the handle of the door and pulled it shut behind her.

They both stood silently for a moment outside the Director's office until Gail started walking.

"Well, you heard him, you weren't meant to know, and any chance of a press badge is out of the question at present. I'll be sure to let you know of the outcome," said Gail, walking briskly towards the elevator. Janet almost had to run to keep up. Gail pressed the lift call button, keeping her finger on it while she worked out the car's whereabouts. There was a ping. They saw the car rise through the elevator shaft, and almost at the same time there was another louder ping followed by the doors opening. The pair stepped inside the elevator car. Gail pressed zero for the ground floor. She turned to Janet.

"I'll just walk you out of the building as it's protocol," she said.

The doors opened with another ping. Gail walked across the lobby to security, and handed in her badge. The security guard looked at her face, his gaze remaining on her until he'd swiped the key card through the terminal.

"Are you both leaving the building?" he asked.

Gail turned and looked at Janet.

"Yes, we're done, she is leaving too," she said.

The guard slid the register towards her, still with the pen nestled in its spine. Gail signed.

"Thank you Ma'am," he said. "See you."

His gaze didn't leave the pair of them until they'd walked through the security barriers.

Outside, Gail turned to Janet. Janet extended her hand and smiled.

"Thank you ever so much for your time today and escorting me around the building," she said as the ladies shook hands. She handed Gail a business card.

"It's been my pleasure," Gail said.

Janet took a couple of steps backwards before turning to walk away, giving a wave as she did so.

"Have you got anything planned for the rest of today?" asked Gail suddenly.

"No, just heading back to the office. You?"

"Oh, I'm visiting my mother later tonight," Gail smiled, briefly lost in a moment of remembering her childhood years. Then, back to the present...

"Bye Janet, you shall hear from me soon."

Gail reached the car park and looked for her car. The ground was covered in varying degrees of leaf fall, and one car parked near the entrance was thinly blanketed in shades of rusty reds and golden browns.

She walked across the tarmac to her car, seeing her windscreen had the beginnings of an autumnal blanket too. She collected up the leaves and let them fall to the ground. She reached into her handbag for her car keys and unlocked her car and got in. She turned the key in the ignition. Nothing. Gail's eyes moved to the dashboard and the instrument panel.

"Oh fuck, goddamn it!!" she yelled.

The switch for the headlights was still in the 'on' position, and a light symbol was faintly glowing on the instrument panel. Gail remembered switching the lights on in the morning, and not remembering to turn them off when she parked. She turned and moved her arm to the passenger seat, and her bag, and Janet's business card. She picked up the card and read it, having not previously looked at it properly. She reached for her cell phone and dialed Janet's cell number.

"Hello, Janet speaking."

"Oh, hi Janet... it's me again, Gail. I was wondering if I could ask a favor. My car's not starting, and rather than me waiting around for the breakdown and recovery, would you be able to drop me off at Mountain View Station? I'll get the Caltrans to Union Station."

Janet was pleasantly surprised and nodded her head.

"I'll be right there. I was only driving around trying to find my way out of this complex, so we can help each other," she said. "I'm speaking to you on Bluetooth now, so stay on the line until I know I'm on the right road back to you."

Janet stopped and drove back the way she'd come. The sun was in her eyes, but she managed to spot the sign "Communications".

"Right, I got you… see you shortly," she said.

Before long, she spotted Gail and pulled up beside her.

"It's not my day today. Thank you so much, Janet, I really appreciate this," said Gail.

"Mountain View Station wasn't it?" Janet asked.

"Yes please."

It was midday now, and the traffic had calmed down. It wasn't much more than ten minutes before they arrived at the station. Janet parked the car at the drop-off.

"Thank you again, Janet. Bye again," said Gail, opening the passenger side door.

"My pleasure." Janet gave a small wave.

Gail climbed out and closed the door.

*****

The tap was running … in theory for a hot bath but not much hot water was coming out.

"Mom, is your hot water out?" called Gail.

"Yes, the boiler isn't working right now," said her mother.

Her mother, Vicky, had just moved into a small condo in LA city, after walking out of her house she shared with her husband.

"Someone was coming out today to look at it. I thought it was them when you knocked earlier. Everything seems an awful lot louder here; perhaps because it's so much smaller than the house," said Vicky. She coughed.

Gail walked out of the bathroom only to almost trip over a box.

Chapter 3

Atmospheric Air Pressure 4.36 PSI

"Oh god, another damn box," Gail growled.

But she couldn't help but notice it was a box which contained her childhood toys and memories. She sat on the floor and opened it.

Among many other things, she noticed a medal and her graduation pictures. It's all from when she was at California Institute of Technology. It's where she'd landed a first in 'Planetary Science'. The medal was at Volleyball. She was an excellent player and won a gold medal while playing in the women's volleyball against Harvard.

Vicky walked over with a cup of coffee and handed it to her.

"Thanks, Mom." Gail grabbed the hot drink with both hands.

"Mom, why have you left Dad?" Gail couldn't help herself but ask.

Vicky shook her head. "He was always working. He never switched off. Always receiving calls. At all hours, day and night. And he'd been having an affair. No doubt with a co-worker. He didn't need me. He wasn't interested in me. I'd wasted enough time on him."

Gail gazed into her mother's eyes.

"I'm sorry, Mom. I'm here for you. And I'm here to help you get settled in."

She picked up the box while telling her mother about the project she was involved with at work.

*****

It was a bright Monday morning. The radio was playing. Janet often listened to the news while driving to work. As she twiddled the knob on the center console, her gaze briefly left the road. As her eyes turned back, she saw a car pull out before her.

Janet slammed the brake pedal, shocked at having been so close to driving into the back of the other vehicle. Her eyes noticed a shimmer from the passenger footwell. She focused and pulled over the car and reached down to pick up what seemed to be an ID card. Janet stared. It was Gail's ID badge from AMES Research Center. Janet turned the badge over and back again and continued to stare at it.

It was the day – the testing of a new method of delivering shuttles into space.

Monday September 11th 2000. Janet decided not to go to the office today but instead turned and headed for AMES Research Center.

*****

There was a click. The kettle. It had boiled. Gail walked into her mother's kitchen and poured the water into two mugs. She was about to leave for AMES Research Center, but not before the two had a coffee together.

"Coffee, Mom," said Gail, as she walked into her mother's bedroom.

While drinking hers, Gail rummaged through her handbag, something she did a lot. She realized she was missing her ID badge. She looked up and rubbed her forehead, also realizing this meant she wouldn't be able to enter the research center today.

"Mom, I'm not going. I haven't got my badge, so wouldn't be able to gain entry," she said.

Her mother took a sip of coffee and replied;

"Oh dear, are you sure? You were really looking forward to all this."

Gail shrugged her shoulders. "I've got my notebook. It'll log into the server to keep track of progress," she said, in a somewhat disinclined manner.

'AMES Research Center' the sign said in bright red lettering. Janet had arrived at the entrance. She headed for Security, at the entry point.

The grass was lush green and neatly kept. Janet pulled over and wound down her window. She had her shades on. The guard at the security gatehouse looked right at her. Janet smiled, and she continued to smile, waiting for the guard to intervene.

"Ma'am, I need your ID badge, please," said the guard.

Janet handed over the ID badge while maintaining a close-lipped smile. The guard has the TV on, the New England Patriots were playing at the New York Jets Stadium. His eyes stared at the TV screen while his hand swiped the card into the terminal. He failed to notice Janet didn't resemble the picture on the badge … he's quick to hand back the 'ID' badge.

"Thank you Ma'am, have a nice day," said the guard.

Janet reached for the badge and pulled forward in her car.

She was now inside the confines of the AMES Research Center, but she had no idea where she needed to get to. She noticed a sign saying observe the speed limits and that other vehicles are moving exceedingly slow, so she did likewise. After a few minutes of driving she spotted a sign: 'Cafeteria N235' so decided to pull in, as they'll most likely be lots of people. Janet parked her car and entered the cafeteria. It was lunchtime and very crowded. The chairs are sky blue and the floor matched. Very in keeping with the nature of the facility. Janet headed to the fridge and chose a sandwich. The queue to pay was stretched all the way around the room. While she stood in the line she heard the group in front mention 'electromagnetic delivery vehicle'. Janet's attention was now focused.

"We've another thirty minutes, guys." It's Chief Engineer Jared Neal from NASA.

Jared, a tall slender figure, towered over the others in the group. His voice was also quite distinct too, a rather high tone. It was easy to hear what he was saying amongst the rest of the crowd. Janet quickly realized she needed to stay with the group, or at least follow them closely behind. She reached the till and paid for her sandwich. The group was sat at a cluster of tables pulled close together as there was not one big enough to seat the entire crowd. Janet took a seat discreetly at an adjacent table, directly behind Jared. The group continued talking, about many other things but occasionally mentioning the program.

A loud, confident voice: "Right guys, let's finish up," said Jared.

The group got up and one by one discarded their litter in the recycling bins provided and headed outside.

Janet conveniently had finished her sandwich and similarly discarded her rubbish.

She followed them outside where the group all boarded a shuttle bus. Janet then had two options: get onto the shuttle bus or follow in her car.

She boarded the bus which gently drove around the campus past many buildings and hangers, until it eventually turned up a road appropriately signposted 'Gamma Lane', Gamma being a form of electromagnetic radiation.

The bus drove through a set of gates operated by guards before coming to a standstill outside a set of large hanger doors, marked with the letters 'N-221'.

Janet patiently waited until the group began to vacate the bus.

"Right guys, can we all head into the building through the hanger doors, keeping to the left side and making sure to observe all signage," said Jared loudly, so that all the group could hear.

They began to leave the bus. Janet got up and followed the crowd. She was now feeling nervous, as trespassing here is a breach of security and can land one in the penitentiary. She left the bus and joined the group waiting just to the left side of the hanger door inside the humongous building.

As she entered, she noticed it was not as bright as she would have expected. She looked up at the ceiling and gazed around. A few seconds passed before her eyes began to adjust to the low light. It was only then that she realized there were many more people here than just the group she arrived with. There must be at least a few hundred people all sat at neatly arranged chairs. All were patiently waiting for an announcement or perhaps a performance. There was a large screen up ahead, suspended from a 'space frame' which the building was constructed from.

There was none of the complex instruments or rocketry she'd expecting to find here. Just a huge overhead projector screen. However, one thing she did spot was a computer server box, on a trolley, with a web of cables connecting it to the 'space frame'. The hanger doors began to shut just as another group of people entered. Janet managed to find a seat. She heard a loud thud. The microphone had been turned on and she heard a male voice.

"Can everyone shuffle up, please," Jared said over the speaker. The seats that are left soon get occupied by a few more who arrive. Jared walked onto a makeshift stage. He raised his hand that held the microphone.

"Well done everyone and thank you for coming; give yourselves a warm welcome," he said.

A certain few began to clap their hands until the whole hanger is filled with the sound of clapping, and echoes of clapping. Jared raised his hand for quiet.

"I'm guessing everyone knows why they're here today. I thought it would be wise and only fair if everyone concerned who's worked hard could have this opportunity to witness the simulation together as one group, before the findings are published." He stopped as there was more clapping.

"This computer simulation will simulate a shuttle... a delivery vehicle leaving the highest point of the Earth's crust, that being the Third Pole: the Tibetan plateau, for example, Mount Everest and K2 summits. This shuttle leaving, completely empty of any rocket fuel, yes... that's no fuel whatsoever, other than its momentum."

He nodded his head, the action adding emphasis to his words.

"... a momentum which it has developed during its rise journey, ... traveling up vertically through the Earth's crust. The thickest part of the Earth's crust is right there, just where it's needed, right below the summits at the great peaks of the Himalayas. The air pressure within the shaft the shuttle shall travel up shall be controlled and equal to the air pressure at its opening at the summit, roughly that at approximately 30, 000 feet altitude, which is approximately 4.36 PSI, absolute atmospheric pressure."

Jared, imagining himself inside the shaft, looked up, and said;

"That is very low air pressure as you are all aware. So, today's test is to determine what the speed needs to be at the point of ejection for this shuttle to continue to travel into orbit without any further assistance – 100 km above sea level being the agreed international definition of space. The shuttle shall be propelled using the electromagnetic technology developed by DARPA and DOD to launch shells at immense velocities. We will obviously be accelerating at speed more comfortable to humans."

Jared took a device out of his jacket inside pocket and pressed a button on it. The screen lit up on the computer software simulation model. He pressed the button two more times and the display showed graphs with multiple numbers displayed to the right side.

"Here we go," he said.

Chapter 4
Simulation

Jared kept his attention on the screen. The numbers began to climb. The silence in the hanger was almost audible. Janet was sure you'd be able to hear a pin drop right now.

Jared slowly folded his arms, frowning slightly. He clearly wasn't comfortable. The graph line was getting higher and longer while the numbers were still multiplying.

He looked away, shaking his head, then looked down, turning his back to the screen. These results were obviously not what he had anticipated.

The numbers began to slow down, some more so than others, until the graph was barely moving. Finally, there was a bleep, a box appeared around one of the numbers as it changed color from green to red. Jared turned around and looked at the display. There was another bleep and another box appeared around another number which turned red. Jared nodded his head. Finally, all the numbers have red boxes around them and have turned red, and the screen then flashed 'CALCULATED' in capital letters. Jared raised the microphone:

"Well, we have the results folks."

It was like announcing the lottery numbers once the balls had fallen.

"Here are the variables. Firstly, we have the graph displaying the best possible design of the shuttle, which looks like a lantern. Secondly, the distance we need for a comfortable acceleration: a vertical distance of 60.654 km. Thirdly, we have calculated the speed: just short of 20,010 km per hour. Fourthly, we have calculated the altitude:

30,290 feet. The fifth is load – here we even have a value for the most efficient load to launch, given all the variables: a tidy 20.1 tons."

A few hands were raised, but he ignored them and carried on;

"This software has been years of hard work in the making, and today we sit here to acknowledge ... to confirm ... beyond all doubts that the great summits are the only place in the world it is possible to launch a multi-million-ton 'Starship' into space. This allows mankind to colonize space, to eventually travel to planets which SETI and Kepler discovered and gave us knowledge of those planets that are potentially habitable and most likely to contain life-form."

The entire gathering began to clap and there was cheering and even the odd whistle. Jared walked off the stage, over to the computer. He began to type as two men in suits walked up beside him.

"Jared Neal," said one of the men.

"No questions now; the findings will be publicized on the NASA intranet," said Jared, without looking up.

"Sir, you need to come with us." The other man pulled out an ID badge.

Jared looked up at the man who is showing the ID, and sees the white and black badge and the letters C.I.A.

He rose from his seat.

"Sir, we are from the Central Intelligence Agency, working under the Deputy Director for Science and Technology, Donald Mann. I'm Agent

Harrison and this is Agent Parker. We believe these findings, the result of the simulation that you have been working on, to be of strategic intelligence. As such, you shall not be publicizing it on the intranet or any other platform. We shall need you and your team to appear at the Pentagon before the Deputy Director Donald Mann, Sir."

Jared's expression was one of disbelief; his mouth moved as if he was about to speak, but it took a minute for him to actually form a word:

"What!"

"Donald Mann would like to meet you, Sir," said Agent Harrison.

Jared looked around, unsure as to what to do.

"Can I at least turn this equipment off first? I'm guessing you don't need me to bring all this along with me?" asked Jared.

"No Sir ... a jet will be waiting for you and your team here at Moffett Federal Airfield tomorrow morning," said Agent Harrison.

Jared looked towards the doors, then back at the two CIA agents.

He nodded.

Beep, beep, beep, beep, beep...

It was 6am, and the alarm clock's tone was insistent, its neon display piercing the darkness. There was no suggestion of daylight shining through the curtains yet.

A hand appeared from under the duvet and silenced the clock before switching on the bedside lamp, casting a shadow the shape of a model-size Saturn 5 on the wall.

Jared had had a late night last night, talking to his team and making sure they'd be ready for the morning.

Jared was nervous and excited in equal measure – he'd never flown on an executive jet before. Being able to just jump onto a plane without the bother of any airport check-in and security. It was exciting to know.

Jared pulled away his duvet, rubbing his eyes. He reached for his cell phone to check for messages or missed calls. He was a little unsure if his team would even all show up.

He stretched and then pushed himself out of bed. His feet padded about the cold hard floor. He'd made extra sure to turn off the heating last night as he wasn't entirely sure how long he'd be at the Pentagon.

Jared's nasal receptors needed the smell of coffee so early in the morning, and he shuffled through to the kitchen.

Jared was a coffee lover and liked his coffee black without sugar, especially in the mornings.

He opened one of the cupboards. One just above head height. He reached in and pulled out a cardboard box of coffee pods, only to dislodge a neatly stacked pile of plates that all tumbled out of the cupboard onto the hard worktop;

'SMASH!!'

The floor was suddenly covered in fragments as the six plates shattered.

"Oh for Pete's sake!!! I'll sort this mess later!!"

He walked over to the light switch and flicked it on. The room is suddenly awash with light. He turned around, exasperated, and walked over to the coffee machine. He extracted a coffee pod from the box and placed it inside the machine and pushed down a button, putting a mug under the spout.

He began to smell the coffee, and all was well. With his mug full, he lifted it and headed for the bathroom.

He ran the hot water and began to lather his stubble ready to shave. He decided that as he'll be before the Deputy Director of Science and Technology at the CIA, he needed to be looking presentable.

The hot coffee was only adding to more steam in the small room, which condensed against the mirror, obscuring Jared's view just as he made his first stroke with the razor.

"Damn it!!!" he swore.

A streak of blood appeared where he had lifted the razor. He'd cut himself. A drop of blood landed in the water-filled basin, dispersing quickly. Jared had a moment of unease over the sight of blood on the day he'd been summoned to appear before the CIA at the Pentagon. But, he remained positive, as was his way. Maybe it was time for a promotion. He rubbed the steam off the mirror and smiled at himself, thinking the only thing I need to worry about is which tie I wear today. He took a sip from his coffee mug before asking Google Home Mini:

"Hey Google, what's the weather like today?"

The device was in the hallway, and replied:

"It will be a blustery day today, with a high of 12°C and a low of 8°C."

He imagined himself wearing a woolly hat and matching scarf. He finished off in the bathroom and headed back into the bedroom. As he walked into the bedroom, he heard the Google device start to speak again;

"I'm not sure what you mean." Jared turned towards it and frowned.

"I'm not sure what you mean," said the device again.

He stopped That's odd, it had never done that before.

Chapter 5
Clandestine

Again, it said;

"I'm not sure what you mean."

The engineer in Jared felt irritated but also intrigued.

"I'm going to find out why you keep doing that," he said in a quiet determined voice.

He walked out of the bedroom and opened the door to a large cupboard which was next to it, and which contained floor to ceiling shelves. He pulled down on a cord which was hanging directly inside the cupboard to turn on the light. He reached up to a box which sat on the fourth shelf and took this down and opened it. It contained screwdrivers. Lots of screwdrivers.

"Let's see..." said Jared.

He walked down to the Google Home Mini and dropped his box onto the floor with a clunk. The screwdrivers could be heard clanging against each other as they hit the bottom of the box.

Jared picked up the device and looked at it closely, turning it over to look at the bottom and its multitude of screws and what sizes they were. His right hand felt around in the box of screwdrivers while his left hand held the device upside down. After pulling out a few wrong screwdrivers, he finally found the right tool to open the device.

He unplugged it from the socket and started loosening the first screw, his curiosity growing with each screw he took out.

He paused. There was one hole without a screw. Why? When he installed the system, all the screws were present and correct. Someone else had opened this device since.

Jared slowly opened the device. There's a lot of electronics and bunches of colored wires. It was too dark to see properly. He put the device on the floor and went to turn on the light.

The corridor is brightly lit up, and when he looked again at the contents of the device, an object caught his eye. It was a microphone. But this one wasn't embedded into the circuit board, intended to pick up sound signals and answer questions and give information. This one was an extra microphone which had been added. He had been bugged.

Jared smashed the whole device to the floor.

"Fuckin' goddamn feds!!"

He walked over to where he left his coffee mug, picked it up and took a sip. It was a little colder than he liked it, so he headed to the kitchen and placed the mug in the sink. He walked back to the bedroom, undressing as he did so. He was now reluctant to use his cell phone. He paused, contemplating the situation.

He dressed. He'd decided to wear a Star Trek themed tie his father had bought him a long time ago, when he was still a student, studying physics and living at home.

"Very appropriate," he mused to himself.

Checking round to see if he had packed everything he'd need, he grabbed his bag and proceeded to the front door. Just as he went to open the door, his eye caught something shimmering on the floor in the corner of the hall.

It was the missing screw from the Google Home Mini.

Jared paused for a moment, concerned with what else they might have bugged, and how long it had been going on. Does an AI decipher what was said or was there an actual person who listened in? Either way gave Jared the creeps. He opened the door and left the house, slamming it behind him.

"Sons of bitches!!" he growled.

He opened his car's trunk and threw in his bag. He turned to look at the house, taking a brief moment to be still – he was feeling a little weary of the events unfolding before him.

Jared had an interest in technology, and ever since he set his eyes on the Tesla motor car, he had to have one – not to mention California was just about the best place in the world to own a Tesla due to the number of charging points available, and the state's readiness for the Tesla's autonomy feature as compared with the rest of the USA.

Jared pressed a button and the car's trunk closed automatically while he got into the driver's seat and fastened his seatbelt.

He began to play about with the control module. On the dashboard screen he touched the letter 'M', then 'O', then 'F' twice, and 'Moffett' appears. In fact, a list of 'Moffett''. He scrolled down them, eventually finding 'Moffett Federal Airfield'. He pressed the option.

It was now a little lighter, and the sun was rising on the horizon; the forecast showed a clear sky today. As there wasn't the need to have his attention on driving, as the car took care of that, Jared's mind was turning over and over the day ahead. One of his concerns was how long he would be away for. He guessed he'd be flown back today. He looked out of the windows at the people going about their day.

Swoosh!

A USAF C-17 airplane took off, while another one, a C-10, came in to land. Jared approached the airfield.

The Tesla drove itself to just short of ten meters away from the security gatehouse, where the autonomous mode self-deactivated.

Jared pressed the gas pedal and brought the car alongside the gatehouse, stopping by the window of the security guard's hatch. He wound down the window.

"Good morning Sir," said the guard.

"Hi, good morning," said Jared.

"May I see your ID badge please, Sir."

Jared removed his badge from around his neck and handed it over.

The guard took it and began typing the details into the system.

"Sir, they're expecting you. Drive up to the airfield car park, it's all signposted. Have a good day Sir."

The guard handed back the ID badge.

"Great, thank you," said Jared.

Chapter 6
Hyperdrive

Jared sped away towards the airfield. As he drove, the surroundings became more open and bare. Before long he spotted a large hanger-style building, and as he got closer he saw its doors were open with a jet airplane parked in front.

There were two black vehicles with darkened windows parked beside the jet plane. Jared slowed down as he got closer to the plane and the vehicles. He gazed out of his front windscreen, trying to see who was in either of the cars or the plane.

The car stopped and he stepped out. The sun was still low and glaring right in his eyes. Two individuals got out of one of the vehicles and came towards him.

"Good morning, Dr Jared," said Agent Harrison.

"Good morning, Sir," Agent Parker nodded at him.

Jared looked at them both and nodded his head, adding a rather belated "Good morning".

"I'm guessing the rest of your team are on their way?" said Agent Harrison.

"That's correct, Sir."

Jared leaned against his car and squinted as he looked around. The sunlight was fierce. Jared turns round and opens the card door, ducking inside to then re-emerge with his sunglasses.

"That's a beautiful car you have there. An excellent car," said Agent Parker.

Jared smiled and gazed up at the sky.

"It sure is one of the century's best innovations, driverless technology. Can't beat it," he said.

"Is it one of your benefits you get from NASA?" the agent asked.

"No, it's on finance, although we do have a reward program which pays out accordingly to our pay grade. For me it covers what the Tesla costs, which is nice."

A humming sound could be heard in the distance.

They all turned to see what was making the noise. A passenger bus. But is it a bus full of journalists? The vehicle continued towards them until it was about 10 meters away, then stopped. The doors opened and a small group of individuals stepped out, somewhat reluctantly, clutching small day bags. They all walked straight over to Jared.

"Good morning Dr William, Dr Fred," said Jared.

"Oh, there's more still on the bus," said Dr William, and just as he spoke a few more people got off the bus, and also walked straight over.

There was Deputy Associate Administrator Danny Allen, Deputy Associate Administrator Dustin Edward, and Associate Administrator for Strategy and Plans Larry Douglas. The three are the most senior chief of staff. Just then, Jared's phone rang. He reached inside his jacket to pull it out of the inner pocket. Agent Harrison said: "As from now, you will be restricted as to whom you may speak with on the phone, Sir."

Jared noticed Gail's name flash up on the screen. Maybe to see where he is. Jared turned to Agent Harrison and turned his phone off, ignoring Gail's call. He realized she might not have clearance, as in security clearance, to be here. He put his phone back in his pocket.

There was not much activity in the field other than the small jet in front of the hanger. Jared pointed to the plane.

"Is that what we are flying in today?" he asked.

Agent Harrison looked at his watch. Just then, in the distance, a military C-17 cargo plane came in to view. A very dull dark green from a distance, once closer it turned out to be gray. Harrison gazed at it.

"That's what we are flying in."

The C-17 was now extending its wheels for landing and lined up with the runway. The loud sound of its four engines completely drowned out any conversation, and everybody stayed quiet. It touched down, and the engines were put into reverse, increasing the noise as they slowed the aircraft down.

The pilots were now visible with their headsets on. Just then, a vehicle emerged speeding down adjacent to the runway. It was a traffic control support vehicle. It parked beside the bay closest to where the two agents and the team were stationed. A member of the Air Force Base stepped out and proceeded to walk in the direction of the approaching C-17. He had an illuminated marshaling wand in each hand with which to give the pilots directions. The plane suddenly stopped with a jolt. The plane's nose nudged down due to the sharp braking. The engines were winding down but still turning as the huge door at the rear of the plane began to open downwards, revealing a ramp.

Agent Parker said, "Right everybody, let's board this plane. Enough seats for everyone, and your life vests are right beside you. It's not going to be a very comfortable ride; however, it's much quicker flying than going by road, as you can imagine."

They all walked up the ramp and entered the plane, sitting down and strapping in.

The interior of the C-17 was rudimentary, merely functional. It was a tool. There were very few crew on board: two pilots (a captain and a second-in-command), and one person who seemed to be cabin crew, who walked up and down to check everybody was buckled up, and then closed the tailgate ramp. It made a humming noise until fully closed, at which point the light beside the door changed from red to green, indicating locked.

The cabin crew person walked to another control panel, turned some knobs, and using a microphone communicated with the pilots that all was secure at the back for take-off.

The captain switched over to the same frequency as the control tower and asked for permission to take off. The engines began to roll again. Air traffic had given authority to proceed.

The captain pushed a lever forward, giving more fuel to the engines and increasing pressure. Engines were now at full throttle. There was an eerie sound of motors moving hydraulics, which was the landing gear being folded away into the airplane. The wings could be heard adjusting to the air pressure and wind direction as the plane prepared for take-off. The sky was clear. Their journey time was approximately six hours. They were flying east, heading towards the sun which was beaming straight through the cockpit window, illuminating the whole plane.

Jared stood up and headed towards the cockpit to see the crew. Agents Harrison and Parker both saw him walking up. He checked his cell phone and realized it wasn't yet in airplane mode, which he proceeded to do. There were no messages or missed calls. He placed it back in his pocket. He looked through the window in the cockpit door. The crew ignored him, carrying on with what they were doing.

"It's clear out there today," said Jared with a smile.

The second-in-command flicked him a glance, but otherwise they still ignored him. He turned around and headed back to his seat and sat down. He picked up his briefcase and opened it. Going through his paperwork, he pulled out a set of papers which he had made notes on: preparation for what he could be asked and answers that he shall give. As he had a six-hour flight, he decided he might as well make the most of the time.

****

Back at Gail's mother's house, Gail continued to scour the NASA website for updates regarding the simulation carried out and was still waiting. She picked up the phone and dialed Jared's number again. It rang, but there was no answer. Obviously at this point, Jared was flying at 30,000 feet on his way to Washington State.

In the plane, Jared sat calmly in his seat, looking at his phone. He turned to Agent Parker.

"Is there any satellite signal in these air force planes? You must have a satellite phone which also has a data link, don't you, Agent?"

Agent Parker hesitated.

"Well, yes, there is, but it's for official, and I do mean official, use only."

Jared turned to look down the plane to see what the others were doing. Dr William and Dr Fred had both got their eyes shut. Dr William was almost certainly sleeping: his head was rolled over to one side, and he was snoring. Dr Fred had his thumbs rolling while his eyes shut. He might have just been resting his eyes.

Derek walked over to the aircraft's cold box at the back of the plane and opened it. Jared saw bottles of water and smiled. Derek took out a few bottles.

"Anybody like a bottle of water?" he asked.

Jared raised his hand.

"Yes please."

Dr Fred opened his eyes and waved his hand.

"Yes, please, one over here."

*****

Back at Gail's mum's house, Vicky was preparing her bag with her medical notes and drugs as she had an appointment today to see a specialist.

"Gail, would you mind dropping me off at my doctor's?" she asked.

Gail was in the bathroom brushing her teeth. She stuck her head round the bathroom door.

"What was that, Mom?" she asked.

"I have an appointment at the medical center. I was wondering if you would be so kind as to drop me off?"

"Certainly. No problem."

Gail walked over to where her coat hung in the hallway, and unhooked it, and slid her boots on.

"Ready to go when you are." she said.

Vicky collects her coat from its hook, and also a scarf, which she holds rather than wrapping around her neck.

"Yes dear, let's go."

The two step outside – Gail first; Vicky followed, and she shut her front door. They walked across to Gail's car, which was parked on the road in front of Vicky's building.

*****

Back on board the plane, Derek drained his water bottle.

He pulled out his phone. No network. But there were two messages from his wife. The first read

'Off to the clinic for the arm to get its x-ray.' And the second, clearly sent before the first and delayed in coming through: 'Gail is here with me. She'll be taking me to the clinic tomorrow.'

Dr William reached for his bag and pulled out a box containing Scrabble. It was a board game which used players' knowledge of words and spelling. Two to four players scored points by placing tiles, each bearing a single letter, onto a board, to create words worth as many points as possible.

"Dr Fred. Let me entertain you, I have something here which you will enjoy. As there's not much else to do. I remembered I put it in my bag last night," said Dr William.

"Oh okay, let's have a look. You're right, there isn't much else to do."

The others didn't take any notice.

The two began to play and were soon indeed entertaining themselves.

*****

The car squeaked. It was the brakes. Gail had parked in the medical center car park.

She grabbed her bag and opened the driver's door while Vicky was reading through her appointment letter, making sure she had the right paperwork ready before putting it back in her bag. She reached for the door handle and opened the passenger door, swinging her legs out first and holding the handle just above the side window as she eased herself out.

"Are you okay," asked Gail.

"Yes. Fine," she replied.

"I'm coming in with you. I think it would be best if you had somebody with you."

"Are you sure? Well, okay – that's very kind of you."

Gail locked the car, pulling at the passenger door handle to double check. She put the keys in her bag before zipping it closed.

They walked together towards the medical center main entrance.

Inside the building, Reception was on the left hand side. They walked over.

The receptionist was busy on the phone but aware that they were there. The call finished and Gail smiled at the lady.

"Can I help you there?" asked the receptionist, returning the smile.

"Yes, my mother here has an appointment today with the specialist. It's for some test results," said Gail.

The receptionist pulled out a book containing a list and while doing so consulted her computer screen.

"May I take her date of birth, please."

Vicky moved towards the counter and leaned on it.

"It's 15th March 1947," she said.

"Ah yes, Vicky White, I've got you here with Dr David. If you'd like to take a seat over in the waiting area just across there –" she pointed – "on any of the green seats, please."

They sat in the green area.

Gail pulled her phone out of her bag, thinking she would ring Jared once more. She noticed something strange on her phone's screen. It flickered for a moment, and she thought she saw Chinese lettering appear on the screen. Maybe it was the phone updating itself. She wondered if it could have been Korean as her phone was a Samsung.

"What's wrong, Gail?" asked Vicky.

"I've been trying to reach Jared but there's no answer. He's meant to be at work."

"Let me see if your father has replied to a message I sent earlier," said Vicky.

Gail turned to look at her mother.

Vicky reached into her bag and found her phone. She looked at the screen for any messages, but nothing. She decided to call Derek. She auto-dialed and Gail could hear it ring and ring before the answer phone kicked in, saying the person you are calling was not available.

"That's strange," said Vicky. "Why is he not answering?"

*****

It was a bright sunny day. Janet entered the CNN building, walking straight to security, clearly in a rush. A colleague waved at her from the other side of the foyer, calling her name. He was another reporter.

But Janet's attention was elsewhere as she strode to the elevator and got in, headed for the 10th floor: Science and Technology Correspondence.

Her department head was a former editor by the name of Timothy, who should be in the building today as she had a message about her being reassigned to a new story which he felt it might be more appropriate for her to work on.

The elevator stopped at Floor 10 and Janet rushed out and down the corridor, oblivious to everyone she passed, not stopping until she reached Timothy's office. She opened the door without knocking and walked straight into Timothy.

"Hi Timothy... really need to talk... I've got something really important you have to know!" Janet was slightly breathless.

Timothy grasped both her shoulders and stood her straight, then took a step back and raised both his hands, pointing both his index fingers towards her.

"You're just the person I'm looking for, Janet. I've got a story to tell you. There's been activity at the university with some ground-breaking..." but before he could say any more, Janet interrupted him.

"No Timothy, you need to listen to this. I was at NASA, and they had some revolutionary new technique to launch a spacecraft into space, which after spending billions has been proven a complete failure due to the need for terrain that we don't have in America," said Janet.

"No, no, Janet. I've got this story, which I want you to work on with me – it will go down a treat. We really need this to happen. Are you able to do this?"

"No, no, no!" yelled Janet. "This is something which I've only learnt about because of effort and perseverance, Timothy. I'm not doing that, no. I've invested myself in this story. It's ground-breaking; it'll change the world. I've been busy, working hard, had my head down only on this, and I just want to do this, nothing else. And the only reason I've got this far is through being proactive, because I am optimistic that it will shake up the world. When it comes to ground-breaking, invested, investigative journalism, I am an investigative journalist, and this is what I want to do, and you need to sit down and listen to what I've got to say."

Timothy looked taken aback.

"Well, okay, I suppose it's worth listening to. What's the harm in that? I give you five minutes, and you've got my undivided attention. Let's see what you have. Put it on the projector screen if you want," he said.

"No, that won't be necessary. Here, look," said Janet and pulled out her phone and showed him pictures.

Timothy gazed at one picture, then the next, and the next, flicking through them all, and then looking at Janet.

"Well, it seems like you were at a NASA facility. How did you get clearance?" he asked.

"Ah, well, you see, I gate crashed. I used someone else's pass to gain access, which I understand is not something to be condoned. But on this occasion it was worth the effort. You are, after all, looking at a new simulation program which demonstrates the only technique we currently have for getting a Starship into space for interstellar travel. For Mars, the moon and beyond, the kind of spacecraft we need is just too big to put up into space using rockets. And that's it. Timothy, that simulation has given them the exact geographic location to make this possible. It's in the Himalayas. On the other side of the planet," Janet explained excitedly.

"So, what was the verdict? What happened? If it failed, what's NASA's verdict? I'm guessing you heard what NASA plans to do in response, right? I mean, it's a lot of money put into research and development," said Timothy.

Janet, overwhelmed, didn't know where to begin.

Chapter 7

"We Can Neither Confirm Nor Deny..."

"Well, of course, it's been a lot of money spent, that ... I also saw two agents from the CIA ... and the Pentagon briefing, the senior scientist there, Jared, he was put under caution not to speak to anybody, but I heard it all. They've all gone to the Pentagon to brief the CIA seniors. Other than that, I'm not sure what is going to happen," she said.

"So, what you're saying, I think..." Timothy walked over to Janet and handed back her phone. "Are you telling me..." he pointed his left index finger at her "... that the CIA has been watching over NASA and told them they need to attend the Pentagon to be briefed, and they have now been flown in, and that's where they are?"

"Yes, Timothy, that's what I just said. They have all gone to the Pentagon. They were flown this morning."

"Well, Janet, on this occasion you've convinced me. This is another biblical scale occurrence. I think the public would love to hear what is currently being said at the Pentagon. I'd like you to make this your priority, and thank you for making me sit down and listen to you. This is worth its weight in gold when it comes to investigative journalism – so, if there's anything I can do to help you concerning logistics regarding travel etc, you just let me know," said Timothy.

"Yes, super, thank you so much!" Janet's smile and enthusiasm were infectious. Timothy laughed.

"And if it means traveling to the Himalayas. Well, it means traveling to the Himalayas. You got to go," he said.

Janet left Timothy's office still smiling. He walked over to the window and looked out, thinking about the conversation he'd just had.

*****

In the medical center, a nurse approached Gail and Vicky.

"Vicky, hi. Follow me to Room One, please. And no more than one accompanying person with you, please." The nurse smiled and nodded at Gail as she said this second part.

The two ladies followed the nurse across the waiting area and down a corridor, to another much smaller waiting area and another corridor with numbered doors. The door labeled 'One' was open and the nurse stepped inside.

"Hello, this is Vicky, and her daughter Gail," the nurse introduced them and then left the room.

The lady sat behind the desk had spectacles which accentuated her vivid blue eyes, and long gray hair neatly tied back in a ponytail.

"Hello Vicky, I've seen you before, haven't I." Dr Charlotte extended her hand and shook Vicky's warmly. "And Gail, nice to meet you." She shook Gail's hand, and gestured to them both to sit down.

"Vicky, I'm afraid I don't have the best news. We have the results of your breast x-rays and blood tests, and I am so sorry to say that you have Stage I cancer in both breasts."

Vicky covered her face with one hand, her other was cradled in Gail's hands. She started crying.

"Oh Mom, I'm so sorry," Gail said softly.

"We have caught it at Stage 1, which is very good. It could spread, but we're going to do all we can to prevent that. It will mean chemotherapy and I will talk you through the details. I've got some documents I need you to sign," said Dr Charlotte.

*****

Timothy had called Janet back into his office to talk more about her trip. He had authorized an increased budget for her, and she was keen to start planning.

"You said you have a source from within NASA?" he asked.

"Yes, I've got a source, but not a very reliable one at this stage." She had in her hand a mug of coffee, from which she now took a gulp.

"Janet, I want you to brief me every day on exactly what you're writing, where you are, who you with, and who you've seen – understood?" said Timothy.

"You've got that Timothy look on your face," said Janet. "You can count on me. I'll give this story 100%, and you will have my 100% attention all the time I'm working on it."

Janet turned her head to look through the glass wall that separated Timothy's office from the rest of that floor, observing her colleagues.

"I assume it goes without saying that this story will remain between you and me. I don't want or need any of the others barging in on my territory. I need to be as covert as possible," she said.

"No, hell no. Of course it stays between us. Loose lips sink ships. I couldn't trust any of the others with this. They'd walk off to another broadcaster," said Timothy.

"Thank you. Nice to know you appreciate me."

"Janet, you are my golden girl," said Timothy, putting his hand on her shoulder and squeezing it. He probably should be more careful, he thought, as these days that could be classed as sexual harassment, and these days sexual harassment could ruin someone's career.

*****

In the medical center, Gail linked arms with Vicky.

"Come on Mom. Let's go; let me take you out for a meal."

Gail smiled at Vicky and reached to take hold of her belongings for her.

"Thank you Darling. I fancy a Mexican. Nachos would go down well." They started walking back towards the main reception area. Just then, they heard a voice.

It was the specialist, Dr Charlotte.

"You forgot the paperwork. Take these advisory notes with you to read at home. They explain what's involved in the treatment and discuss likely side effects and how to deal with them. If you have any questions at all, don't hesitate to give us a ring on the number at the top of the first page."

*****

Back inside the cargo plane, the only sound was the humming of the four jet engines in the background. Everybody in the cabin except Jared was asleep. Jared was playing a game of hangman.

At the far end, the door to the cockpit was closed, and the steward was currently nowhere to be seen. Jared stood up and walked around. There were pallets fastened tight to the floor with straps. They were all locked with seals on. Jared tilted his head to read a label on one. It had a date on it, and some file numbers.

"God damn – CIA had also been snooping on my research," he muttered. He was thinking all the documents must have been printed off and copied and filed in the boxes he turns around and nodded his head. He could understand now what they might have been up to. He headed to the bathroom, and was inside the cubicle when someone tried the handle, attempting to get in.

"I'm in here; I won't be a moment," Jared shouted.

*****

Rather inappropriately, Janet put down her empty coffee mug on Timothy's desk, on its polished wooden surface before waving at him and making her way to leave his office. He raised his hand to stop her.

"Hang on, Janet. How about I take you out for lunch today?"

"No, Timothy. I really want to start organizing my travel itinerary. I will be sure to forward it to you as soon as I'm done," she said.

Timothy stood looking at the floor for a moment. He looked disappointed.

"I have something for you." He walked over to a cupboard which he opened and took out a box. Inside it was a silver pen which had been in his possession for 20 years. It was a gift when he first joined the CNN news team, and he had kept it in his office ever since then.

"There you go, Janet. It's a gift from me to you. I'm sure you'll take care of it, and I hope it measures up to the great work you do," said Timothy, handing it to her.

Janet took it with both hands and inclined her head.

"Thank you Timothy. It's lovely," she smiled.

She opened her bag and put her new gift into it and walked out of the office.

"Bye Timothy."

*****

Jared opened the toilet cubicle door. Stood in front of him was the aircraft crew member. He noticed the man's surname was printed on his overall. Beck. Jared walked out of the cubicle and stood to one side so Mr Beck could get past.

*****

Gail and Vicky were back in Gail's car and driving towards town, when Gail said,

"Mother, I know a nice Mexican. It's the one I went to last year. I know where it is. We'll go there."

"Oh dear, I just can't understand how this happened. But I suppose, life goes on. People have lived to tell the tale." Vicky wiped teary eyes with a tissue.

*****

Janet closed the door of Timothy's office, reading its sign, 'Timothy Whyte' as she did so. She walked through the office, ignoring her name being called by several colleagues who were trying to attract her attention, and remaining focused on her task in hand.

"Hey Janet, what you up to? Where have you been?"

"Janet – weren't we supposed to meet up?"

She sped up as she got closer to the elevator. Once there, she pressed the button and soon there was a 'ping, ping, ping,' as the elevator arrived. Janet stepped inside and looked into the mirrored panel in front of her inside the elevator car. She pulled out her hairbrush and brushed her hair. The elevator descended right the way to the ground floor without stopping.

*****

Inside the cargo plane, as Jared turned around to look at Mr Beck as the crew member entered the cubicle, he felt uneasy. It was a feeling of mistrust as he felt he was being snooped on. Or was he just being paranoid? They were all just doing their job, but he couldn't help feeling unsure as to some of the group's motives.

Beep, beep... Gail's reverse parking sensors warned of an obstacle. She and Vicky were in the car park of 'Penrino's', the Mexican restaurant Gail had been to before. A big neon sign announced the restaurant's name.

"Lovely. I'm looking forward to my nachos. I think I might as well enjoy whatever I fancy, given my circumstances," said Vicky in a slightly grim tone.

"Hello dear ladies. May I take your coats?" the waiter asked them. 'Penrino's' restaurant was known for its excellent customer service.

"Yes, thank you. Here, let me take my coat off. Mom, you okay with yours?" Gail handed her coat over and Vicky did the same. They were then escorted to a table where the waiter pulled out a chair for Vicky to sit on and then for Gail.

Both ladies were smiling because Gail knew the restaurant's menu and knew they were in for a treat, and Vicky was looking forward to nachos. She went straight to them in the menu, whereas Gail pondered through the menu to see what she fancied this time other than nachos.

*****

"Meow... meow!" it was her cat. Janet bent down to her.

"Hello, my lovely kitty," she said.

It had been a few days since she'd been home, and she felt guilty for neglecting the poor animal. She now made sure the litter tray was empty and freshened and there was enough food in the bowl.

Janet switched on her laptop. She must arrange her travel itinerary. She needed to book some flights as she had an idea about how to get to the bottom of whatever was going on at the Pentagon.

She booked on the next flight out from L.A. to Virginia, which was at 18:00 and would get her there in the early hours of the following day. She scrolled down and saw further flights but decided to just go ahead with that one with Delta Airlines.

She was a frequent flyer and so collected points. She proceeded to the payment stage. She had her card details already saved to her account, so it took a mere click of the mouse to pay. The screen showed payment confirmation and she received an email confirmation.

"Right, I had better get packing. Toiletries, passport, what to wear... now where did I put my new sandals...?"

Soon, Janet had her holdall and another handbag ready to go. There was leftover takeaway on her desk from yesterday, which she picked up and finished off.

*****

Inside the C-17 aircraft, there was the humming of jet engines. It was now approaching 1700 hours and there was just one hour left of the flight.

"Listen folks, it's the pilot here. We have approximately an hour left of our flight to Washington DC. If you'd like to start getting yourselves ready, you'd be one step ahead." That pilot's name was Dave Manning.

Agent Harrison said, "Folks, just to let you know we are scheduled to arrive at the Pentagon tomorrow morning. We've got you booked into hotels. Be sure to remain together as a group when we get to Arrivals once we've landed, as you will be briefed by my colleague."

*****

Beep, Beep. Janet's house alarm responded to her typing in the code to set it. She grabbed hold of her bunch of keys and put on a hat and scarf, then picked up her coat – something of a balancing act with her handbag and holdall both over her shoulder. She shut the door and turned the key, hearing the door lock.

"Dammit! I forgot to call an uber..." Angry with herself, Janet pulled out her phone to make the call. It was the convenient way to travel, and no more expensive than airport parking. The Uber app was showing five minutes. Then it dropped to three minutes. Janet selected the ride and walked to the road, looking at her watch. Time flies, she thought, and at the exact moment a bird flew over her head. She smiled to herself. The uber appeared, with the app displaying one minute to reach her.

*****

Gail raised her hand. Vicky did too, thinking two hands better than one. The waiter spotted them and walked over, pulling out his order notebook as he arrived.

"How can I help you ladies?"

"Nachos with chili sauce for me and Peri Peri chicken please," said Vicky.

"Actually, same for me. I'll try something different. And for dessert, the ice cream. That's all thank you," said Gail.

The waiter wrote the orders down, nodding his head and asked, "Would you like anything to drink?"

Yes, Gail was thinking she'd try something alcoholic.

"A pitcher of your bestselling cocktail, thank you," replied Gail.

"Super, Madam, thank you. I'll take your menus if I may."

They handed them to him and he walked away.

Gail spotted a wall hanger with newspapers and went and selected *USA Today*, and motioned to Vicky whether she'd like one. Vicky shook her head.

She walked back over to her seat and sat down while reading the front cover.

Chapter 8
Chinese
Fortune Cookie

'China's ambitions for quarrying on the moon.'

Gail turned the newspaper around to Vicky.

"Hey Mom, have you seen this?"

"Oh my lord, that's up your street. Seems like there's a competitor out there," replied Vicky.

*****

Janet had just passed through check-in and had a 20-minute wait before boarding commenced, so she decided to go over to the retail outlet where she found newspapers to browse.

She lifted the one she usually read, *USA Today.* As she walked over to the counter to pay, she noticed a heading;

'China has ambitions to quarry on the moon.'

"Hell, that's odd. What a coincidence," she muttered, thinking that it was almost as if they were living in parallel worlds. Well, I guess we are all human and we all have the same agenda, she thought.

*****

The door to the cockpit on the cargo plane opened. It was dark outside now, and the lights on the wing tips were flashing.

The pilot announced;

"Can everybody now take a seat and buckle up. We are due to land in approximately 10 minutes. The time at landing should be 1815."

Jared had already sat and done up his seat belt. There were a multitude of clicks heard as the rest of the team buckled up.

The pilot was heard again: "Can we make sure all devices are in airplane mode please – as protocol requires."

The sound of the jet engines changed as the aircraft descended and lost altitude.

There was a clunk. The landing gear had been deployed from underneath the plane's underbelly and from the nose. Within a few minutes, there was a sudden jolt as the back tires hit the tarmac runway, followed soon after by the front tire touching down. The crew member asked for everyone to remain seated, just as the pilot once again asked over the tannoy for the same.

After a little taxiing on the runway, the aircraft came to a stop, and there was some commotion as everyone unbuckled their safety belts.

The door at the rear end of the plane started to open, descending slowly. Everyone stood up: Jared, Derek, Dr William, Dr Fred, and Agents Harrison and Parker. Immediately the ramp touched the tarmac, they started disembarking. Right by the plane was a waiting convoy of three SUVs with blacked-out windows. They were ushered into the vehicles, with the agents both getting into the first one.

"Well, it makes a change to having to go through the usual airport security – no need to have our passports or luggage checked," Jared said to Derek.

"Jared, we're not at Washington DC airport here. This is a military airport," Derek said.

"What was that, Derek?" Jared looked out. Nothing but military aircraft and vehicles. "Oh, this must be..." he started, but was cut off by Agent Parker;

"Davison Air Force airfield, Sir."

The vehicles drove over some speed ramps before slowing for a check post, though almost as soon as they slowed the barrier is raised, and they were free to continue.

After about 10 minutes, Derek asked;

"How long we got and what hotel we are staying at?"

"Sir, just another 10 minutes and we'll be there. You're staying at the Doubletree Hilton Hotel, Sir," replied Agent Parker.

"Remind me to get a newspaper. I'm guessing being the Hilton, they'll have one available as part of room service," said Derek.

Everyone suddenly jolted forward as the vehicle stopped. They had arrived at the hotel. Agent Parker instructed Jared while they were sitting in the car;

"Sir, can you please be ready downstairs in the lobby area tomorrow at 8 AM – we will be here to pick you up. Can you please brief the others in your team."

"Sure. Thank you," said Jared while finding the handle on the door. He pulled it and the door opened. He got out and walked round to the truck. Agent Parker was already there, unloading luggage.

"There you go. Help yourself to yours," he said.

They all walked towards reception.

"You are all checked in under your surnames," called Agent Harrison – he was still sitting in the SUV, with the window wound down. Jared turned round and gave him a thumbs-up in acknowledgment.

At reception, Jared asked Derek;

"Did you want a newspaper?"

"Oh, of course. Excuse me Ma'am, could I please have a copy of today's *USA Today*? I'm room number 113," asked Derek.

"No problem, Sir. I have requested it on the system, and someone will be over to your room in the next 10 minutes with a copy. It will be added to your room bill," replied the clerk.

Derek and Jared took the elevator to the first floor and headed to their rooms. The others were still in the lobby checking in. Derek touched his key card against the door lock, and there was a click as the door unlocked. He turned the handle, opening the door. Jared's room was on the other side of the corridor. Once inside his room, Derek dropped his bags and headed straight for the kettle thinking just how much he could murder a strong brew right now.

There was a knock on the door and Derek turned his head towards it, wondering for a second who it could be, before remembering about the newspaper. He headed for the door and opened it.

"Good evening, Sir. Your newspaper."

"Thank you very much, much appreciated," replied Derek. He immediately looked at the front page where it says;

'China has ambitions to quarry on the moon.'

He shut his room door before growling, "Goddamn Chinese quarrying on the moon!! That's just more to go wrong – a recipe for disaster with the Chinese in space!"

Derek rushed out of his room, leaving the door open and headed straight to Jared's and knocked on the door.

The door opened and Jared stood there with a towel around his waist.

"Yes Derek, what on earth is it? I was about to take a shower."

Derek turned the newspaper front cover so it was facing Jared, and pointed his finger at the article, poking it.

"Look at this, Chinese ambition to quarry on the moon! With them being in space, there's just more to go wrong. A greater chance of collision. We won't know where they are and what they're up to. Goddamn Chinese," said Derek.

*****

It was the next morning. Jared was brushing his teeth. He had the radio playing. He used the radio as his wake-up call as he enjoyed waking up to the news – it was gentler than the beep of an alarm clock. The news that morning, unsurprisingly, was focused on the headline about the Chinese and them preparing to launch a rocket containing a lunar rover into space and beyond, towards the moon. This lunar rover, which now had a successor known as a space exploration vehicle 'SEV' was something which analyzed and assessed data to give a real understanding of what was out there and if there was anything of interest. It was window shopping, and once they had something of interest, they went to take a closer look. One didn't go window shopping unless there was the ambition to acquire something.

*****

Beep, beep, beep... the alarm clock on the phone was insistent. A hand appeared from under the covers to pushed the screen slider to 'off'. It was Janet's phone.

She slid herself out of bed, heading towards the window. She briefly looked out of the window as if needing a glimpse of daylight to confirm in her mind the time of day and not just rely on an electronic device. The light outside confirmed it was time she got up, and she headed for the bathroom. She pushed the door open and clicked on the switch. It was suddenly very bright on her still-waking eyes. The extractor fan was humming away. She looked at the toiletries on the side of the basin. Each of the items had the name of the hotel printed on it: 'Doubletree Hilton Hotel'. Yes, she was at the same hotel as Jared and his team.

Chapter 9
LAPD Officer

She picked up her toothbrush, and after squeezing a generous amount of toothpaste onto the bristles began to brush. She looked at herself in the mirror, thinking about a contact she had in the Los Angeles Police Department. She'd give him a call. He owed her a favor and she needed to call it in. She went back into the bedroom and picked up her cell phone from the bedside table. Scrolling through the contacts, she found 'Jeff LAPD' and pressed the dial button.

He picked up on the fourth ring.

"Hey Janet, how are you doing? Good to hear from you."

"Hi Jeff. I'm fine, thanks. Just working on a new story. It's a huge one as it would be, and I wanted to call in that favor you owe me, remember?"

"Of course. You gave me a few contacts. Your beautiful looks came in handy," he replied.

"Well, I need to locate an individual. He's working for NASA on its strategic project. I'd like to speak to him. Can you give me his location? It's early morning. He should be at his hotel. That's all the information I need. For now."

"Listen, Janet, I could lose my job for this. The technology you are asking me to use is for counter-terrorism; using it like this is a misappropriation and a serious felony. This is unreasonable. I could lose everything."

"Listen, Jeff. I understand that, and I wouldn't ask, but I have a career here that I live and die by as well, and I need to speak with this individual. If this comes back on you, you can call me on it, okay.

You can trust me. It's literally to see which hotel he is staying at so I can interview him."

There was a long silence. She could almost hear Jeff's mind wrestling with itself.

"Just this once. Read out the number," he said.

"8.3.3.6.2.4.0.1.1.2."

"Right, I'm just going to read it back to you to check. You've given me 8.3.3.6.2.4.0.1.1.2. – is that correct?"

"Yes, that's it, that's the one, and his name is Jared. Okay, I'll leave that with you. Give me a call back in the next two minutes. Speak to you shortly," said Janet.

She went back into the bathroom, proceeding through her morning ritual of pampering and carefully going through each of those complimentary toiletries provided by Hilton hotels.

*****

The kettle was boiling and the steam rising, hitting the ceiling. In Vicky's kitchen, where the steam caused a little condensation on the kitchen ceiling and the temperature had dropped, and the steam had turned to water again, a drop fell onto the floor. Vicky was making coffee.

She wondered if Gail would like a drink if she was awake.

"Gail, are you up. Would you like a coffee?"

"Yes please."

She picked another cup off the rack. She knew it was black coffee, no sugar.

*****

Janet's phone was ringing. She rushed to pick it up.

"Hi Janet, it's me again. I have a location for you. Jared is showing to be right on top of the Doubletree Hilton in Washington. And where are you right now?" Jeff's voice had a smile in it.

"Ha, ha, same place, same hotel. How bizarre. Okay, let me go down to reception and tell them of a lost key. Thank you Jeff!"

"Janet kept hold of her phone and rushed down to reception.

Vicky walked into Gail's room with her coffee.

"Here you go, Love."

"Thank you Mom, my ID card hasn't come to light. I'll have to go to security to get a new one. That's my first port of call today."

*****

In Jared's room, he was getting dressed, and had just put his trousers through the trouser press. He picked up the phone receiver and dialed 116 for Derek's room.

"Hi Derek, just checking you were awake. I'll meet you at the Fourier in half an hour."

"Hi, yes – awake and up. The lobby, okay, catch you later," said Derek.

"Hey, by the way, the trouser press is worth using if you need to. Works very well. I'll see you later," said Jared and put the phone down.

*****

Janet arrived at the reception lobby and walked across over to the desk. She was in her pajamas and dressing gown, and the clerk behind the desk saw her and smiled, his expression suggesting he assumed she'd locked herself out of her room and she was not the first guest to do this.

"I am so sorry, I've locked myself out of my room. It's booked under my husband Jared's name. Are you able to do me a spare key please?" she asked.

"Ma'am, I'll need to know your room number; I'm not authorized to give out a key otherwise," replied the clerk.

"Well, I just followed my husband and last night I had a little too much to drink and I didn't take much notice of which room it was. And he is not here to ask now. Which is why I'm hoping you can help," said Janet.

"I'm sorry Ma'am, I cannot help you there – you will need to get in touch with your husband."

"Okay. Well, I also need to speak to an individual who is staying at this hotel too. I just need to know the room number. I'm a reporter from the CNN."

"Well, that I could help you with, I guess. What's the name?"

"It's Jared," replied Janet.

"Now let's see... yes, he checked in last night, and it's room 113 on the first floor. You can call from here, or I guess if you're staying here, you might as well go and knock on the door. Feel free," said the clerk. But Janet was already dashing off to the first floor in her pajamas and gown.

Jared was making himself a coffee when he heard the knock on the door. He didn't have his trousers on as they were still being pressed. He put a towel around himself and went over to the door to open it. As soon as it was open a notch, Janet leaned her head to the side to try to see past it, and had to hold herself back from impolitely pushing her way in.

"Hello, Jared isn't it? We haven't met before. I'm a reporter with the CNN. I cover science and technology, and I believe you intend sending space vehicles into space. I would really appreciate it if you'd be willing to give me ten minutes of your time to interview you," said Janet.

Jared smiled but shook his head.

"Listen." He shrugged his shoulders. "Listen, I really can't. I have been summoned to appear at the Pentagon and been told under no circumstances may we speak to anyone else outside. Certainly not news organizations. It's something which is of national interest. Significant and strategic and needs to remain secret."

"Listen, I represent the people," said Janet. " The general people out there paying taxes must have a right to know where their money is going. Just think of the millions of people out there who tune in to CNN. I'm not hiding anything. I would just like to be having sole access to whatever little bit of information there is. Surely there is something you can give me."

"How did you even get to know about this and where I was," asked Jared.

Janet looked up at the ceiling. "It's my job to know. It's what we do and get good at in investigative journalism."

"How much do you know?" he asked. "Look, I need to get ready. We're being picked up by the CIA this morning. I don't have time to speak to you I'm afraid."

Janet was very tenacious. She didn't want to give up...

"I'm just asking for your help. I'm just trying to do my job." She waved a hand in frustration.

"If you need to know more, you will have to follow us, but being the CIA I'd like to know how far you'll get," said Jared. He started to close the door, signaling time for Janet to go.

"When are you leaving this morning?" she asked.

"In about 15 minutes."

Janet headed back to her room. She needed to get dressed and get herself down to reception.

*****

Derek was in his bathroom, trimming his beard. He went into the bedroom, put on his wristwatch and checked the time. Time to go.

Putting his shoes on and grabbing his coat, he headed out of the door.

*****

The traffic lights were red. Agents Parker and Harrison were in the front SUV, with Agent Parker driving. Tap, tap, tap, tap... Parker was tapping away on the steering wheel with his fingers. He had a tune in his head from the previous evening when he'd been watching a video of the last time he'd been at a dance event, singing with his wife. Just then the lights turned green, and all three SUVs headed towards the hotel to pick up the team.

"Did you get up to much last night?" Agent Harrison asked.

"Well actually, funny you should ask. I was at home watching some old videos of when I went to a dance contest with my wife – going through the old moves." The SUV rolled up the ramp towards the hotel.

Janet was rushing around her room, hopping on one leg while she got the other leg into her tights.

She almost fell over, and sat down on the bed for a moment.

"Oh, for God's sake, come on Janet!" she muttered to herself. "Now do these tights match the skirt?"

She hurriedly got herself ready, leaving out the make-up and rushed down to the lobby. She only had her cell phone on her. She didn't have the chance to grab her handbag. There before her in the lobby was Jared. Above them hung crystal chandeliers. It was quite a grand entrance at the hotel. Quite impressive art decor. It was right underneath the chandelier that they were all waiting. Janet had her sunglasses on and sat beside the group with her back turned.

It dawned on her that the best thing to do may be to wait outside because when the vehicles arrived to pick the group up, she could maybe get into an SUV before the others leave, hence not being spotted, and get a ride in without the others noticing.

Janet walked calmly out of the building. Just as she was standing by the steps up to the main doors, the three SUVs arrived and parked up close to each other. Agent Parker and Agent Harrison both vacated the front vehicle and moved into the hotel building. As they were dressed in stereotypical CIA dress code, together with the black SUVs, Janet realized this was them and decided to casually walk over to the third SUV. She opened the back door and sat inside. The driver turned around and looked at her.

"Good morning Ma'am."

He assumed she was one from the group. Janet smiled back at him and nodded and returned his 'good morning'.

Just then all the others in the group left the hotel building and walked towards the front two cars and got in. Jared and Derek got in the front one and the two doctors walked over to the middle one. That was all of them? They had all got into the vehicles. The three-vehicle convoy was just protocol. A protocol that Janet benefited from as, apart from the driver nobody saw her. The two agents climbed back into the first car, and they drove off. They were heading to the Pentagon with Janet sat calmly in the back seat of the third SUV. Remaining unnoticed once they arrived at the Pentagon, however, would pose far more of a challenge for her...

*****

Gail rummaged through her handbag, making sure she had her forms of ID that would be required by security.

"Yes passport, yes driving license. Yes, utility bills. Everything I need," Gail muttered to herself, ringing the bell on the counter at reception.

After a few moments, a security officer appeared clutching a clipboard and a list of some kind.

"Yes Ma'am, how can I help you?" The guard's name is on a badge pinned on the top left of his shirt as Gail was looking at him. 'Federico'.

"Yes, I'd like a new security badge. My badge has either been misplaced or lost," said Gail.

"We require two forms of ID, two forms of proof of address and a letter from your Head of Department stating you are still working in the premises," replied Federico.

"Well, that would be Jared. I'll try and call his number again. I had some difficulty before."

Gail tried to dial Jared, who at this moment was being driven to the Pentagon.

There was a dial tone, and Jared's cell began to ring. He reached inside his jacket pocket to pull out his phone and swiped up the answer button.

"Gail, hello, how are you doing?"

"Jared, I've been trying to reach you. I've lost my ID badge and I really need another one. Security needs authorization from you as head of my department. I have everything else I need other than a letter from you. Are you anywhere where you are able to email something through?" asked Gail.

"Well, you're not going to believe this, but I am in a vehicle with the CIA who are taking me to the Pentagon. Derek's here, and so are Dr William and Dr Fred, the chief scientist and chief technologist," Jared said.

"Did you just say CIA and the Pentagon?" queried Gail.

"Yes, yes, I did; the CIA is driving us to the Pentagon right now. They want us to debrief them on the entire project and what our findings are."

"Okay. Keep me posted. I can't gain access anywhere on the facility without the badge. I'll speak to you soon," said Gail.

Chapter 10

100-foot room

"How long are you planning on staying here?" asked Mr Khan.

"I'm here in this region for another few weeks, but I am here in the country for an indefinite period. In a few weeks I want to move into the Himalayan region. The area surrounding mountain K2, perhaps. Am I correct that situated in Pakistan are five of the world's highest mountains?" asked Jackson.

"That's correct, Sir. Here in north Pakistan you will find the envy of the world. Some of the best vistas and of course some of the highest mountains on Earth, which I assume is right up your street. If you need any assistance, I'm your guide. I can show you the best guest houses; give me a call," said Mr Khan. "I am going to have some more equipment shipped over by airfreight into Islamabad Airport; then it was going to come across to Gilgit Airport, but I think I'm going to redirect it to Skardu Airport, as it's closer to the mountain K2," he continued while he tried to start the car once more, and he turned to look back at Jackson.

Jackson reached into his pocket and pulled out a wallet. He opened it and inside were a bunch of photographs. He pulled out one of the photographs: it was a picture of Janet and Elijah. They were on their honeymoon. One would wonder why Jackson has a photo of Janet and Elijah in his wallet. Well, a closer look at Jackson, who now has his face covered with a beard. He has been given a new identity.

Mr Khan turned to look at what Jackson was holding.

"So, what's that. Who is that in the picture?"

"Oh, it's nobody, just somebody in the past," Jackson replied.

*****

Inside the 100-foot long room at the Pentagon there were many representatives sat around the table. Starting at one end, there was the Deputy Director of the CIA, Mac George; then the Chief Operating Officer of the Agency, Gerry Townsend; then the Deputy Director of Analysis, Todd Gordon; next is the Deputy Director for Operations, Andrew Lopez; then the Deputy Director for Science and Technology, Donald Mann. Finally, across from Donald, we have the Director of the Agency, Sheila McDaniel.

Sheila McDaniel was a 51-year-old woman standing at 5'5" in height, with brown hair and a bigger than average build. She was seriously committed to the CIA cause and had been with the Agency for 20 years. Her father, now passed away, was of Scottish descent, and also served the Agency. Recently, she had been on edge. Her husband had left her for a younger Filipino woman, and she was very bitter. She was a mother to one daughter, Silvia, who was away traveling.

Next to Sheila sat the Deputy Director of Support, Bobby Singleton; then, the Chief Scientist and Chief Technologist, Dr William and Dr Fred; after that, Chief Engineer Jared Neal; and finally, we have Derek White, Director of Communications.

It seemed there was only three of them from NASA, but further along, there were a few more sat. There was Colin McCormick from 'Search for Extra-Terrestrial intelligence (SETI), Institute of Technology and Security, and adjacent to Colin there was Seth Beck, the Director of Development at SETI.

Agents Harrison and Parker were sat in the back together with a few more personnel from the CIA.

Sheila McDaniel was chairing the meeting. She pulled the microphone close to her mouth while she placed the glass of water back onto the table from which she has just had a sip of water.

"Good morning ladies and gentlemen, we're here today to discuss one of the gravest dangers to our national security. Our establishment and the scientific organizations whose leadership is present have made a discovery which will have profound implications for this world.

"Just a few days ago on 11 September, software that was developed specifically for the purpose conducted a theoretical experiment which concluded that the Himalayas is the only location on earth from where we can launch a ship, commonly referred to as a 'Starship', meaning big enough for interstellar travel – that's to say, Mars and beyond.

"As you are aware, this region is surrounded by nations that are nuclear powers which have intercontinental ballistic missiles and some sort of space program.

"We have been following the progress of the development for quite some time and have decided to conduct a meeting today where we can all sit together and agree on a consensus of how this will affect the United States of America."

There was astonishment and surprise on some people's faces, complete disbelief and shock on others. A few hands raised, but Sheila pointed at Donald Mann.

"Good morning, I'm Donald, Deputy Director for Science and Technology, and I think it would be a good idea if Jared, Chief Engineer, would talk us through the software and the discoveries which have led to this meeting taking place. Over to you, Jared."

"Hello, good morning. I'm Jared, Chief Engineer at NASA and myself and my team have been working on this software for a few years now. The software was to give us results when it comes to the best location on Earth to launch a 'Starship' into space. We knew the thickest part of the Earth's crust is at the Himalayas, which is also the highest at 30,000 feet. But the experiment was to see whether if we played about with the shape of the shuttle – if it was to not involve as much height and therefore not require as much depth – would that make a difference in terms of being able to launch it from another point, such as maybe within the

United States. Ideally, we want to build this thing inside the US, as it's a costly project. In fact, one of the most expensive ever undertaken by mankind. Unfortunately, the results came back indicating that it's only possible to launch a shuttle without rocket fuel using electricity and magnetism at almost 30,000 feet above the sea and it needs depth to accelerate up to an altitude of 197,000 feet. Also, the results calculated the most efficient payload, which was 20 metric tons. This geological set-up is not available in the US. Fortunately, there is one, and only one, place on earth it does exist. The Himalayas. It might have not existed at all, but millions of years of plate tectonics, the shifting plates of Europe and Asia have pushed the rocky surface high and low, and there is a location that gives us a foundation and launchpad to put a 'Starship' into space. We can do this. But we have to do it in the Himalayas.

Jared paused for breath, running his fingers through his hair and then flexed his hands before clasping them together, indicating he still had so much to say but just could not find the right words. Donald took over;

"So, as you can see we're in a situation where if we don't take action, and soon, we are sure to lose the global leadership we have today. The Chinese will almost definitely take over."

"Well, the indications are they already have ambitions to send probes to the Moon and Mars and have ambitions to quarry and mine above there," said Sheila.

"Well, given what you've just referred to, no doubt the Chinese will be constructing this launchpad, given that the Himalayas is within their country, the west of Beijing," said Mac George, the Deputy Director.

"Is there no way we could lease the territory for 100 years, like the agreements that exist with shipping ports?" Todd Gordon interjected.

"Such is the importance and scale of this, if we're not there, then we are finished. 100 years is not good enough; it would mean leaving the Chinese with the capability to render us obsolete. We need to annex those territories, to keep them out of reach from whomever has them right now, whether it be China, India, Pakistan or someone else," said Sheila. She reached out to lift her glass of water.

A few started to whisper at one another, and Mac George said something to Sheila. She seemed to nod in agreement.

"Over at the far end, Colin McCormick and Seth Beck. You're both from the SETI Institute. Could you explain in a few words your understanding of the situation?" asked Mac.

Colin stood up. He walked around to the dry-wipe board and drew three big squares, big enough to draw in.

"Ladies and gentlemen, here we have three windows. If we look in the first one, I'm going to draw Goldilocks and the Three Bears: Mummy bear, Daddy bear and baby bear. If we don't act, Goldilocks will be staying at home with the three bears. In the second box, we have Snow White and the seven dwarves. If we don't act Snow White will be staying at home with the seven dwarves, and in the third box, we've got Buck Rogers. During the 1960s I remember there was a comic book character, space detective Buck Rogers. The name is synonymous to the American way of life and identity. Well, if we don't act, there is never going to be no goddamn Buck Rogers."

Colin walked back to his chair.

"Thank you Colin, for your rather elaborate explanation of the situation, but I think it's about a little more than Walt Disney and comic book case studies and setting a precedent on a cartoon character," said Mac.

Sheila looked up and nodded her head in agreement.

"We need to make our pitch now before it's too late, before the goddamn Chinese take over this planet, so we are going to devise a solution which will not leave this room. Mac turned his head to Andrew Lopez.

"Andrew, can you give us your verdict."

"Well, in my opinion, we need to get our electorate, our masses, the people, to overwhelmingly agree upon an attack on foreign soil due to us having sustained a heavy loss and heavy casualties by what would seem an aggressive action by a foreign entity. It would be portrayed that way by media as they would not know any better or any more of it then need to. It would give us a reason to enter the region and get our foot in the door."

He looked at the faces around him. Some appeared in disbelief and shock, while some agreed and acknowledged the countermeasures. Sheila nodded while she took notes.

Bobby Singleton spoke up; "Well, the weakest link we have in the region is Afghanistan. It's an age-old problem, never progressing – we've been at war for most of the century. It's somewhere where we could conduct operations from what would be an ideal staging post, and it even borders China at the foothills of the Himalayas: we'd be going straight up the back door, straight up the Khyber Pass."

A few began nodding their heads while trying to disguise the fact that they find it funny and ironical.

"I will authorize this so we can conduct what we need to, " said Sheila. "I shall be drafting a list of people from this room today who are to attend a meeting, code-named 'Spaceport Himalaya', and we shall be discussing the timeline and logistics of the operation. I'd like to ask Jared one more question. Can you give me a specific location which would be best suited to launch the shuttles from for the development of a 'Starship'?"

She asked this just as Jared took a large gulp of water, resulting in him swallowing fast and coughing.

"Yes, sure. It's within a cluster of five of the tallest mountains and is also where the thickest part of the Earth's crust can be found. The summit of mountain K2 which borders China and Pakistan is almost 30,000 feet high," said Jared.

"Thank you. That's all for now right. I'd like to close this meeting, and I'd like everyone to leave the room apart from Mac, Gerry, Todd, Andrew, Donald and Bobby. Agents Harrison and Parker, could you please escort the others out of the room. Thank you," said Sheila.

The group from NASA and the couple from SETI were looking at each other. They picked up their coats and after a little shuffle left the room. Agents Harrison and Parker were waiting at the doors, which they closed after the last one leaves, which was Jared. He stood at the door, turned and looked at Sheila as if he was about to say something.

"That will be all Jared, thank you," said Sheila.

"Sir, can you leave the room please," said Agent Harrison.

He did so, with the agents behind him. The room was left with just those people Sheila had asked to stay behind.

"We'll go and have some lunch, and then I want you all back here in this room for a briefing about how we are going to get our teeth into this mess. I'll meet you back here at 1 PM when we can draft out exactly what we will need to do this. It's now 11:47 AM; I'll see you here at 1 PM," said Sheila as she closed her file and stood up.

Sheila headed off through another set of doors into what presumably was her office. The others made their way out individually.

*****

Janet arrived back at her hotel room. She had just walked in, slammed the door behind her, thrown her bags onto her bed and before sitting down headed straight for her phone to pull out her police friend contact at the LAPD.

Janet inadvertently saw her police friend cover up the crime scene when she was reporting on an alleged break-in at a technology company in Silicon Valley. It was due to him receiving a payment for work, which was not ethical and was a violation of their code of practice. It was going against protocol and the values they stand for as a police force to remain impartial. Her cameraman was also seen. So, she had never expected the day to come when the two of them would join forces and work together and help each other to achieve whatever they desired to. But, she was sure that he had good intentions, and that these tech companies were as guilty as sin.

"Hey, it's me again. Janet. Are you okay to talk? I need your help again."

"Hey, I thought that was the end when I gave you the location of phone. You can't keep doing this to me. You're killing me!" said Jeff.

"Listen, Jeff, if I don't have this story… The editor has the details on file, which would automatically lead to the next story in line. It's there as a contingency if I failed to bring in a story that's your story, so I'm afraid you're going to help me with this. We will work together. What I need is a direct link to his mobile phone and what was said today," said Janet.

Jeff exhaled in disbelief.

"Is it the same number," he asked.

"That's correct, same one, registered to a Jared Neal," she said.

"Right, hang on there and give me a moment..." said Jeff.

At the station, he was thinking and looking around to make sure nobody was watching him.

"Right, I'm going on the server and typing in my authorization password ... right, I'll just get the number off my notepad, just a moment."

"I've got it right here if you need it again," said Janet.

"No I'm okay, I've got it. Right I've got the recording here. I'm just going to put my headphones on, so I won't be able to hear you," said Jeff.

Jeff played around with some recordings and comes across one which left him in shock. He turned around, took his headphones off and dropped them on the desk, and turned to his phone.

"Janet, are you there?"

"Yes, I'm here."

"Well, I've just heard the last recording. He was talking to somebody, discussing a meeting that he'd just come out of at the Pentagon, and the meeting apparently concluded with them having agreed to pay blue on blue friendly. From what I understand that's when you kill your own people for a specific reason. What on earth is going on? I mean, this is something with which I need to get the police involved. That's what we do right? The LAPD?" said Jeff.

"No, no, no, no," said Janet. She shrugged off any suggestion of getting involved with this. "You've got to trust me on this. Jeff, it's something concerning national security."

"Janet, what you mean national security, dammit? I've just heard someone tell somebody else that, from what I gather you're telling me, our government is going to organize a true blue on blue. That's a murder. That could be you, your family, me," said Jeff.

"Well, Jeff, one thing you can do for me, if you would. You can keep a tab on my location, because if ever I get hurt or go missing, at least you know where I am and will be able to send help. I'm counting on you." said Janet.

"Yes I'll do that for you, Janet, you got my word there. It's done every day. The system will update and save your location onto our drive, no matter where you are in the world. We can save and record your calls as well. This is a system which has been afforded to us under the prevention of terrorism, but it seems as if our own country is the terrorist." Jeff remarked.

Janet took out her diary and made some notes. She had concluded that the United States of America was to carry out an attack on foreign soil as a means of gaining access to some part of the world which it needed to launch spaceships.

*****

It was getting dark now, and it seemed as if the world was closing in on the two men sat in the Toyota jeep driving towards the valley in the Himalayas.

"How long till we get to the guest house, Khan," asked Jackson.

"Sir, you see that ridge over the other side of the river?" said Mr Khan.

"Yes, I can see it well."

"Well, that is a stone marking 1 km to the town."

"Well, that's good, because I don't like driving in the dark, especially looking over our shoulder down these valleys traversing cliffs ... awful when I can't see them. It's bad enough in the daylight," said Jackson.

Slowly but surely, as they roll over the reach, the town is clearly visible ahead.

"Mr Jackson, that's your hotel right there. It's known as a guest house in this part of the world. We mustn't afford it. The credit of a hotel, sir," said Khan.

There was a crunching sound of tires rolling over stone as the Toyota meandered through the car park of the guest house until it crunched to a halt. Khan took the key out of the ignition and turned the engine off. The two got out of the vehicle, and Khan headed straight to the back. Khan opened the back door, and Jackson reached to pick up a bag, but Mr. Khan put his hand over Jackson's wrist and held it tight.

"It's okay, sir. I'll take care of the bags, please."

Jackson turned to look at Khan, but after a dull stare, insisted that he was going to pick up the bag. He lifted the bag, threw it over his shoulder and headed off to reception. There wasn't much left in the vehicle for Khan to take other than his own possessions. He quickly grabbed his little bag and closed the door before locking it and pushing himself to the lobby. He found Jackson there, sat waiting.

"I have arranged two rooms and am just waiting for the keys as soon as these registration forms are done."

It had just turned 1600 hours and the pair of them were hungry and looking forward to lunch in this part of the world. They liked their rice with meat, lightly spiced with some light mixed fruit and berries, not unlike a biryani.

Jackson handed the forms to Khan to pass to the reception clerk.

He checked in his bag to look for his passport, before pulling it out of his pocket. He turned and asked the clerk;

"Will you need to make a copy of my passport?"

Mr Khan muttered something to the clerk. The clerk then turned around and leaned his head over to see Jackson as Khan is stood in the way.

"No, sir, that'll be fine. You're staying for one night, correct?"

"Yes, that's right," said Jackson. There is a sound coming out of the office.

"Sir, I need your passport," said the clerk.

"Damn it, that's what I asked you in the first place. Will you need my passport and you said no."

Jackson walked over and handed the passport to the clerk and remained in the spot until he received it back.

The clerk walked into the office with the document, presumably to make a copy, and after a minute comes back out.

"So, you are an American citizen," said the clerk. His name badge read 'Faisal'.

"That's quite right. It's got the United States of America written on my passport which surely makes me an American," said Jackson.

"So, I hope you have a wonderful time and would like to take this opportunity to welcome you to the Valley. We have guides here, and we have horses here if you would like to go horse riding. Also, this part of the country is famous for the highest polo tournament ground on Earth. If there's anything else you need, don't hesitate to ask us."

Jackson took a couple of steps back before sliding his passport into his pocket and nodded his head before walking away.

"Thank you," he said.

"Your room keys are here." Faisal slid the keys over the counter. Khan picked them both up and passed one to Jackson. The numbers 16 and 17 were written on them. The two men headed up to the first floor.

*****

It's 1300 hours and at the Pentagon, the team were returning to the 100-foot long room. Sheila was walking back from her office. The others were sat at the table. Those present all CIA senior figures: deputies and heads of departments.

"So, we have established that Afghanistan is the weakest link and we need to establish reasonable grounds to gain access to the region. What remains uncertain is how we go about conducting an operation which will give us those reasonable grounds," said Sheila. She opened her file, writing down the date and time, in readiness for what each of the individuals facing her had to say.

"So, we'll start with you, Mac. What are your thoughts?"

Mac held his hands together and is rubbing his fingers into one another.

"Well, the idea of a rogue element of the Russians. Some house supplying the local militia in say Afghanistan, so it's the Taliban, a missile which can shoot down one of our passenger airlines flying over the region," he said.

Sheila nodded, made some notes in her file and then nodded to Gerry.

"There's the option of releasing a chemical or biological agent. Some sort of capsule or phial, most probably tiny in size and easily transportable, somehow gets into the hands of the Taliban, and it's released at a given time and date amongst the residents of Manhattan. We could perhaps control who is in the vicinity at the time, but I'm guessing you'd need to have a death toll to give an impact of the magnitude that would be required," said Gerry.

Sheila made more notes and then looked at the next person, Todd.

"Hide them. We'd either go along the lines of hijacking an airplane and perhaps attempting to flee into a third-party country such as maybe Jordan," Todd said.

More notes, and Sheila shook her head.

"Not very imaginative, but nevertheless okay, point taken."

"Hacking into an airline has always been a possibility. For years Boeing has made a point of highlighting the issue and advising us, and it's high time that we use that to our advantage. Hack into an aircraft and when we know no one is in or behind the cockpit, take the plane out. If there were any hijacker or hijackers involved, the evidence would be eradicated, so we have to recreate that scenario," Andrew said.

Sheila put a tick next to that suggestion.

"Well done Andrew, very imaginative," she said, and turned to look at Donald.

Donald stood up and walked over to the white board located just behind him. He drew the Pentagon, the New York Twin Towers, a bridge of some sort, and a collection of airplanes and then put down the marker pen.

"For this to go ahead without any questioning of our intent, and any thought of whether there is a hidden agenda, we need to make this as brazen and brash as humanly possible. The Chinese would not allow us to conduct operations on their doorstep. I'm not talking about nuclear or chemical/biological weaponry because we can't control it; I'm talking about it spreading to areas other than where it's targeted. So, I think we'd need to hack into a fleet of US aircraft and fly them in coordination. They would need to happen simultaneously and the Air Force would be deployed to take out any opposition once these airlines are listed as a threat. We take out the Twin Towers. And the Pentagon. We ended the manifest to make it seem like the shady characters were on each of those planes. In fact, they could have been given an invitation to a specific job opportunity which you could never turn down, and from there, the airline bingo! As for the airline, it's remotely controlled as it's now been hacked, and the coordinates of the towers and the Pentagon are uploaded onto the onboard computer, making it easy to then work out the trajectory it needs to intersect that location," said Donald.

All around the room, mouths were wide open in shock. There was silence until Sheila started to nod her head, indicating approval.

"Certainly, Donald, that seems like something we need to do, and I notice you're the only one who mentioned how profoundly objectionable the Chinese will be in this. A nation turning up at the doorstep does need a valid reason like you suggested, and we will gather a consensus of a few dozen countries from around the world. We'll call it the coalition of the willing.

Sheila turned a few pages over and proceeded to make more notes. She then looked at the others and pointed her pen at them.

"On a given date and time, each of you will need to brief those high ranking officials in your departments whom you consider your most trustworthy co-patriots. I'd like to emphasize the word patriot. They'll need to attend as we will discuss the operation in greater detail. We'll most likely go ahead with the idea Donald suggested. The idea is of strikes across multiple locations using US aircraft, hacked remotely but made to look as if there were hijackers involved. So, let me repeat: you need to bring along the relevant bodies who you believe are best suited for us to conduct this mission as secretly and as effectively as possible without causing suspicion, meaning it must never get contagious.

Thanks, everyone. This meeting is terminated at 13:36."

She stood up, gathered her paperwork and walked away from the table towards the door leading to her office.

As everyone began to gather up paperwork ready to leave, all eyes turned to Donald.

"Well, folks, don't look at me like that. I'm sure their deaths will not be in vain. If they're true patriots, they shall sacrifice themselves for the greater good of the nation. Just think of and repeat the words of Abraham Lincoln, or any other great leader. We can interpret them and translate them to whichever way we need to for the greater good of the country, and I am a true patriot," said Donald.

Chapter 11
Shigar Fort Hotel

Jackson was in his hotel room. He wanted to go and have some food, but first had to unpack his equipment and baggage. He pulled out his holdall and from inside takes out what looks like an ID badge. It was his old ID badge together with a passport. He opened it, and there was a picture of a man, cleanly shaven, with the name Elijah Moses. The picture was of Jackson. Jackson was Elijah Moses. His old ID was from his role with the CIA, which gave him diplomatic immunity.

There was a knock on the door. It was Mr Khan.

"Mr Jackson, would you like to join me for dinner? The chef has prepared the traditional dish of North Pakistan today. Mutton biryani. My favorite. I'm sure you will love it."

Jackson put everything away quickly into his holdall and threw it onto a shelf in the cupboard.

"Hang on, I'll be with you in a second." he said.

Jackson quickly changed into something more comfortable, then joined Khan.

"Okay, let's get something to eat," he said.

They went downstairs. A table set for two was waiting for them. Mr Khan must have had some words with the catering staff.

In the middle of the table sat a large oval dish. It's laden with rice flavored with green saffron, cardamom leaves and ginger. Also on the table were cashew nuts and a large quantity of mutton.

"Sir, please," Khan gestured to Jackson that he should help himself.

"Oh, thank you. I'll just get a plate," said Jackson.

Jackson reached for a plate and began to carefully help himself to the rice, making sure that he had a taste of all the different ingredients. He turned to Mr Khan.

"So tell me, Khan, how's your family keeping? Which part of the country are you living in?"

Mr Khan turned and smiled at Jackson.

"Well, sir, I'm just a poor person trying to make an honest living. My son has leukemia. You understand, in Pakistan we don't have the medical resources here like you do in America. And my wife also is not very well these days. She sells woolen scarves in the market, but she is easily exhausted because she has a bone disorder. Her bones are slowly deteriorating. She only just makes it to the market once a day and back home, but, mashallah! She sells a few scarves through the day to make ends meet, should I say correctly. We are from a town in northern Pakistan. It's the town of Skardu, which sits in the valleys of the Himalayas. It has its own airport, which can accommodate large-sized passenger scheduled flights such as the Airbus A330. So, for example, Pakistan International airlines will fly there daily."

*****

There was a knock on Sheila McDaniel's door.

"Yes, come in," said Sheila.

A man entered her office. He was in military uniform.

"Ma'am, got a delivery for you," said the officer.

Sheila stood up and walked across to him. Her expression suggested she was expecting whatever this is.

"Thank you officer." She signed the consignment note and took the package with both hands. She walked over to her desk and proceeded to sit down and open it. The office door closed as the officer left the room.

It was a tablet device. She placed her hands on it and her face 30 cm from the screen, and it engaged... Once logged on, she had a list of contacts; she selected the first one down, which was Mac George.

"Hi Mac, I guess you received your package. Listen, this is the most secure way of communication. Our call here is encrypted, and only these devices can communicate with one another. There's seven of them, and it's impossible to add another device, so the others will be aware soon as they read my message. From now on everything we say or do regarding Spaceport Himalaya shall be done on these devices. We will refer to it as the code name 'shield', and will soon be arranging another meeting to discuss the exact timeframe and logistics of operation 'Spaceport Himalaya'. That'll be all for now. Thank you Mac. Goodbye," said Sheila.

She scrolled to messages and began to select video messaging and repeat pretty much what she'd just said to Mac. The camera was now activated, and her face was visible on the screen;

"Hello everybody. From now, all communications we have with regards 'Spaceport Himalaya' will be conducted via this device, referred to as the 'shield'. The 'shield' is encrypted to a very high degree. It's the most secure means of communication, and these seven are interconnected such that communication can only take place between the seven, and when communication does take place, it acts like a conference call – all the others will see the message simultaneously. Your 'shield' will require a login fingerprint and face recognition, so the risk of it falling into the wrong hands is almost eliminated. I'll be in touch very soon to discuss the operation," said Sheila.

Sheila swiped the selector across, and there was a bleep. The video was now saved and uploaded to the timeline call log. It was now able to be viewed from all seven devices. The 'shields' had been delivered to seven individuals in total, including herself. Mac George had one, Gerry Townsend another, Todd Gordon a third, Andrew Lopez a fourth, Donald Mann a fifth, and Bobby Singleton a sixth.

The packages were slowly but surely unwrapped, turned on and authenticated by each member of the group, with each of the devices acknowledging that Sheila's message had been read by each.

*****

It was early morning as Gail came rushing into Jared's office.

"Hey Jared, good morning. Hope you've done that little favor for me. I need it right away to get my ID badge reinstated, so please tell me you've got it done."

Jared nodded towards the tray but was reluctant to turn his head and look at Gail.

"Yes Gail, it's ready for you, on the top of the top letter tray. Help yourself," replied Jared.

*****

Downtown Los Angeles. Janet was sat at a table by the window in a diner. She checked her watch to see how far past the hour it is. She had agreed to meet Jeff, the police officer with the LAPD.

She saw a patrol car pull up outside the building.

Janet was relieved as the door opened and Jeff walked in.

*****

"Hey Federico, I got a letter from my department saying to come and collect my ID badge," said Gail.

"Be with you in just a second," said the security guard.

Gail put down the letter she had received so she could pull out any other information that she might be asked for, such as ID or proof of address.

"Good morning Ma'am," said the security guard as he walked over.

He picked up the letter, turned it round as it was facing the wrong way and walked over to his computer terminal. He typed something and then filed the letter away, but not before scanning it and emailing the security dept so they had a copy on electronic file as well. He opened and checked the e-version, and then went over to Gail again and picked up the two forms of ID and proceeded to scan them into the system as well.

"Ma'am, that's all done for you. If you'd like to take a seat and look at the camera, we'll take a fresh photo, and you're good to go."

Gail faced the camera. There was a flash. Picture done.

*****

Back at the diner, Jeff and Janet were sat side by side at the table by the window.

"There's something I meant to tell you about the newspaper headlines," said Janet. "Just today they showed that the Chinese have ambitions to go into space for mining and exploration."

"Janet, I'm just an everyday normal LAPD police officer. This is all above my head," said Jeff.

He ran his hands through his hair, his expression one of bewilderment tinged with concern. He sat back on his chair, shaking his head at the magnitude of the situation.

"Jeff, you're going to have to stay quiet with this, and not share it with any of your seniors, or you might find yourself reassigned or even worse out of a job. This situation is being handled by another agency, so we have to do our best to seem unaware, you okay with that?"

"Yes, I'm sure as hell keeping quiet about it. It's not like I can make an arrest, is it."

"So, what I need from you is a full manuscript of everything said by Jared, and hopefully we'll be able to work out what is going on. Is that okay?" said Janet.

"Well, I've got this, which is exactly what was said. It's been typed up using Dragon software, which the agency uses, and you can see the conversation. You take this copy. I will keep you updated, and let's say we meet tomorrow, same time, to catch up," said Jeff.

Janet pulled the sheets of paper over to her and had a brief look.

"Yes, sure, here same time tomorrow. I'll just run through with this and see why. What I can make out of it," said Gail.

*****

"Ma'am, I have your ID badge here for you," said the security guard.

Gail smiled and walked over to the front desk to collect her new badge. She then headed for Jared's office. She wanted to know all that she'd missed at the simulation event because of not having her badge. As she walked down the corridor to his office, she caught a glimpse of him through the glazing, and he spotted her and waved. She opened the door to his office and went in.

"Hi. I got my ID badge. Thank you. What on earth were you talking about when you mentioned CIA and that you'd been to the Pentagon?" she said.

Jared shook his head and looked at the ceiling.

"Well, wait 'til you hear this – the simulation was being followed by the CIA. There were two agents present: an agent Harrison and an agent Parker. The simulation result showed beyond doubt that the only place on the planet where a starship could be launched into space would be the Himalayas – that region and only that region, due to the altitude, and the length we'd need for a vertical run to accelerate the shuttle delivery system."

Gail nodded her head slowly.

"I suppose the CIA have their own jobs to do and if the Chinese are able to deliver a starship, and we're not... It has strategic implications as well as national security, and this is what the CIA is acting on, from the vibes I got. And their initial talks didn't sound pleasant either," said Jared.

"Yeah? What do you mean?" asked Gail.

"I'm sure from what I understood they're talking about blue on blue: that is to say, causing casualties amongst our own for the cause of gaining access to the region. From what I gathered…"

Gail was open-mouthed, her expression one of alarm. She shook her head in disbelief.

"That's bloody awful. We're really looking to build at literally any cost?? I always viewed these projects as performance targets, and it was a program, but I guess with all the money the agencies are receiving, the Heads are looking for answers and don't want to hear a no."

Jared stood up and headed over to his door, which stood ajar, and softly closed it. He walked back to his desk and sat restlessly right on its edge, half his bottom hanging off the edge. He looked at Gail.

"There's more. This CNN reporter, who was caught out by the CIA trying to gain access by sneaking into their vehicles. On that same morning you rang. Do you know anything about her? Have you met her?"

Gail gazed around the room, and then down towards Jared's feet. She began to nod her head;

"Yes, that's right, it was that morning I went to Derek's office to brief him with regards to our simulation. I bumped into her outside the building. I had dropped some paperwork and she picked it up and handed it back to me. She introduced herself and later that day gave me a lift as well as my car failed to start. Janet. Janet from the CNN newsroom, that TV news organization. She is a science and technology correspondent there. Why are you asking?"

"Well, because the CIA has briefed us that we are to speak to nobody outside the organization, and certainly not the press. So, whatever she knows is certainly not because anyone has said anything, in theory. All we can do now is hang on and wait for instructions. Until then, just do your job," said Jared.

Gail's expression suggested she was remembering something which worried her.

"Yes, of course, that's exactly what we can do. Thanks again for my ID card. I'm heading off to my office and to catch up with the others as it's been a while since I've been around." Said Gail.

Gail turned and left Jared's office, closing the door softly behind her and heading straight to the bathroom. She entered and walked over to the wash basins. Behind her, the soft-close door was squeaking before the 'thud' of it shutting. Gail's eyes turned to the door to make certain it had closed. Then she took her mobile phone out of her pocket.

The dial tone could be heard, then a voice. The line crackled and Gail pulled the phone away from her ear slightly as it was uncomfortable.

"Hi Gail, I'm so happy that you rang. I was so looking forward to hearing from you. Is everything okay and have you managed to sort your car out?" said Janet.

"Yes, my car is fine. I was wondering if we could meet up soon as I have something I'd like to share with you; something which I shouldn't be saying over the phone."

"Of course, any time you want me, just say and I'll come straight over. You're the most valuable person I know right now ..." Janet sniggered.

"You know the food diner opposite the LAPD building?" said Gail.

"Yes I do."

Chapter 12
Brainstorm

"8 o'clock this evening."

"Gotcha, I'll be right there," said Janet.

At the Pentagon, Sheila was at her desk. She selected meetings on her shield and created a video of herself. She tilted the device so it has her face clearly visible, and pressed start.

"Strategy meeting, the first of many. I want you all here tomorrow morning, and I hope you've now sourced all your patriots," said Sheila.

Without even a hello, good morning, hi or any form of greeting, Sheila hit straight to the underlying message, it's a cold, ruthless organization, the CIA.

Her video had been uploaded and was now available for viewing by the others on their shield devices.

It was almost 8 PM in the evening, and an uber was stationary at a set of traffic lights in downtown L.A.. Janet was sat in the back with her mobile in her hand. She was following herself on google maps, on her mobile device and trying to establish how far she was from the diner where she was meeting up with Gail.

The Uber drew up outside the diner. It was a classic red and white diner which had had students eating there since the 1950s, although it may have been revamped since. With all the blinds rolled up, all customers inside were clearly visible from the outside. Janet thanked the driver, climbed out of the vehicle and headed towards the door to the diner. As she entered, there was a bell-like sound. A face turned to look at her from behind the counter.

A fifty-something lady with curly hair, chewing bubble-gum. She turned to look at the wall clock after seeing her enter.

Janet walked over to the counter as she didn't spot Gail anywhere.

"Hey there, are you Janet?" asked the lady behind the counter.

"Yes."

The lady pulled out a note from under the bar and slid it over to her.

"I've got this to give you."

Janet took the note and opened it. 'There is a lobby bar at the Renaissance Los Angeles Airport hotel as my flight is running late be there. Gail'

Janet looked up at the ceiling, and sighed. She took out her phone and selected the Uber app. She began to type 'Renaissance'. It appeared: 'Renaissance at LAX', Selecting it as her destination, she saw it display one minute to arrive.

"Thanks very much," she said to the lady behind the counter.

Janet walked outside and decided to light a cigarette while she waited, but she only managed one breath of smoke before her uber ride appeared. It was a white Toyota. She dropped the cigarette on the pavement and opened the car door. It had a black leather interior, which was a sharp contrast to its white paintwork.

"Renaissance LAX?" asked the driver.

"Yes, yes, please. Quick as you can." said Janet.

Ten minutes later the car reached the airport hotel. She thanked the driver and opened the door the moment the car stops, jumping out and rushing into the lobby. As she entered, she noticed it was newly renovated, and looking very modern and chic, reminiscent of an artist's studio. Certain features seemed Venetian. She spotted Gail, who was in a pink dress. She was at the bar with a man. Gail felt as if she was known to this man and Gail and he were having a discussion. Janet walked across, and Gail noticed her.

"Oh, am I glad to see you, Janet!" said Gail.

"Who is your man?" Janet asked.

"Well, let's first sit down, find ourselves a table," said Gail.

Gail found a corner sofa and a chair with a couple of tables. There was even a power socket built into the sofa unit. Jeff sat in the chair. Gail sat on one side of the sofa while Janet walked around to the other side, On one of the tables Gail put down what looked like a manuscript of some sort.

"Janet, this is Jeff. He is an officer with the LAPD, and he is with the special task force which combats organized crime. He can access phone records and conversations of calls of anyone in the USA. What I have here are transcribed conversations of individuals within NASA, and other such organizations. What's alarming is that you to chatter seems to be giving the idea that there is going to be a blue on blue attack," said Gail.

"Blue on blue. I'm guessing that's our defense organization harming our own people or military personnel?" said Janet.

"That's correct; we spoke about this before, so Jeff here has printed out the transcribed files," said Gail. "We have a whole bunch of recent telephone conversations that have been recorded and transcribed by software from the audio file to a typed document."

Janet picked up the pile of papers bound together and started to look through them. After a moment, her eyes widen. Specific keywords had been highlighted, words that emphasize harm, death, and destruction, intent and guilt in a threatening nature, or one being threatened, et cetera. Then, suddenly she spotted a name: Derek White! Her mouth opened wide.

"That's... that's your father," exclaimed Janet.

She was looking directly at Gail, and Jeff, and she repeated the words as though the pair never heard it the first time.

"That's your father, Derek White!"

Janet looked back at the transcript and read it out loud.

"We cannot have the goddamn Chinese up there with a starship above our heads, waving their damn Willies down at us. At US!"

"Is that what your father said?" said Janet. "Oh my god!"

Jeff reached out and put his hand on Janet's arm.

"Ma'am, I can assure you, these are official audio transcripts which have been obtained by the LAPD, Special Crimes Taskforce. And yes, that's your father, Gail. However, nothing more of this will be said."

Gail reached out and grabbed the transcript and looked at Derek's name with her own eyes. Until then, she was in disbelief. She spots the name Derek White and turned to look up at the Venetian ceiling with its ornate art decor.

"Mom was right, he is a sleazy bastard."

"This sort of information we've been collecting helps us to paint a picture, and so far, all indications are pointing at that the agencies are planning on sending many scientists across from different organizations to Afghanistan and Pakistan," said Jeff.

"And why would that be?"Janet asked.

"Well, I'm guessing for the simple reason of carrying out research into the geology, terrain and simply what's in the ground," said Gail.

A waiter came round with a tray, tidying up the adjacent table which had empty glasses left on it and walked over to the three.

"Good evening, may I get you anything?" he asked.

Gail put her hand up.

"May I have some sparkling water please, lemon and ice. Thank you," she said.

Janet turned to the waiter;.

"And one for me too; in fact, make that three, and also a whiskey and Coke please."

Janet reached into her bag and dug out her purse, from which she took her CNN issued credit card and handed it to the waiter by placing it down on his tray.

"Oh, Janet. Are you sure?" said Gail.

"Yes, it's all fine. My news agency has upped the credit limit on the card, so the least I can do is offer to get drinks for you guys."

Janet put her purse back in her bag and pointed her finger at Jeff.

"And talking about credit limit, I think it's high time that I fly across to Afghanistan and Pakistan with my cameraman… second thoughts… actually … leave the cameraman out. I'm ready for anything that might arise, which from the look of these transcriptions won't be long in coming? I'll make some hotel reservations tonight and book my flights."

Jeff gazed to her and was lost for words somewhat, reluctant to say any more. But he guessed that was her job. She was playing a dangerous game, being an investigative journalist.

"Just make sure to keep in touch. It's good to know you're safe and sound. You never know with these people – you could well be the next target," said Gail.

Jeff nodded his head in agreement.

"Well, if you're heading that way, I'm a great admirer of the Serena Hotels brand, they're run by the Aga Khan Trust. They're renowned for the best quality service in that part of Pakistan, the northern areas," he said.

Janet smiled and nodded her head while clutching hold of her handbag.

"May I, may I have these?" she asked.

Jeff quickly put his hand over the transcriptions he'd brought along and shook his head vigorously.

"No, certainly not, I'm sorry but like I said I'm afraid this is all classified, more than my job's worth. This is not even supposed to be printed."

Janet nodded her head. She knocked back her whiskey and Coke, and loaded the Uber app once more on her mobile phone and booked a ride.

"Thank you very much, Jeff, for your help. It's been a pleasure meeting you, and hopefully we shall meet again soon. I'm going to have to take off. If there is anything more, just email me – you'll find my email on the CNN website on the science and technology page. I really need a cigarette before I get my cab. See you soon."

*****

Skardu airport. It was a tiny airport with domestic flights arriving from the major cities of Pakistan. There were very few of the facilities you would find in larger, busier, more international airports, as it was literally the size of a ten Pin Bowling Alley and attached car park.

Jackson was waiting at the conveyor. He was waiting to collect baggage as he had just flown in from the capital city Islamabad. While he was waiting, he pulled out of his pocket a marketing leaflet showing a hotel. It was a hotel set in an idyllic location in the valleys of the Himalayas.

It was a former castle, which had been converted into a hotel by a charity organization known as the Aga Khan foundation trust.

Apparently, 90% of the profits are donated back to the local population, and only 10% retained by the heirs. He turned the page around, and its name was in bold letters at the top: Hotel Serena, Skardu.

Just then the conveyor belt started to roll. Jackson put away the leaflet and was waiting patiently, his gaze fixed on the incoming baggage.

He spotted his holdalls, their yellow and black North Face branding, 70 liter and 90 liter in size, two of each. He edged his trolley forward and picked them up one at a time in a hurried manner so as no not let one go by. He began to leave the small airport baggage claim area and was soon outside, where he saw the clear blue skies and the lush valleys.

The mountains were clearly visible in the distance, seeming much closer than they were due to their size.

He was told by Mr Khan that full-sized commercial airlines landed here, which was the case, as he had just arrived in one. Mr Khan was traveling up by road with his Toyota off-road jeep, so Jackson was getting picked up by the hotel's complimentary transfer service. Just then, he spotted a silver looking minibus with Serena Hotels written on the side. The driver saw Jackson and approached him right away, guessing correctly from Jackson's western clothes and appearance, and knowing his name was Jackson, that he was a foreigner.

"Hello, Mr Jackson, I am pleased to see you," said the driver.

He came forward with his hands outstretched to take the holdalls.

"Thank you, be very careful. There are electronics and instruments in those bags. Hello! You heard what I just said! Gently!" exclaimed Jackson.

Once in the vehicle, the first thing the driver made Jackson aware of was the journey time.

"Sir, our journey to the hotel should take us about one hour; there are two check posts on the way. In the meantime, make yourself comfortable in the back."

"One hour! Hey, that's a lot longer than I thought it would take! I'm guessing due to roads meandering around the valleys and the mountains and not traveling straight," said Jackson.

*****

Back inside the 100-feet long room at the Pentagon. On the table were everyone's shield devices.

Chapter 13
The Doctor

"Catching up from where we left off, you were to bring along trusted aids and patriots... Andrew, I see you've brought someone along with you. Can you please introduce him to the group. I'd like to hear what he has to say," said Sheila

Andrew turned to look at his aide beside him.

"This is Dr Ishmael, who has been conducting research on hypnosis. So today I have asked him to come along with a presentation of his work in his field, which I think would be very useful in the so-called blue on blue spectacular. Dr Ishmael, if you will, please," said Andrew.

"Good day ladies and gentlemen. I am Dr Ishmael, I am a specialist in the field of hypnosis. Hypnosis is the induction of a state of consciousness in which a person apparently loses the power of voluntary action and becomes highly responsive to suggestion, or direction. Its use in therapy, typically to recover suppressed memories or to allow modification of behavior. Let me plug this USB in the monitor, I have a recording which I would like to play for you."

He walked over to a monitor on the wall which has a USB port on the side. There's no computer, eliminating any possibility of hacking, exchanging or even stealing data. It's turned on, the USB drive was pushed into the side by the doctor, and of the options that appears on the screen the doctor picked a video file named experiment number 123.

The video began to play. A man was sitting in a chair. He was being interviewed by a man in a white coat. There was a camera and a microphone in the room, but nothing else.

"Can you look out of the window, Charlie, and tell me what color the sky is today?" said the man in the white coat.

"It's pink, Dr Charlie," said the man, referred to as Subject:123.

The doctor nodded his head with approval, and said;

"That's right, Charlie, can you now tell me where we are going today?" asked the doctor in the white coat.

"Yes, I can. We are flying to the moon, Doctor," said Subject:123.

"Charlie, can you show me your boarding card?" asked the doctor.

Subject:123 walked over to his coat, which was hanging on a hook on the wall and pulled out a boarding card which he showed the doctor. The camera focused on it, and it was clearly visible on the monitor screen. It showed a flight number, flying to the moon.

"Yes, I see your boarding card. That's good, thank you, Charlie. Now, what would you like to have for your dinner? And anything to drink?" said the doctor. Subject:123 went to put his boarding card back in his coat pocket, and replied;

"Steak and kidney pie with chips would be nice, or maybe lasagna, and to drink, a bottle of red wine and some still mineral water. Thank you."

The video now stopped, and Dr Ishmael walked back to his chair, where he sat down. He turned to look at all the group members before looking straight at Sheila.

"Subject:123 is a perfectly normal, healthy, fit man of around about 40 years of age. He has undergone hypnosis and is programmed to carry out specific instructions. He believes the sky is pink as you can see. Once he arrives at the airport, he is boarding a flight to the moon. In his subconscious, his own mind, he has no idea he has being hypnotized or gone under hypnosis. He has a concept of taking a flight to the moon, which is perfectly normal, and he's just a passenger, just like all the others and will sit in his seat and do no more."

Sheila turns to look at the rest of the group.

"Very ingenious. I must say I am impressed, Andrew. What do you suggest?" she asked.

"Well, we can carry out this process with a dozen or so subjects who travel as passengers on various flights from across the country. These subjects will be of Middle Eastern origin. Using the airline hacking facility envisaged by DARPA we remotely operate these flights to specific targets such as New York, the Pentagon, etc. To the general public these individuals will seem as though they were the hijackers."

Sheila turned around to look at Donald.

"And what's your verdict on this, Donald? I'd like your feedback on this notion."

"Andrew, and Sheila, this is superb. If we can get these bodies in the planes and they're all of Middle Eastern origin, and all the planes come down, our problem is solved. Once the flights are downed, passengers' names shall be searched on the flight log. Let's have handed to us by agencies working closely with us a group of middle eastern operatives who are all known to have sympathies for jihadist organizations! We're all cooking on gas, and I'm with that 100%."

"Well, listen guys, I'm going to select September as the month, and let's select a date. Any suggestions?" said Sheila.

Sound mutters from the other side of the room. It was Todd.

"What was that Todd?" she asked.

"I said it would be ideal if we can match a date with something which is commonly spoken on the telephone as it won't get picked up by law enforcement and won't be so alarming. For instance, our date of independence or Christmas Day, or Thanksgiving, or even 911. That would work. 911. September 11, so we call it '911'," said Todd – his Head of Analysis 'hat' firmly in place.

While looking on a calendar on the shield device, Sheila pointed at Todd while nodding her head and then slapped her hand down on the table as if she's swatting a fly.

"I like that! Yes! Thanks, Todd will go ahead with that 911 idea, people. It's not just about the Porsche car or the emergency services responding, but more to do with the Jewish calendar. Even more, looking on the calendar, that's the kind of day which I wanted, does anybody know why?" said Sheila.

Everybody looked at each other, all trying to guess and see if anyone else guesses, but nobody did.

"Marvelous, Todd – let's go with that," said Sheila.

Sheila held her arms out wide, looking all everyone...

"Come on guys, we got to make sure that no goddamn Jews are around that day. We can't be harming no Zionists. Otherwise we'll be in right up the shit street. The guys have got their fingers in everything... goddamn fucking MOSSAD," said Sheila.

That was the Israeli secret service, MOSSAD: it stood for 'HaMossad leModi'in uleTafkidim Meyuḥadim'.

Everybody looked at one another; a certain few tried to hide their reaction, while others managed to look as though nothing alarming had been said. Mac George put his finger up and said;

"Tuesday, September 11th is in. According to the Jewish calendar, Tishri 5779. It's when candles are lit, they cook a dish on the evening of the second day of Rosh Hashanah, that sort of thing, I guess."

Donald put his thumb up and nodded his head while looking at Dr Ishmael. He now pointed his finger towards Dr Ishmael, and Dr Ishmael started to nod his head too. There was an acknowledgment. He was pleased he was due to get approval for funding.

Dr Ishmael had been working on the hypnosis project for some time. The agency was due to cut its funding next month. But as of today, the scales had tipped.

"So, Tuesday September 11th will be the day as they'll be off celebrating their customs, whatever, and out of government buildings, so it won't be an issue. Are we all in agreement?" said Sheila.

The room was quiet, and Sheila pointed at Donald and Andrew before saying;

That's it for now, folks; I've selected that as the date, so can you all reach for your shield devices and acknowledge the date set. That concludes our meeting. Thank you."

*****

Outside 601 New Hampshire Avenue, north west Washington, DC 20037 there was an emblem of a green palm tree with a pair of swords laid beneath it, resembling a cross, surrounded by a gold circular frame with a star-like outer rim. It was the emblem of the Saudi Arabian Embassy.

Massive iron gates opened and a series of US administrative vehicles drove in, all with government number plates. A long driveway led the cars to the Fourier where they stop.

The doors opened and out stepped Mac George, Andrew Lopez, Donald Mann and security staff.

The team had entered the lobby and were waiting for further instructions as to the whereabouts of the ambassador. Just then, doors opened, and a voice could be heard;

"Gentlemen, if you would like to come this way," said a man in traditional Saudi attire.

There was a tray of refreshments offered to the CIA team, and also hand towels which were slightly damp and fragranced. There was a second tray which had dates.

They were now all sat in a massive room with neatly arranged sofas around the perimeter. Everything seemed very sparkley and was very light in color. The decor was Arabian bling, yet the building itself was of Georgian architecture. Doors opened, and the Saudi ambassador Mahmood walked in fashionably late. He approached the CIA team and began to shake their hands.

"Hello Gentlemen, I am delighted to be at your service. I have been looking forward to meeting with you. May I thank you again for the vital defense cooperation and trade we have, or shall I say you have agreed to offer us in exchange for our oil."

Ambassador Mahmoud walked around and took a seat on the end sofa. He must speak up a little as the room was so big.

"So, gentlemen, what has brought you here today?"

Mac George looked at his deputies before proceeding.

"Ambassador Mahmoud, we have today come to request from you some assistance in helping us to improve further our bilateral relations, in particular with regards defense. What we already have between our two countries concerning intelligence, we'd like to extend."

The ambassador nodded his head.

"Ambassador Mahmoud, prevention is better than cure. So, what we propose to do is embark on a new program, not just where we share information and intelligence which we gather out in the field. We start with having access to all those who are detained by your country, in the prisons, in the camps. I understand that you have a program whereby you de-radicalize them and put some on the correct path by offering them access to facilities such as entertainment, sports and their own rooms etc.. What we would like is to fly a team of our own specialists over to interview them, just to gather information which you might have missed, and to learn from any findings with regards changes we can make in our country too. As you know, here in the USA there are over 2 million incarcerated. I'm sure you'll agree it's not asking much to want to reduce that number."

"That seems fine as we are working together, with a duty to aid each other as best as we can. If interviewing or interrogating our subjects offers you reassurance, then it shall be," said the ambassador.

He was smiling, his large teeth sparkling just like the very grand Swarovski Crystal chandelier right above his head. He nodded his head and began to laugh. His waved a hand to his aides, indicating they should offer the visitors more drinks. A man came forward with a tray of crystal glasses filled with what seemed like flavored water. They all at least try it, as it would be rude to refuse.

"Please, try the dates, they're fresh from Saudi Arabia, just arrived today," said the ambassador.

"Mr Ambassador, you need to give us a contact in Saudi Arabia, who we can arrange to meet when we travel across. We are looking at possibly flying over next week with a team of about a dozen people. What we ask for is we are given the opportunity to interview each subject individually and privately, as any distraction, coercion or threat would render the interview pointless. Is that okay?" said Todd.

"Sir, whatever you need, we will provide for you. I will speak to the Minister of Interior and make sure the General Directorate of Corrections is informed. I will endeavor to make sure he understands what you need and is expecting your arrival. Are you okay for accommodation?" said Ambassador Mahmoud.

"Yes, we'll have our embassy arrange accommodation. Although, it depends on the location of your sites. Perhaps we could confirm this with you at a later point?" said Mac.

"CIA deputy, Mr George, whatever your wishes – you can call me if you have any issues or concerns, and I will make sure everything is resolved speedily. You have my word. You have my promise," the ambassador replied.

Just then, Andrew reached into his Filofax and pulled out a USB stick, which he passed to Mac;

"Is it possible, while we are here, that you can give us the details and locations of all your facilities in Saudi. Where these inmates are being re-educated and reintroduced to society, and society's expectations?" asked Andrew.

The ambassador walked across to Mac and took the USB and then walked over to his aide and whispered a few words at him. His assistant nodded and walked away.

The room went quiet while the ambassador poured himself some tea. It was black tea with some leaves in it, possibly mint. After helping himself, he walked back over to his chair, and gestured to the tea;

"Please, do help yourself. I have sent my administrator. He will be uploading the information and should be down shortly."

Just then there was a call to prayer. In the Arab and Muslim world it is referred to as the Azan. Everybody in the building other than a few security personnel gathered in a straight line in an adjoining room to conduct an orchestrated prayer ceremony, consisting of standing in a line shoulder to shoulder. There's bowing with both hands on the knees and kneeling down with the forehead and nose touching the earth, while hands flat on the floor. This sequence is repeated numerous times throughout the prayer, until at the end, the head turns once to the right and once to the left, while saying twice 'peace be upon you'. Andrew Lopez is fluent in Arabic and understood everything being said.

"I'm guessing you, Andrew, followed that easily did you not?" asked Mac, turning his gaze away from the group performing the prayer to look at his colleague.

"Yes, I understood it all," said Andrew.

After a short while, the same administrator who left with the USB stick returned and handed it to the ambassador. While doing so, he whispered a few words, and then left. The ambassador, now smiling, took hold of Mac's hand and put the USB stick into it, closing Mac's fingers around it.

"You have what you came for; you will find everything on here. If there is anything more I can do, just ask," said the ambassador.

*****

Gail burst through the door and slammed it shut behind her. She was in Derek's office. Derek was stood by the window with his back to Gail, trimming his little bonsai tree.

"I thought you'd be coming down; I had a sneaky feeling," said Derek.

"Father, what is the agency up to? I have a sneaky feeling that the research we have conducted and the findings we have discovered have led to increased hostility and will lead to even more so – possibly even harm to people!" said Gail.

She walked over and sat down on a chair in front of the desk. Derek turned around and gazed at her. He had his specs on that were not bifocal. He wore them on the edge of his nose and looked above them to look at her.

"My dear. You know all the work that we do here is closely scrutinized by central government. After all, it must first be assessed, and only then can we be authorized to leak the findings to the press. As you are quite well aware, we are not to disseminate, disclose or publish anything unless it has been authorized. So, on this matter, I can't say any more."

Gail cradled her head in her hands, and she closed her eyes as though fighting a blinding headache.

"Dad, it's something about blue on blue. What on earth is it all about?" exclaimed Gail.

Derek was about to walk towards his desk when his gaze suddenly turned to Gail. He had this nervous, guilty look.

"I don't know, Honey. If you look up at the sky, it is blue, the future is bright and all ahead of you. You have your whole life ahead so go find yourself a husband and start a family."

Gail was fuming. She looked around as one doing a recce of a room to see what was available to throw – on this occasion, at her father.

"Dad, Mother was right. You are a sleazy bastard, I'd hate to think what's going on in your head right now. Just imagine, you will die with all that guilt and sin. I don't want to be in the same room as you anymore. And isn't that Mother's bonsai tree!"

Gail stood up, looked at the bonsai tree, shook her head and went to walk out of the room. Before opening the door she turned to her father one last time;

"Asshole!"

"I'll just pretend I haven't heard anything," said Derek.

Outside the CNN news agency, Janet was marching up to the main doors on her way to visit Timothy. After a few moments, she arrived at the floor, where she gets accosted by a few work colleagues who are keen to know what she has been working on. Maybe rumors have spread that her monthly expenditure budget has been increased.

"Hi Janet, it's good to see you. We were all wondering if you'd like to join us for Joe's stag do tonight. We could really do with your company," said Sharon, news journalist for sports coverage.

Janet had a bag of nachos in her hand, soon as she heard Sharon utter those words, would you like to join us, Janet takes out one large nacho and puts it in her mouth and begins to crunch on it, drowning out in her head the sound of her colleague's talking.

"No, I can't. Too much on my plate," said Janet with a mouthful of nachos.

She certainly did have a lot on her plate – those nachos which she now handed over to Sharon. Janet walked off to Timothy's office. The door was ajar. Janet walked in and quietly closes the door, then waited patiently for Timothy to acknowledge her presence.

"Hello Janet, nice to see you. I'll be with you in just a second."

He finished off signing that night's editorial listing, then turned to Janet.

"Janet, progress update please – have you got anything yet?"

Janet walked around the room, giving Timothy minimal eye contact.

"Well, I have been told of official audio files which have been transcribed into written format, and these I have seen and read through. Unfortunately, I couldn't obtain the actual copies, but it gives me without a shadow of a doubt suspicion that something sinister is being planned. Coupled with all the knowledge we have, and the information I have put together, I will be packing my bags and heading for exactly where I don't know yet, but I'll start with flying to Islamabad. Because I think it's good to get in early and create contacts, friends, and I am sure all this will prove to be fruitful later.

"Well, Janet, the best advice is, follow the money!" said Timothy.

"So, this is what I've come to see you about, Timothy. For an indefinite period I want to be stationed in that part of the world until I see any other viable option."

"Super, well, looks like you'd better get your bags packed then!"

Janet smiled and walked over to Timothy, extending her arm. They shook hands.

"Just before I go, there is one more thing," said Janet.

She had a dress pin attached to her blouse. She pulled it apart, and exposed a small microchip which she put on Timothy's desk. She passed him a USB adapter;

"Insert that chip into the adapter, and plug it into your computer. You will see the transcribed files which I wasn't able to obtain. I purchased this device with the limit on my credit card. I felt it was worth $5000. That's your first prize."

Janet gave Timothy a thumbs-up and with a smile left the room, looking confident giving the impression she was a sexy diva and an attractive woman who could flirt her way out of anything. The door closed behind her as she vacated the CNN building.

*****

It was 50°C in the scorching desert heat and it was already taking a pounding on the entourage. The team was headed by Mac George, except he was not there. They were at Riyadh international Airport in Saudi Arabia, also known as King Khaled International airport.

As the team had just left a C-17 military cargo plane, the passenger docking facility afforded to scheduled and charter commercial airlines could not be utilized. So, the team from the CIA and the scientists headed by Dr Ishmael walked out and climbed into a convoy of black SUVs which have blacked out windows. Dr Ishmael got into one, and his aides join him, while Todd and Andrew entered another one. There was also a whole host of other individuals not to mention security personnel. All in all, there are six vehicles, all SUVs, which were the preferred choice of car in this part of the world. The American Embassy here in Riyadh was one of the biggest in the world.

The team drove in a synchronized manner, keeping in a straight line and maintaining a single file, as they traveled to the terminal.

Inside the building, it resembled more a five-star hotel lounge than an airport, with an abundance of marble and chandeliers. Marble rather than glass due to the intense solar radiation emitted by the sun in this part of the world. There was a whole array of water fountains dotted around the terminal building, while the building design itself is of geometric shapes decorated in geometric patterns.

The team passed through an area designated for diplomats and VIPs. The entire crew had been afforded the privilege of a USA diplomatic passport, thus eliminating the need for a Visa and giving unhindered access to the US Embassy building in Riyadh.

Due to the diplomatic status, the entire entourage would be free from the risk of prosecution and arrest.

One by one they walked up to the counter at passport control and had their passports scanned.

"Assalamualaykum, good day Sir," said Todd.

His passport was handed back to him. He walked past, and Andrew walked up. The passport got scanned... until the entire team, within a few minutes of arrival, had their status processed and had cleared immigration control.

"Well, Hilton Riyadh here we come," said Andrew.

The entire entourage had now collected their baggage and was heading out of the airport towards the Hilton Hotel in Riyadh. It was expected to be a 30 km drive, taking approximately 22 minutes.

The driver turned around to Todd;

"Sir, as per our itinerary we're due to head to the Hilton Hotel Riyadh. Is that correct?"

Both Todd and Andrew turned to the driver and briefly interrupted each other;

"Yes, that's correct."

Andrew pulled out his Filofax. Inside, he had a web page printout of the amenities that the hotel had to offer. He carefully ran his finger down the list, searching for something. He saw the phrase 24-hour bar;

"I sure as hell hope they're offering alcohol as I am dying for a Jack Daniels," said Andrew.

"Well, I have been trying to become teetotal for years. Just hasn't worked out for me. I don't think it is going to, either!" said Todd.

The entourage was driving along the highway through a desert-like landscape. It was just the odd palm tree and grass only where it had been nurtured. Halfway through the journey, there was a vast university complex. The University Princess Noura Bint Abdul Rahman University. It was renowned for its education throughout the Middle East and the world. There were a certain few within the CIA who have studied here too, as the agency liked to recruit from a wide array, broadening the range of ability, and knowledge and experience of the outside world that staff had.

The first on the list was known as the Mohammed bin Nayef counselling and care center, based on the outskirts of Riyadh. Its history goes as far back as when the Saudi Prince Mohammed bin Nayef bin Abdulaziz, son of a deputy prime minister and a deputy minister for security was keen on addressing the issue and took the initiative of inaugurating the program in the year 2007. This after a series of terrorist attacks, which also included kidnappings and bombs.

The satnav is saying five minutes to the destination.

"Hey, I was wondering if they'd be doing cocktails in the minibar? In this rehabilitation center," said Andrew.

"Yes, sure, just not your type," said Todd, smirking at him.

"Hey, driver do the other vehicles' occupants know we're going to the Hilton Hotel first?" asked Andrew.

The driver's gaze remained on the road ahead as he replied;

"That's an affirmative, Sir."

Later, after the group had checked into the hotel, the plan was to visit the center. It was a facility in Saudi Arabia intended to reintegrate former jihadists into the mainstream of Saudi culture. The Center is in an old resort which got converted and is complete with swimming pools and other recreational activities, afforded to these once enemy combatants.

Just then a large Hilton Hotels sign appeared, and the vehicles turned off to the right, onto Abu Jaffar Al Mansoor Street, the hotel and other residences now clearly visible. There were two towers, both colored white with an abundance of glass. Each tower was in the shape of a triangle. The cars passed through security barriers and drove onto a raised entrance which led into the hotel foyer, which is shaded and almost half covered by a canopy which extended from the inside of one of the towers, out across halfway onto the entrance. The sunlight was shimmering off the panes of glass, causing it to appear colored, from sky blue to a subtle bronze further down as the sand reflected off the façade. An array of palm trees completed a rather majestic, picture postcard scene. And there were people walking, many in pairs, in brilliant white attire, head to toe.

The vehicles all entered the foyer and came to a halt.

Andrew left the SUV he was in and headed for the rear car containing Dr Ishmael.

"Hi folks, you'd better check yourselves in as you got a long day ahead of you."

The hotel was a five-star, and had a five-star service. The concierge gestured for luggage trolleys to be brought out, and four porters appeared each with a trolley. Just as the SUV in which Dr Ishmael sat had its tailgate opened, one of the porters started unloading luggage. One of the bags fell on the floor, from which there emerged a host of paperwork – what looked like a list of flights detailing airline names, flight numbers, departure and landing times.

"You fool, can't you see what you're doing!" Dr Ishmael exclaimed.

He rushed across and grabbed hold of the paperwork and hurriedly stuffed it back in the bag.

"Sorry Sir, sorry Sir, sorry Sir," said the porter nervously, while he rearranged his hat.

With his hat straight, he was confident enough to start to load the bags once more. He seemed of Bangladeshi appearance, as is usually the case. Seldom do you find a Saudi citizen working as a porter in a hotel?

Once at the check-in desk. The group soon realized that the deputy directors get the presidential suites when staying away, which is perhaps why they were checking in to a five-star hotel. So, Andrew, Todd and Bobby checked in at the platinum desk, while the others make do with queues at the regular (wood veneer) desk.

*****

Back at NASA we're at Jared's office. Just as he was checking his emails, he noticed one from the CIA. It was making him aware that he has been put forward and shortlisted for a promotion, which involves relocating out of town with the incentive of a 300% pay rise plus expenses. Relocation was not an issue – he was single and didn't have children. He nodded to himself, smiling while raising his wrist to look at the time.

"This calls for a celebration," he exclaimed.

Then, further down in the email he spotted something a little nerve-wracking. It stated that he needed to get his immunizations done – his polio vaccine, etc.

Well, no time like the present. He picked up the phone handset and dialed his doctor's surgery.

"Hello, it's Jared Neal."

"Okay, just hold on a moment and let me find you," said the receptionist at the surgery.

There was a brief pause, and Jared used the time to continue reading the rest of the email.

"What is it you're ringing for?" asked the receptionist.

"Oh, immunizations. I'm going abroad."

"Okay, I see, well, we've got tomorrow afternoon. 4:30 PM, with the nurse. Can you make sure you arrive 10 minutes early to fill in some forms."

"I shall do so. Thank you very much."

Jared hung up.

*****

Janet was sitting in her car looking out of the windscreen at the Starbucks she has just been in. She took a mouthful of her bagel before calling Timothy, her editor.

The phone was ringing.

"Hi, hello there, how are you getting on Janet, my lovely?" Timothy greeted her.

Mumbling as she had just taken a mouthful, she just about managed to speak;

"I just thought I'd let you know I've submitted my Visa application and handed my passport in," said Janet.

"And what embassy is that with, may I ask?" he inquired.

"Pakistan, Thought I'd start there." She said.

"Okay, that's the spirit; remember to keep me posted. You're my golden girl, Janet."

Janet took one more large bite out of her bagel which she was holding in one hand, while the other hand holding her phone managed to drop it in her handbag, hanging up on her editor in the process.

"Shit!" She grabbed the phone and redialed Timothy's number. He answers immediately;

"Yes, Janet?"

"Just one more thing – the normal time for processing a visa is 10 days, but it's extended to 30 days for some bizarre reason. It still says 10 days on the website, but I was notified that due to extenuating circumstances it's 30 days, so I'll just do some research on the region while I'm at home."

"Oh, I see. That's bizarre," said Timothy.

Janet proceeded to hang up the phone and throw it back in her bag, and as she did so, stuffed the remainder of her bagel in her mouth.

*****

Later that evening, the team sat in the bar in the lobby of the hotel in Riyadh.

"Listen, Todd, I've got some investors interested in short selling, I guess when all this eventually takes fruition, the markets will be very jittery and it could be a good time to make the right move before the spectacular," said Andrew.

"Well, I guess it's a vicious world out there, and the boys with the money are ruthless. I wouldn't be surprised one goddamn bit if you're right. However, if you choose to show confidence in certain markets, do not be too specific, and I repeat again you must not be too specific – and there's then nothing the agency nor central government can do to stop us from having freedom of speech in all respects," replied Todd.

Andrew smiled. He took his Jack Daniels and downed it – his mouth opened as he felt a burning sensation at the bottom of his throat.

"That's it, Todd, you've got it, it's 'I scratch your back, you scratch mine'," said Andrew.

Chapter 14
Saudi Rehabilitation Center

It was the next day at the Hilton hotel. Dr Ishmael and his aides were enjoying their breakfast in the early morning before their first trip to the rehabilitation center. It was just approaching 8 o'clock when they all began to gather at the reception lobby.

Dr Ishmael was dressed in gray khaki top and trousers with a slightly darker shirt containing many pockets. The deputy directors were not due to attend the facility as there was no need. All arrangements had been made so the psychiatric team led by Dr Ishmael could conduct its research over the next few days.

One of the members of the psychiatric team turned to Dr Ishmael with his hands in front of him;

"Dr Ishmael, about our package. While we haven't had a pay rise as such, the salary we were getting has been tripled, plus expenses, so we were assuming it applies to the all of us including you?" said Dr Jacob.

Dr Ishmael shook his head, affirming his disapproval of this discussion.

"Listen to me folks, or may I say, doctors – as we all are aware, we've had this discussion before! Our salaries remain the same, but we are all on a 300% pay increase while we're conducting research overseas, including expenses such as our stay at this hotel. So, now that we are all here, let's make a move."

All four doctors were dressed casually, a couple with baseball caps on. They could be mistaken for tourists going off to explore.

They all headed outside where two SUVs were waiting, afforded by the US taxpayer and complete with security, bodyguards and armor plating – it was all protocol as they were embassy vehicles.

Once strapped in, the teams soon sped off down the ramp heading out of the hotel straight onto the highway. It was known as Dammam Road. It was only a twenty-minute drive to the rehabilitation center which was located in between Naif Arab University for Security Sciences and King Fahd Security College.

As the vehicles arrived, they got checked in and passed through to an area used to identify bombs hidden beneath vehicles. This involved a security force operative moving a mirror under the vehicles.

They continued forward as they've been told to head straight to the main entrance, where Dr Abu Talib will be waiting for them. As they approached the main building they slowed to a halt, and the team began to get their belongings together before opening the doors.

The four entered the building. It's a beige-colored building which has been rendered and painted in beige, with not much glass visible. As the team entered, Dr Abu Talib approached them and reached forward with his hand to shake the hands of all four in the team.

"Doctors, I would like to welcome you here to our country. I wish you to have a warm and welcoming experience to the kingdom of Saudi Arabia. We can have some tea and my favorite baklawa biscuits. I'm sure you will like them."

They walked across to a cafeteria where it seemed refreshments and an array of biscuits known here as baklawa were available throughout the day.

Dr Talib began to eat.

"Please help yourself and take a seat, team," he said.

He passed across to the others tea in small ornate cups which were more akin to something you would put in a display cabinet than actually drink from, holding as they did very little liquid. After taking a few sips, Dr Talib put his cup down and handed over a leaflet to the team about the center. It looked more like a brochure for a holiday resort than an institution, let alone a prison.

"So, doctors, this care and rehabilitation center is one of a few institutions or facilities in Saudi Arabia. Its single outcome is to reintegrate former jihadists into the mainstream, not only Saudi culture but what is expected of one in a civilized human being throughout the world at large. As you will see in the brochure I have just given to you, it's what I wrote."

Dr Talib was all smiles;

"It is complete with swimming pools and all other recreation facilities such as badminton and table tennis, snooker and so on. We have suspected terrorists enrolled on our program, who have either been caught by Saudi security forces or surrendered themselves, and even Guantánamo detainees. We aim to return these so-called extremists to the true Islam, pure and uncorrupted in its simplest form. We have here Mullahs who deploy intensely religious instruction, deconstructing extremists' perceptions and interpretation of the holy Koran, which might be obscuring their understanding. As well, we have Islamic scholars and clerics from Saudi universities who regularly attend, and have established a foundation and a curriculum which we use and follow. So, I am sure you will have many questions, but I'm guessing you're here for a few days,"

The four doctors were all giving signs that they understood now what the facility had to offer.

"Yes, that's correct, possibly up to two weeks depending on our findings," said Dr Ishmael.

"So, gentlemen, let's first go to the restaurant, as around this time they will still be having their breakfast. You will see that even the restaurant has some recreational facilities because we try to make everything as easily accessible as possible." Said Dr Abu Talib.

He stood up and waited for the others to get up. He began to walk, passing through doors, each needing him to key in a code on a pad. He approached a final set of doors which had a keypad to its right. He began to type a code. It seemed to go on for a while, quite possibly at least a dozen digits long. Finally, a light changed color, possibly alerting that the magnet had detached, and he proceeded through after pushing the door forward. The doors led into a large canteen with multiple tables. It was a cafeteria, complete with a hot food counter. In the distance, there were table tennis, snooker and pool tables visible. While some were tucking into their morning breakfast, others were already occupied with recreational activities.

"Gentlemen, you can try the food here, it's exactly what we eat as well. It's prepared by excellent chefs, and there's lamb today. It will be served at lunchtime, at 1 PM. My favorite, with the rice and the raisins. It's beautiful, and I highly recommend it. Please try?" said Dr Talib.

A few in the group shook their heads while expressing their appreciation, but it's a no.

"Oh, we're good, thanks. We had the Hilton breakfast back at the hotel," said Dr Ishmael.

Dr Talib looked at the group and nodded.

"So, you've all eaten... that's good," he said. "In that case, we must continue."

He headed straight down a corridor which has doors, but no restricted access as they were already inside the rehabilitation center facility. They continued alongside a veranda, which was along the outside of the building parallel to a garden. Yet the massive walls were visible just to the far side of the gardens, until they approach a separate building which housed what seemed to be the swimming pool, as there were shimmering blue reflections visible through the glass windows. Once through the doors, it became apparent this was surely a semi-Olympic swimming pool. The fact that it was a resort in the past becomes very evident as having a swimming pool in prison is one thing, but a semi-Olympic pool is a big deal.

"Gentlemen, doctors – you see the pool here. We certainly have not cut corners when embarking on the facilities afforded to the inmates," said Dr Talib.

He continued through to the other side of the swimming pool, leading them into an outdoor area which consisted of tennis courts. Walking past the tennis courts, they head back around what seemed to be where they set off from, except it was more of a station where the professionals are based.

"So now we have had a good look at the facility, do you have any questions?" asked their guide.

"No, I'd just like to know when we are able to meet the individuals in this facility, and where we'll be able to interview them," said Dr Ishmael.

The doctor looked round at his aides who were now stationed in the general office, and looked up at the roster to see what their duties were for the remainder of the day.

"Yes... Saleem and Hassan will guide you through. They will bring out the individuals and stay with you throughout your time here today."

"Wait, I think there has been a misunderstanding!" exclaimed Dr Ishmael.

Dr Talib looked confused.

"What do you mean?"

"Well, we have been promised unhindered, unsupervised and uninterrupted private access to all these individuals. It's the only way we can be sure that what you're telling us is the truth and is a credible basis we can learn from. Our findings need to be based on something which we believe to be right and not just been handed over to us!" said Dr Ishmael.

"Ah... in that case... let me make a phone call; I'll be just a minute," said Dr Talib.

He walked through into an adjoining room, past the general office, and was clearly visible through the glass. He closed the door behind him and lifted a handset, dialing some numbers... It seemed to take forever, but he finally got through to the person he needed to speak with. His facial expression showed that he had been admonished. He put the handset down, and after dwelling for a few moments with his back turned, he began to walk back to the general office. He was looking straight at Dr Ishmael and held his gaze for a moment, staring at him before he softly closed the door behind him.

"I see, I have spoken to my seniors and they had to confirm to me once again you are right. It's what was agreed. Therefore, Saleem and Hassan will remain in the communal areas while you interview the inmates as you wish, Sir," said Dr Talib.

Dr Ishmael, holding documents in one hand and a mobile phone in the other, had been on edge until now, but now nodded to Dr Talib, grateful the situation had now been resolved. Otherwise, he had been about to call his seniors at the CIA.

He now turned to his team;

"Well doctors, there you go; the matter has been resolved. Thank you Abu Talib. You guys can now begin your work – let's get cracking.".

"Once again, Sir, please accept my apologies," said Dr Talib.

Abu Talib left, leaving his aides, Saleem and Hassan.

Dr Ishmael followed his finger down the list and came across a name of interest.

"Mohammed Atta: he's Egyptian, right?" he asked Saleem.

"Yes, that's correct."

"Well, I'll start with interviewing him, while Dr Jacob will interview Hani Hanjour, he is of Saudi citizenship. Then we'll continue down the list." said Dr Ishmael.

"I'll go and get them for you," said Saleem.

Just then the other man, Hassan came forward;

"Who would you like after that? I'll make sure they're ready for you."

Dr Ishmael went through the list;

"Well, there's Abdul Aziz, who is Saudi; then you have an Ahmad al Haznawi..."

Hassan walked away down the corridor, as many of the inmates had gone to their rooms.

Just then Saleem returned with the first on the list, it was Mohammed Atta, the Egyptian.

"As-salāmu alayka, pleased to meet you, Mohammed Atta," said Dr Ishmael.

Mohammed Atta looks uncertainly at Dr Ishmael. He takes a moment before speaking anything.

"Wa alaykumu as-salām," said Mohammed Atta.

"Well, as you might be already aware, we are conducting research and would like to learn from this facility, which you are making good use of, I'm guessing. Maybe we can adopt the same measures back at home in the United States of America when it comes to reintegrating our detainees into society when leaving penitentiary. So, I just need your approval for our interview?" said Dr Ishmael.

"Yes, I think I'm happy with that," said Mohammed Atta.

Dr Ishmael gave him a thumbs-up.

"Okay, good. Saleem, have you found me a room yet?" he asked.

"Yes, we have, the north side of the building, which has rooms... empty from when it was our resort facility. I'll open the conference room for you there."

Saleem began to walk, and Dr Ishmael and Mohammed Atta followed.

All in all, there were 19 people on the list they were due to work through.

Once inside the conference room, It's only Dr Ishmael with Mohammed Atta. There was a table with chairs round it at one end of the room, and Mohammed sat down on one side of it, while Dr Ishmael moved to the other side and sat down opposite him.

*****

The Toyota HiAce came to a stop. Jackson's complimentary airport transfer vehicle had just arrived at his hotel after passing through two check posts which were as undisruptive as they could have been – security merely peered into the windows of the vehicle!

The side door slid open as the driver pulled the handle. Jackson looked up and noticed striking features of the building. It was set amid the wilderness, the mountain landscape, with stunning views. Made from warm earth tones, coupled with locally inspired designs and touches such as wooden floors, exquisite woodwork and native stone and finishing – there are pagodas, and verandas, all decorated in local art painstakingly restored by local artisans.

It wasn't long before the staff at the hotel came out to the vehicle and helped with unloading Jackson's baggage. This time they seem to be a little more careful as to the contents.

"Be careful, I have instruments and electronics inside my baggage!" he said.

As he was being shown the way to the reception, he is approached by a man in a suit.

"Sir, a warm welcome to you, Mr Jackson. I will show you to your room and get you settled in. If I could just get you to sign here," said the man.

This was the guest relations manager. The name on his tag was Abdul.

Jackson picked up the pen which was placed on the printed sheet of paper on the wooden shelf just outside the office. There wasn't exactly a lobby, nor a reception – more a hole in the wall. The Serena Shigar Fort was unlike other five-star hotels; it was a more boutique kind.

"Excellent, Mr Jackson, let me take you to your room, if you'd like to follow me... you're in our heritage suite. The hotel's heritage suites originally served as the Chambers of the royal women and the Raja's midseason quarters. We have a complimentary tour which we offer to all our new guests. It's every morning at 10 o'clock. If you're interested, I'll meet you just outside the restaurant in the courtyard. It's for one hour, about the hotel and its history. I'm sure you will find it very interesting," said Abdul.

Jackson smiled at Abdul.

"Yes, as I'm here, that would be a treat. To get to know the local history and the origins of this majestic building. It's a museum in its form, while a functioning form."

Due to the altitude causing low air pressure, it didn't take long for Jackson to start needing to breathe a little harder and faster, and it taking more effort to do so. It wasn't an altitude his body was accustomed to. After climbing a few stairs ranging from local stone to timber frame, and turning many corners around the exterior of the fort, they finally arrive at the heritage suite. It was a rather small looking door seeming to be of original wood, with a handmade clasp and shackle securing it against the stone wall. Instead of a keyhole, it had a padlock, a rather large one with an old, clunky -looking key. The key and padlock seemed to be dated itself. Abdul unlocked the lock. Released the door away from the shackle and it swung into the room. Once inside, Jackson took his shoes off, following Abdul. He walked around the room, showing him the views from each window. And, the direction of the Qiblah, that's the Holy Mosque in Mecca. Not that he would need it. Then finally the bathroom, together with something which was a surprise to Jackson: an extra bed in a tiny adjoining room which was for servants and security of the Raja in the early years.

"Is that all okay, Mr Jackson?" asked Abdul.

"Yes, that's fine. Oh, evening meal, of course; what time does the restaurant open?"

"Sir, the restaurant is open now, and everything is made fresh up until 10 PM tonight," said Abdul.

Jackson nodded his head, licking his lips while looking at the room. Just then, two men with slight builds, both smartly dressed, with greasy hair waved back, entered the room, as the door was wide open. They were both dressed in beige attire with Serena Hotel embroidered on the front of their tops at chest height, together with the hotel logo. They were carrying Jackson's baggage which was placed gently down in a neat straight line on the floor. They then left the room.

"That's nice, I think I'll come down in a little while to have a look at the menu. I fancy a curry," said Jackson.

"Very well Sir, I'll be off; I'll see you in the morning at 10," said Abdul.

Jackson closed the door to his room and began to make himself comfortable. He decided to freshen up, and while doing so he admired the complimentary toiletries in the bathroom. He noticed the sanitary ware was of a western brand. There was a logo engraved into the basin tap: 'Grohe'. That was a German brand. He couldn't resist smelling the fragranced moisturizer in one of the miniature tubs; the others contained shower gel and shampoo.

Once he was done, Jackson dressed in something a little more comfortable and went down to dinner. It was a rather small dining area which consisted of no more than six tables. A waiter came in through a set of double doors with a pen and pad in hand.

"Hello Sir, good evening. Can I get you something to drink?"

Jackson was still observing the menu but he nodded his head, looking at the list and flipping it over.

"I'll have a pomegranate juice please, and to eat... you see the lamb ginger curry... I'll try that, together with Keema naan... Yes, no, in fact, I'll go for the local Peshwari naan. That's it, lamb ginger curry with Peshawari naan, thank you," said Jackson.

There were a few newspapers neatly placed in a rack which caught his eye, and he stood up, walked over to the rack and picked one up. It's an English newspaper, the *Dawn News*. It's Pakistan's national newspaper which is published in English. The headline states Pakistan Chinese relations improve further. Bilateral talks take place in the capital to further strengthen investment and cooperation between the two nations.

Jackson was flicking through the pages when the waiter enters with his pomegranate juice. Jackson put back the newspaper and sat down again to enjoy his beverage.

Before long, his main dish arrived. The doors swung open and the waiter entered the dining area, while another held the doors open. The waiter was carrying a tray with a variety of dishes on it. He approached the table where Jackson was sat and began to lay down the assortment, starting with the main dish in what looks like a tiny wok known as a karahi;

"Sir, your main dish: lamb and ginger balti, here are your Peshwari naans, and our complimentary salad and side dressing. If you need anything else, just let me know," said the waiter.

Chapter 15
911

It was a new morning with clear skies, yet the blue in the air was still not yet visible as the hour was still early. The Earth was at the initial stages of the illumination of the lower atmosphere, as the sun itself was not directly visible due to it being below the horizon. Sunlight was scattering high above in the upper atmosphere, thus illuminating the lower atmosphere so that the Earth's surface was neither wholly lit nor completely dark. A sharp point was visible on the distant horizon, creating a silhouette. It was the summit of Mount Everest.

An eerie sound could be heard bellowing through some funnel and a clatter of brass. It was coming from a monastery which lay in the foothills of Mount Everest. It was Rongbuk Monastery. There was an array of colored flags fluttering in the breeze, like linen hanging on multiple washing lines, forming what resembled painting in canvas. The monastery lay on the north side of Mount Everest at 4980 meters above sea level, at the end of the Dzakar Chu valley. It was claimed to be the highest elevation monastery in the world.

Gazing through the doors into the dark, where there was the heavy scent of incense, a haze was seen in the distant, where a multitude of the infused sticks were smoldering and releasing a smoky fragrance.

There seemed to be a group sitting around in a circle on the floor. The congregation was of Buddhist monks that were of a young age, all dressed the same with cleanly shaven heads, mentored by one who was much mature. The monk leading opened a book, which appeared to be very old, with the ancient transcript handwritten.

"It is known that mankind will endeavor to find hope in colonizing other worlds. It is from the giants before us, and only from these giants before us, that mankind will be able to travel upwards, in such numbers as to meet other beings from other worlds. As the law of the universe is written, revealed to us in this book for us all. That is the only way we can leave the constraints and physical forces this planet exhibits, pulling us down."

Said the wise old monk.

He now held his hands up in the shape of a mountain before drawing them together to form a summit and then lifting them into the air above his head to emphasize the ancient script.

The correlation between ancient text and modern-day scientific discoveries become clearer – intertwined to make revelations even more profound.

Back in the conference room which Dr Ishmael was using to interview the inmates and detainees at the rehabilitation center.

It's just the doctor, and sat opposite him is Mohammed Atta, an Egyptian national.

Mohammed Atta reached into his pocket to pull out a cigarette. Here they can smoke openly, far stretched from the constraints and confines of conventional prisons around the world.

"Are you Muslim?" asks Mohammed Atta.

"No, me, I am Jewish," said Dr Ishmael.

"Yes, I see, it's also a Muslim name. You see," said Mohammed Atta.

By now he was exhaling smoke, and it was obvious somebody in the room was smoking.

Dr Ishmael opened his documents and pulled out some pictures. He placed them on the table and asked the detainee if he could identify which plants were in pots and which were in the ground. It led to the detainee forgetting he had a cigarette in his hand until;

"Ahhh! Oh-Oh!! Who put a cigarette in my hand!" exclaimed Mohammed Atta.

The cigarette fell out of his hand onto the floor. Dr Ishmael stood up and walked to where the cigarette had fallen, and picked it up before extinguishing it and disposing of it in an ashtray on the table.

"Mohammed Atta?" said Dr Ishmael.

Mohammed Atta was now looking at him. His gaze was blank.

"Mohammed Atta, do you hear me?"

The detainees eyes did not move from the doctor.

"Well, if you hear me, can you put your right hand up?"

Mohammed Atta's right hand lifted straight up above his head.

Dr Ishmael nodded his head. He moved the plant pot pictures away and pulled out a flight number: American Airlines 11, it says. Flight 11 traveling from Boston to Los Angeles, abbreviated as LAX.

"That's okay, now you can put your right hand down," he said.

Mohammed Atta's right hand came down to rest on the table.

"You will be traveling from Boston to Los Angeles on Tuesday 11 September 2001. You will be boarding American Airlines flight 11. I repeat American Airlines flight 11. You will not need to meet anyone, see anyone, talk to anyone, hear anyone, do you understand?" said Dr Ishmael.

"Yes, I do," said Mohammed Atta.

"Repeat back?" said Dr Ishmael.

"I will be flying from Boston to Los Angeles on flight American Airlines flight 11, on Tuesday the 11th of September 2001."

Dr Ishmael turned some pages in his notes and ticked off a box adjacent to the name Mohammed Atta. Then he walked back over to Mohammed Atta, taking out a cigarette from Atta's pocket, lighting it with a cigarette lighter out of Atta's pocket and putting it back between his fingers.

Dr Ishmael pulled out a picture of some plant pot with colorful flowers in it and shows it to the detainee sat in front of him;

"Come back, you can see the plant pot. Now the plants are in the plant pot, where they belong."

The cigarette in Mohammed Atta's fingers went straight into his mouth to take a draw of nicotine. He never realized for a moment that the cigarette had been missing from his fingers. During these three minutes, he had been under hypnosis. He was now back in his subconscious and has a concept of flying to Los Angeles from Boston on the Tuesday 11th of September. 2001.

And yet, until then, he will have no recollection of this event.

"You see that cigarette in the ashtray? I'm sure I didn't see that when I walked into this room. Strange," said Mohammed Atta.

Dr Ishmael now repeated the whole process again with the same flight, allowing Mohammed Atta to travel from Saudi Arabia to America, with the next inmate, Abdul Aziz al Omari, a Saudi citizen. Then further again with Wail al Shehri, Waleed al Shehri and Satam al Suqami, all Saudi Citizens.

The plan was to intercept Mohammed Atta and the others after their release from this rehabilitation center and before the flight dates, when they were familiar with the flights that were booked and had boarding cards to hand in their possession – tucked away in their belongings where they were able to retrieve them.

Dr Ishmael's counterpart in the team was interviewing the others. While there were a further two psychologists not questioning but coercing, or even, to put it mildly, hypnotizing and embedding pockets of memories which, upon such a time will become apparent, active and be implemented upon – all as part of the program which was developed by Dr Ishmael.

The process of visiting the rehabilitation center and secretly hypnotizing the inmates lasted for a total of three days. All the dates the detainees fly out will need to coincide with the spectacular which will happen on Tuesday, September 11th, 2001.

In total, nineteen inmates at the rehabilitation center had undergone the memory transplants under the hypnotism program.

The team will make sure that all the inmates concerned and enrolled now have all the details ready upon their arrival to the United States embedded into the deep mind. Also, during the hypnosis, any relevant information right down to the number of the E visa was implanted and transplanted into their memory for easy retrieval, upon request by the authorities.

Mohammed Atta and the others are seen at least half a dozen times by at least two of the doctors to make sure everything is touched upon and covered, and all information has been processed by the so-called terrorists.

The team gathered for lunch at the restaurant at the Hilton Hotel. A couple got engaged. The man knelt on his knees and proposed to a young lady beside him. Just further along, the CIA deputy directors, Andrew, Bobby, and Todd sat in line with the four doctors.

"I am finding this stake rather chewy. Wouldn't you say, Todd?" said Andrew.

"Certainly indeed," said Bob.

Dr Ishmael has just passed over to Andrew a sheet of paper signed off by him and at least one other doctor stating that the nineteen had gone through the entire process which had gone according to plan: memory implants for boarding those flights allowing them to reach the United States, and domestic flights thereon, on the day the spectacular is planned.

Andrew nodded his head:

"Well, gentlemen, it looks like we're good to go, I can't see it being too long before I'm able to tuck back into my Texan rump stake."

"So folks, as soon as we finish lunch we're heading to the embassy. That's all of us, as we need a secure setting. It's the only place where we can discuss anything meaningful," said Andrew.

Bobby just finished his second glass of wine. He was licking his lips;

"I'm sure this damn wine has been watered down. It can't possibly be Chardonnay."

Todd took a sip followed by a further two, then looked at Bobby;

"You gotta remember it could have been left out in the heat. I guess the drinks kind of lose the flavor a little. It's sweltering out there."

An hour later, following the meal at the Hilton, the entire entourage is now at the US Embassy in Riyadh city. Sat in the secure room, they placed all the documents each of the doctors had on the table.

"So, Andrew, like I said, including Todd and Bobby, we have followed the procedure, and we can all agree between the four of us that the inmates which we call terrorists have all been briefed, and the information which they require is safely and securely embedded in their deep thought; i.e. a memory specific to that moment in time. So they're referred to as sleeper cells.

"Great, so as I said, folks were good to go. I shall speak with the ambassador Mahmoud and the minister again to allow the inmates concerned to have their records available to us; to make available to us a continuing update and to maintain a process in which we can monitor the behavior and see any signs of radicalization not diagnosed as planned. Due to our program of works on learning and sharing information, we obviously require keeping the inmates' progress on check so we are reassured and confident that the program is working and to help us to implement this back in the United States. I guess, almost like a tag. Thus, allowing us to intercept them and make sure they're able to board the flights to do the damage, I guess," said Andrew.

Dr Ishmael reached his hand out and slid four USB sticks over to Andrew.

All the interrogations or interviews, whatever you want to call them, have been recorded and saved on these USB sticks in video format recorded with the tiniest cameras the doctors wore.

Andrew looks around at the doctors, unsure how to respond.

"I don't think we need those; goddamn evidence could end up in the wrong hands. I think we are confident with your work, Dr Ishmael, thank you very much," said Bobby.

"In fact, I think we might as well destroy and dispose of these, while we are all here," said Andrew.

Andrew got up and picked up the four sticks and threw them on the floor, proceeding to stamp on all of them until there were no fewer than a dozen fragments left of each USB stick. He continued to sit down, and the broken plastic bits are left on the floor.

"Right, we can all disband now; let's take a break. I'll see you back here in one hour, and that's all of you," he said.

Andrew left the room and headed for an adjoining room with a phone in it. He needed to be connected to Ambassador Mahmoud at the Saudi Embassy in Washington. There is a long wait, then he is told to put the phone down and wait a while and he will be called back on the same line.

He stood up and walked over to the door;

"Hey Bob, could you please get me a tea; I'm stuck on the phone?"

Andrew gave a thumbs-up;

"Yeah, sure, two sugars right?" said Bob.

Bob went off to the canteen while Andrew sat in front of the desk waiting for a call. It was a spare office. It was once an office for a female diplomat who'd decided she'd had enough of working in Saudi Arabia. There was a mark on the wall where a picture frame once hung over a hook: a rectangular patch much cleaner than the rest of the wall.

Bob walked through the door with a cup of tea, just as the phone began to ring. Andrew grabbed the phone with his left hand, while using his right to take the cup of tea off Bob.

"I got it, thanks Bob," he said, before holding the handset to his ear.

"Hello, Andrew Lopez speaking."

"Hello, Andrew, As-salāmu alaykam, peace be upon you, it's Ambassador Mahmoud."

Andrew took a few sips of his tea, and from the expression on his face, it was just how he liked it. He placed the cup on the table beside him.

"Hi Ambassador. Things are going well here. We've learnt a lot. My doctors have been doing good work with the inmates, and it's all great, except we need to keep on monitoring their progress. Otherwise, the whole effort has no meaning. As you can understand. But from what I gathered, the nineteen detainees are doing very well, and have transitioned successfully from the state of radicalization. So, what I need from you is: number one, we need to be sharing their whereabouts as I'm sure you will be placing a tag on these detainees; number two, I need to know who else is in contact with them, such as any other agencies or security forces; and number three, if they're seeing family members we need to know exactly who, when, and where. That should be enough for now. Just to let you know, I shall put this down in a written request."

The ambassador began to cough. Cough profusely. Such that Andrew pulled his ear away from the handset. He rolled his eyes and frowned, and picked up his teacup to drink a little more, while the ambassador cleared his throat.

"Of course Sir, we can do all that for you. I will speak with the minister, and we shall forward you a link which will connect you and allow you to access everything there is to know about the 19 detainees... you did say 19?" said the ambassador.

"Correct."

"Yes, so the 19 detainees. You will have a link to each of those individuals allowing you to access their timeline," said the ambassador.

Andrew is drinking his tea while nodding his head.

"Well, that's all I wanted to discuss. I'll put this forward in written correspondence to yourself just now. Otherwise, everything okay?" said Andrew.

"Alhamdulillāh, it's all great, by the grace of Allah," said the ambassador.

*****

It was night-time. It was dark in the room. Janet was in bed fast asleep. She was tossing and turning and she began to mumble. She was shaking even though she was asleep. She was having a nightmare. Then she begins to utter the name 'Samantha'.

"Samantha, honey, come here... everything will be fine... Mommy's here." It was Janet talking in her sleep.

Suddenly there was a scream. It was Janet. She was now awake and began to cry.

She was reliving trauma in her past. She had lost a child. A six-month-old baby. The weather had been bad all day – wind and rain – and that evening Janet had stepped out of her front door to grab her cat and the wind blew the door shut and it slam-locked. Just inside the house there was a table and on it an ashtray with a still smoldering cigarette.

The wind somehow caught the cigarette and it fell onto the carpeted floor. Next moment there were flames, which took hold quickly. Before the door lock could be broken, the room was overwhelmed with fumes and smoke, which the baby choked on. Ever since that night, Janet had been haunted by the nightmare of the sight and smell of her home burning with her child inside, and occasionally was visited by these nightmares, reliving that night. It caused the breakdown of her marriage, as her husband couldn't forgive her, and felt that he couldn't love her anymore. It was one of the reasons she was willing to do the most dangerous jobs in journalism: she would never lose the need to punish herself for what had happened. It had taken from her the two most important people in her world.

*****

Janet's husband now had the new alias of Jackson, and also has something of a death wish, as the CIA field operative operating in northern Pakistan – who at this moment is wiping his plate clean of lamb and ginger curry.

He put his hand up to call the waiter; "You know, my wife used to love this curry. We always used to go halves on the dish as it is rather calorie intensive, but she mostly ate the naan," said Jackson, beginning to laugh. Then tears began to appear around his eyes. He didn't wipe them away, but let them roll down his cheek.

"Sir, is everything okay?" asked the waiter.

Jackson nods his head and then rubs his tears away.

"That's a damn nice curry, and a scorching one," said Jackson.

He slid his chair back.

"May I sign whatever I need to sign, please; got a long day ahead of me tomorrow."

"The waiter walked to the counter and collected Jackson's bill, grabbing a pen and walking back to him.

"Just on the dotted line please, Sir."

Jackson signs his autograph and hands back the bill and pen.

*****

Back in Janet's bedroom, Janet screamed, the sound is deafening. With such a high pitch she woke herself up. She sat up in bed and swiveled herself round 90 degrees so she was sitting with her legs out of bed and her feet on the floor. She sat with her face cupped in her hands and her elbows resting on her knees, and stayed like that for about a minute.

Eventually, she turned to look at the clock on her bedside cabinet, 3:50 AM. She turned back her head, and covered her eyes with her hands; elbows still resting on the knees.

Right now, if there were any drug which could get rid of the past, erase the pain, stop these visions which haunted her, she would not hesitate to give it a chance.

She walked across to the bathroom and turned the light on. She looked at the little cabinet on the wall with the mirrored door. She opened the door to reveal an array of drugs. She knew exactly what she wanted, and her hand moved straight for a dose. After knocking back a handful of pills and a glass of water, she headed for the kitchen. She filled the kettle with water and flicked it on, and then prepared a mug with a teaspoon of coffee ready for when the kettle had boiled. Walking now to the fridge, one can't help but notice a few pictures on the fridge attached using magnets. Samantha. Janet held the fridge door, about to open it, and paused for a few moments, thinking at what could have been. She decides she will be visiting the cemetery today.

There was a click. It was the kettle. The water had boiled. Janet pulled the fridge door open to help herself to the milk. After making the coffee, she headed back to her bedroom as it was way too early to head out. It's not even remotely light outside.

Later, that day, Janet knelt, clutching some flowers. She must let go, she had to. She placed the flowers on the tiny gravestone. Written on the stone: 'Beloved Samantha'. She began to weep. It resembled a grave just like any other for a child who had if they had died at such an innocent young age. Littered with teddies and toys of all colors of the rainbow. She often spent an hour or more there. When she found the courage to turn up.

Janet's cell phone began to ring. She had spent close to an hour just clutching a soft teddy. In her heart she felt that Samantha was almost certainly in a better place.

Her phone continued to ring. Finally, she slid her hand into her pocket and pulled it out. It was Jeff from the LAPD. She decided to answer and somewhat reluctantly held it to her ear;

"Yes," said Janet.

"I've got something you're really going to want to see, Janet. This is shit hot!" Exclaims Jeff.

"Janet softly puts the teddy down while nodding her head, the tear which rolled down her cheek has already dried.

"Right, right. Sure, five stars tonight," said Janet.

"I finish at 7 PM so let's say 7:30 PM just to be sure. See you then," said Jeff.

It had just gone 7:10 PM and the uber taxi pulled up outside the five-star bar in downtown Los Angeles. Janet tipped the driver via the app for excellent service, and got out of the vehicle.

The bar exterior was brightly colored, reminiscent of Latin America... with a few lights shining upon the façade, while the inside is very dark and dreary, displaying a few colored lights to try and rather failing to give the venue a music theme and carnivalesque feel.

Janet walked through the door and had a good look around for Jeff. She walked over to the bar where she saw Gail and ordered herself a drink before greeting Gail with a firm handshake.

"I'd like a whiskey and coke. Where's Jeff?" said Janet.

"Oh, he's here, he's just gone to the bathroom," said Gail.

Janet turned to the bartender; "Excuse me, could you make that a double whiskey and Coke."

The bartender smiled at her while reaching for the whiskey bottle.

"Sure, I can do that for you."

Just then the door to the bathroom swung open, and the sound of a hand dryer continuing to blow away could be heard as Jeff walked out. He momentarily turned to look at the bartender before turning his gaze back to Gail, then spotting Janet. His eyebrows lifted;

"Hey Janet! Fashionably late. Nice to see you made it. Boy, have I got something to tell you."

Janet's double whiskey and coke was sat on the counter. She lifted it to her mouth, about to take a sip when Jeff put his finger on her arm and said;

"You know Bill Gates, the billionaire Microsoft owner, has become a philanthropist? Well, the program he has set up has over the last few weeks seen an exponential growth in medical personnel applying for visas to Afghanistan and Pakistan."

Janet put her glass down firmly on the bar before turning to Jeff.

"Well?" said Jeff.

He turned to look at the bartender before turning back to the two women.

"Let's go and sit down.

Excuse me, could the music be turned down a bit please?"

The bartender frowned at him;

"Well, it is a rock bar!" he exclaimed.

She turned the volume down by one notch.

They all walked over to a corner table which had a seating arrangement à la church pew in style, circling it.

"I see, well, it's something which I will look into and see where all these job applications were advertised, if in fact they were at all; where the individuals applying have previously worked and are there any connections; also, whether or not they have any links to the Secret Service," said Janet.

She pulled out her diary and began to take notes.

"Gail, this is where you're going to have to pull your finger out and use your initiative to help us out. See if you can, by any means necessary, find any useful information, whether by extracting it from Jared, or the NASA space institution servers et cetera. This will all be kept confidential in the event of any backlash in years to come. Nothing will be publicized until agreed. But the people have a right to know, especially where taxpayers' money is getting spent.

"Listen, I've already tried... it's like getting blood out of a stone and eventually all that will happen is that I most likely will lose my job, not to mention having a lawsuit against me for breach of conduct, as we've all signed a disclaimer," said Gail.

"Guys, you should both know that I've sent my passport in to Pakistan's embassy in Washington for a Visa application," said Janet. "When I get my passport back, I am moving over there indefinitely as I feel that it will be the epicenter of much activity in recent years to come. I have asked to be stationed over in the northern Pakistan region and become the CNN correspondent covering the region. Currently, there isn't even a correspondent in Afghanistan, so I guess it will have to be me, which has all been agreed with by my editor as you know. I also have so much to escape from over here," she said, her voice breaking.

She began to sob.

"Hey, Janet, you okay? Is there anything we can do to help?" said Jeff.

Neither Gail nor Jeff was aware of Janet's past and her losing a baby or of the circumstances involved.

Gail touched her head with both hands and began to shake her head, turning to look at Janet and then Jeff.

"Oh, hang on, there is just one thing. Jared is a scientist in our science and research department. He's the computer programmer and specialist in physics. He's been offered a promotion, which he briefly mentioned to me. It involves him going for an immunization, so I presume it will be an overseas mission. I didn't give much thought until now. I haven't had the chance to ask him about it in more detail. Until now when all this information which seems to be coming from all directions. I can only assume he will be heading in the same region. Oh my god!" Exclaimed Gail.

Jeff pushed his beer glass away from himself to the middle of the table, and sent an angry look in Gail's direction.

"Hang on, you're just mentioning this to us now? Don't you think it's something you could have mentioned earlier! Knowing what your colleagues are doing and where they are is a good enough reason, wouldn't you say! It looks like he's heading off to the same region, would you not agree?" Jeff rolled his eyes, shaking his head.

"Well, it only just came to my attention. I didn't think much of it at the beginning. Initially, I thought it was just a promotion, but then as soon as the immunization was mentioned it rang alarm bells, but I haven't spoken with Jared as it's best to play it dumb right now," said Gail.

Gail turned to her drink to wash down her sense of feeling rather foolish.

"Well folks, if I do receive my visa and my passport, this will be our last meeting in person, and I hope, I sincerely hope we can make something out of this, and our efforts don't go unnoticed," said Janet as she pulled out her cell phone to request an Uber rid.

*****

The vacuum cleaner was sucking away and drawing up dust from the carpeted floor of the conference room in the US Embassy in Riyadh. The cleaner came across the broken pieces of USB sticks scattered about the floor. They too got sucked up and enter the vacuum cleaner. The cleaner looked Bangladeshi in appearance. In this region of the world, many people are working under a labor program from South and South East Asia.. Later, in the cleaner's cupboard when the contents of the vacuum cleaner were being emptied out, he decided to collect all the insides of the USB sticks as he thought he could use them for his own personal use to send photos home to his family, and vice versa.

The cleaner's brother was working at the Hilton hotel as a porter. His brother was due to fly home next week and would be able to take photos on the USB stick with him.

Later, that evening, when the cleaner was at home, he decided to plug in one of the sticks to the computer. As there was hardly any plastic casing left on the flash drive, it was a case of inserting it in the PC with a pair of tweezers.

The screen popped up showing the available saved files. It showed videos which the cleaner was not interested. As he scrolled across to delete, he had one thought enter his head: 'Why not have a quick look at them before I remove them...' Curiosity got the better of him.

He clicked on and proceeded to play one of the videos. Just then he could see it was a specific individual in what seemed like an interrogation room, and another individual who appeared to be a professional. He soon realized that the first individual was under duress and not entirely in control of his actions. It wasn't something which he usually watched for any form of amusement but decided to play a little more. It was when the hand was raised, and the cigarette burning the individual's finger was spotted that he realized that there was hypnotism involved. He decided to keep that one and send it home to his family and use another one for his personal photos which he began to copy across. Nothing was deleted.

*****

Inside the seated waiting area of the Consulate General of Pakistan, Los Angeles, Janet was patiently waiting on one of plastic the chairs provided. She had come to pick up her passport with what should be by now her passport with a Visa. She had a token in her hand showing a time of 11:45 AM. It was the time the passport collection office opened. Right in front of her were two booths with glass screens: kiosks numbers one and two. She is sat on a chair looking out of the floor-to-ceiling window onto Santa Monica Blvd: the consulate is at number 10700.

Just then a light flickered on and a man appeared behind one of the screens. However, it wasn't quite time yet, and he didn't even make eye contact. Janet continued to peer out of the window. Across the road a tall tower caught her attention. It was the Los Angeles California temple, and right above the temple, there was a gold statue. She began to think of her daughter once again and enters a state of inhibition. As the sun shimmered off the golden statue, she can only start to wonder what it must have been like when Samantha was burning in the inferno. Janet was wholly lost in thought and sad memories when suddenly she saw a hand wave in front of her face;

"Excuse me, Ma'am, but have we met before?" asked Jared.

Janet turned to see who the voice belonged to. She was so far gone from the present that it takes a while for her to readjust and realize this man who stood in front of her was that scientist from the big experiment at the hanger: that big building Janet crept into and listened in on the NASA simulation in the hangar.

"This oh, yeah... I think we have. You're a scientist, right?" said Janet.

"And didn't you try to get into my hotel room? The reporter, right? Who got flung out of the CIA vehicle?" said Jared.

Janet adjusted her eyes to look at kiosk number two behind Jared. There was a man sat there trying to look busy, merely pen pushing while peering to see the two of them catching up with each other.

Janet stood up and strode over to kiosk number two. Jared right after, turning to the other kiosk, where somebody had now just arrived. He walked over and slid his token under the screen into the booth.

It transpired that both were due to collect their passports today. This was due to a spike in diplomatic visas applied for, one can only guess these were for US civil servants. The tokens were a way of identifying and locating the passport of an individual. Janet was handed a receipt together with an envelope which she assumes contained her passport.

"Appreciated, thanks," she said, quickly opening the envelope to confirm her passport was in there, which it was, together with some other documents folded inside the passport.

"That's super, great, thank you."

Janet turned around, and she was all eyes and ears now. Yes, it was the scientist Jared. She soon realized where they'd met when he was stood right next to her.

"Lady, you certainly are tenacious. You just don't know when to give up. At this rate, you do realize you are going to get yourself in a whole load of deep shit." said Jared.

"Listen fella, I'm just doing my job, and you can just carry on doing yours. I'm sure you're damn good at your job, And I for that matter am good at mine. So, I take it you're off to Pakistan?" said Janet.

Jared frowned.

"It ain't going to take a genius to figure out that one, given the exact location we're at right now..."

His hands went to his waist and he rolled his shoulders back in an effort to relax. He was getting slightly annoyed with this mischievous character.

Janet smiled.

"Listen, if it's any consolation, it's nothing personal. I just have reasons for wanting to go somewhere far away from it all. It's why I'd even consider volunteering to do such a dangerous job as an investigative journalist and stick my neck out."

"Oh yeah, well, what might that be then? And might that be a reason why you might not be in the best frame of mind? A security risk?" said Jared.

Janet looked down in despair for a moment, bringing a hand up and grabbing Jared's arm.

"Hey, as we are both flying out, we might as well fly out on the same flight? and at least I could tell you a little bit about my experience?" said Janet.

Jared turned around and looked at the ceiling for a moment.

"I'd be intrigued to know what your motivation is here... I'm due to fly out tonight at 18:25 with Turkish Airlines via Istanbul. It's the shortest connection," he said.

Janet nodded while looking into Jared's eyes. She began to smile, still clutching his arm.

"Well, I don't even have a flight booked so I best get going and check for availability, don't you think?" Giving Jared a smirky smile, Janet lets go of his arm.

"Well. Hope to see you on board then. We'll have plenty of time to discuss your experience as the flight is over 21 hours in total. See you later," he said.

Jared left holding an envelope in his hand: his passport. Janet stood still for a few moments, dwelling on déjà vu.

*****

In the general office at the rehabilitation center Dr Abu Talib is about to make a phone call. He has today decided to release two dozen individuals from the center. Most of them are the 19 which had been visited and monitored by the psychiatric team led by Andrew, Todd and Rob from the CIA. The phone was ringing, and Dr Talib drew it up to his right ear so he could keep the phone cord away and be able to carry on with his work. He is adding a few signatures the documents required.

"Good morning, deputy director Andrew Lopez speaking."

"Oh, hello Andrew, I hope you're doing well? It's Dr Abu Talib here. As-salamu alaykum. I thought you'd like to know that today we are releasing two dozen inmates here who have met our program criteria. They have met their goals, and all the 19 which your team had a keen interest in with following up with their progress are included in the two dozen. You can now check their progress on our intranet which you have a link to, I presume?"

"Oh, yes we do. I'll be sure to check up on that. And I'm really grateful you've rung me as we'd like to keep our monitoring up to date and not miss a moment," said Andrew.

Well, okay, it's 3 PM here with the release time. We have a bus here, which takes some to the station and we will leave them with $1,000 in cash to help them on their way."

"One more crucial thing – their geo-tags. Have they got a tag and are they monitored location wise?" asked Andrew.

"Most certainly Sir; you will be able to access their location via a link when you go into their file. Just select 'locate an individual' at the top in the menu."

Andrew was sat beside Bob when without making too much of a ruckus he had a smile appear on his face and gave Bob a high-five.

"We will be sure to locate them and keep a close eye; and thanks again for letting me know," said Andrew.

*****

Janet was at Los Angeles International Airport. She is facing a counter, it's the Turkish airlines ticketing desk, and she's brought along all her baggage in the hope she will be able to get on tonight's flight.

"Excuse me, I was wondering if you can sell me a ticket to Islamabad on your flight leaving tonight at 18:25 hours?" she said.

The lady sat at the desk is dressed in red attire with a smile on her face.

"Yes Ma'am, let me check for you," said the lady.

According to her name label, she was called Maria.

She typed away on the keyboard with a very loud click on each strike of her fingers touching the keyboard.

Janet is nervously waiting although she managed to keep a smile.

"Ma'am, I only have business class," said Maria.

"Lovely, that's fine. I can pay for that now," said Janet.

Janet slides her passport out of its envelope, which was in her bag and hands it over to Maria with her credit card even before she is given a price. Just then;

"Ma'am, including taxes that comes to $5,550," said Maria.

"That's fine, please charge my card," said Janet. Janet has a finger on the card and slides it close towards Maria with her passport against her thumb.

"Sure ma'am, just give me a moment, and I'll process this for you. Won't be a moment," said Maria.

There was a noise of dot matrix printers going off in the background while Maria was busy typing away data, just like a data processor. Maria's face turned towards Janet's passport, and she opens it to the first page so as she could see Janet's name as it appears on the passport while she continued to type. She then turned to look at Janet's face, making sure it's the same person

"Ma'am, do you have a visa for Pakistan?" asked Maria.

"Yes, yes, just had that done," said Janet.

Maria handed back the passport and proceeded to charge Janet's card by sliding it through the machine and then typing the card number into the online payment system.

Once complete, Maria handed Janet her ticket. It was a paper ticket. As it was done last minute it cannot be an e-ticket. Maria turned to Janet and handed her her credit card.

"Ma'am, checking begins at 16:00 hours, and as your business class you are able to use the executive lounge, so make yourself comfortable and feel free to use. Also, you have the dedicated check-in counter at your convenience so feel free to use it," said Maria.

Later that day, after getting a light bite, Janet is the first to arrive at check-in. Once checked in, the first thing she did was check her seat number.

"Excuse me, is it possible to move me to a seat closer to somebody else on the flight?" Said, Janet.

The check-in steward doesn't look at Janet.

"I can check for you, what's the name?"

"It's Jared, Jared Neal," said Janet.

There's a brief wait – she looked around while she began to bite her lip.

"Ma'am, you're in business class. But Jared is further back towards economy, and there is a seat available. I can move you there if you want, but you won't have the amenities available that you would do in business class, such as legroom, enhanced meals, newspapers and Wi-Fi," said the steward.

"Oh, that's fine, just move me. Thank you, I'll be happy to lose those."

"Ma'am, I'm sorry. I physically can't do that; the system won't allow me as you purchased a business class ticket. It's something we never get asked. However, I'm sure you will be able to move around once the aircraft takes off as it's not a busy flight."

Janet looked a little bemused but nevertheless remained hopeful. She took away her boarding card with her handbag over her shoulder and proceeded to head towards departures.

Once in departures, she noticed that the executive lounge was available and fancied getting herself a light bite and a black coffee, so headed off.

One week earlier;

It was a beautifully sunny, hot day and the vehicle's air conditioning was running while the engine was idling. It was a black SUV. It was parked outside the rehabilitation center. If one were to peer through the tinted glass of the vehicle, you would most likely get a reflection as the front two occupants were both wearing dark shaded glasses. It was the two CIA agents, Agents Parker and Harrison.

"You want gum," asked Agent Parker.

"Nah, I'm good," said Agent Harrison.

"Anyone want any gum?"

A hand reached forward and pulled out a stick of gum. It was Dr Ishmael, sat in the back together with a few more agents and counterparts in the field of hypnosis.

"When in the bloody hell are they are getting out! I sure hope we are not waiting around for the whole day," said Dr Jacob.

The whole entourage had their eyes focused on the exit to the rehabilitation center. Everyone waited patiently. The agenda was to follow, intercept and apprehend or even abduct under duress to hypnotize. And eventually, fly them out on the next available flight to the United States.

Jaws dropped as the gates now open! It's a minibus, and it drove out containing at least a dozen people.

"Roger one to Roger two we are good to go, now pulling off. Take your position," said Agent Harrison.

Most likely, if going to plan, the minibus was due to drop the individuals off at the bus station. The SUV containing the entourage began to pull off and to follow the minibus. It was keeping a set distance apart of approximately 100 m. Just then, a further six vehicles started to pull out of side streets. A display in the other cars allowed the others to monitor the exact location of the SUV carrying Agents Harrison and Parker. Therefore, no need to be conspicuous or to cause alarm, or be close to the minibus as only the one vehicle was required.

As per Dr Abu Talib's instructions, these detainees were now free to go and would not, therefore, be under armed guard. Hence the vehicle they traveled in, the minibus, should not have any armed personnel.

They reached the bus station car park where the minibus stopped at the drop-off. The inmates began to leave one by one, and just then at least six cars arrived – mainly the same ones that joined the route as the SUV drove past them. These all stopped in parking bays, dropping off individuals in a vaguely coordinated fashion – as if it had been orchestrated to seem as if the individuals who have been dropped off have been so randomly and are not connected with each other. The individuals headed straight for the former detainees who have left the rehabilitation center.

Certain code words were mentioned to the individuals leaving the minibus. The former detainees respond to the code words as though they've just had a mood swing. These were words which have triggered their embedded memory and engaged it as reality. The detainees followed the individuals. These individuals with code words were CIA field agents. The minibus driver failed to notice anything and was too busy rolling his tobacco to light his next cigarette, before pulling away.

All the released have now paired up with their CIA field agents and have left in different directions.

The released would get further pockets of memory implanted in them and given guidance: flight times, a timeline, etc. All this in aid of achieving the spectacular.

*****

In the waiting lounge at Departures at LAX airport, Janet was pouring herself a black coffee. She was at the self-service table which was laid out at the business class section. It was only another 15 minutes to the flight boarding time.

"Turkish Airlines flight TK10 for Istanbul is ready to board at gate 151."

Janet stopped pouring her coffee and decided the half-a -cup would do. She was on the sixth floor, at the Star Alliance lounge, and a rather comfortable hour had just flown by as there was so much to read and also Wi-Fi to hand.

It's September 10, 2001, a Monday. Janet gathered her baggage and headed off to gate number 151 which is located on the south concourse end of the Tom Bradley International terminal.

*****

Back at the rehabilitation center, the parking spot where the SUV was previously parked was now occupied by another SUV – again with tinted windows. As former inmates were randomly being released, agents inside the SUV were identifying them with binoculars and DSLR cameras with zoom lens, then following them in whatever vehicle they were picked up in. By now there were at least half a dozen individual private cars parked up outside. One could only assume they were family or friends of former detainees being released today.

*****

Janet was walking down the south concourse as she approaches gate 151. She focused her eyes on the information display, which read 'Istanbul, flight TK10'. That was her flight, and now for the fourth time she pulled out her passport and her boarding pass and proceeded to wait in a queue, along with the other passengers.

There was no priority or privilege queue for business class customers, so Janet was with all the others.

*****

Back outside the rehabilitation center, another SUV, identical to the others, drew up and parked up at the exact same spot where the other two left from.

The occupants again, CIA field operatives waited patiently. They all had cameras and binoculars, and were also equipped with a digital catalogue of photos of the former detainees which have undergone Dr Ishmael's hypnosis program. The facial recognition software assists in identifying without much effort needed with pointing equipment at the released detainees.

One week forward again.

At LAX, where Janet was patiently waiting to board her Turkish Airlines flight TK10 to Istanbul. There are a few individuals who had already scuffled their way to the gate door which is at present closed. Just then, two stewardesses from Turkish Airlines arrived at the desk and made an announcement.

"Ladies and gentlemen, we are now commencing boarding. Would all passengers seated in business class please make their way to board the aircraft."

Janet put one hand over her handbag, and the other on the holdall over her shoulder and made her way over to the double set of glass doors at the gate. As she walked past the stewardess, the lady checked again to make sure Janet's boarding card had business class written on it by cross-referencing it with the seat numbers.

When everyone had finally boarded the aircraft, all the passengers underwent the routine safety announcement;

"Ladies and gentlemen, we would like to take you through the onboard safety procedures; we ask that you kindly listen carefully."

Further down the aisle. The air stewardess began to move about her arms and gave an example of how in the event of an emergency to engage and utilize the lifejacket. Janet paid no attention, as she'd flown that many times she'd grown numb to the thought of it all.

It all ended with a message regards flight mode. Just then, Janet remembered, she pulled out her phone and instead of engaging flight mode, she switched her phone off as it was a rather long flight.

Today, there was an easterly wind which meant that the aircraft could take off at a reduced and lesser ground speed due to the headwind, as there was a higher flow of air over the wings as a result. The engines began to scream in harmony and it wasn't long before the aircraft was facing easterly on the runway and beginning to prepare for take-off. Just then, there was a sudden blast of thrust-like sound. It was like a coordinated twin hurricane bellowing along the two sides of this fixed-wing aircraft. Right then, Janet began feeling pinned down into her seat, feeling the g-force pushing her back into her chair.

It was September 10, which meant it was the season of autumn. The trees were entirely golden brown, with hardly any blowing around on the floor at this stage, even though it was a windy day.

*****

In Washington DC, the Air Force Memorial was not far from the Pentagon in the state of Virginia.

A phone rang, so a hand reached into a pocket. Very inconveniently, it began to rain. A second person opened an umbrella. It was the deputy directors Andrew Lopez, Bob Singleton and Todd Gordon from the Central intelligence agency who had come out for a walk.

"Andrew speaking."

There was a brief null. While Andrew patiently listened to what was being said. He began to roll his eyes;

"That's good news, terrific."

Andrew put his phone away and then looked at Todd.

"All former detainees on the program are now engaged," said Andrew.

Todd now took out the 'shield' tablet and authorized all involved to conduct their objectives: hacking into those specific flights, but only once they had confirmed the passenger lists to establish those released detainees who had undergone Dr Ishmael's program had made it onto those flights as per the mission.

Todd also took out his mobile phone, and called a special operative in the agency.

"It's good to go, I'll authorize the strikes on the 'shield' device. Make certain you check the individuals are on board before the strikes, as per plan."

The special operative was an agent embedded in the ground control and maintenance facilities, tasked with installing the devices into the aircraft which would enable those specific flights – those with former detainees onboard – to be remotely operated and therefore led to targets, such as New York's Twin Towers, the Golden Gate Bridge, the Pentagon and the White House.

The hardware was the same as was used in Aerial Reconnaissance Vehicles (ARVs), also known as drones. These controls were built by corporations such as Lockheed Martin and BAE systems as well as others. Once installed into those commercial airlines they would allow it to be operated just as the ARV or drone would – thus, being controlled from a ground shipping container, containing a smaller cockpit.

Chapter 16

The Operation

There was a ping and Janet looked up instantly to see if the seat belt light had gone out. It had.

"About time too... I need the damn toilet," she muttered.

She undid her seatbelt and as she had an aisle side seat she got up and headed straight for the lavatory.

Just then there was another announcement informing all passengers that the crew would be traveling down the aisle with light refreshments.

The cabin crew were passing down the aisle with the trolley just as Janet left the lavatory. She walked behind the cabin crew and trolley at a snail's pace back to her seat. She looked behind her, but it was only business class all, and Jared was going to be at the other end of the aircraft, in economy.

After having had a good look at what was available refreshment wise while she was walking behind the trolley, she finally got to sit down in her seat, just in time for needing a refreshment.

"Excuse me, black tea for me. I'm just about to take a seat here. Two sugars, please. Moreover, while you're at it, whiskey and Coke!" exclaimed Janet.

Janet pushed right back into her seat, making herself comfortable. Her attention is on the cabin crew making her drink. There was one making her hot drink while the other prepared her whiskey and coke, which came first.

"Ma'am, your whiskey and coke," said the stewardess.

Janet was really in need of something to wet her mouth. The drink in her hand had almost gone by the time the tea arrived.

"And, here's your tea Ma'am," said the second stewardess.

Janet took her time to let the tea brew before adding the milk. She liked milk in her tea. Maybe it's because of her British ancestry, as there are not many countries in the world that add milk in their tea.

*****

At Logan International Airport in Boston, a United Airlines aircraft was undergoing routine maintenance. A flight technician removed a cover containing electrical avionics. It seemed like general maintenance until a device is placed inside, clipping onto existing electronics and on to electrical wiring as he disconnected current wiring. The device was now embedded into the circuitry. This device would enable the aircraft to be remotely operated when it is engaged. The devices would control a multitude of faculties within the plane, this one the avionics. He proceeded to add another one to the electrical circuitry controlling the jet engines, and so on. Eventually, once completed, he screws the aluminum panels back in and vacates.

"United Airlines flight 175 system engaged. I repeat United Airlines flight 175 hardware installed and good to go."

The technician was a field agent and a part of the operation involved in the set-up process for the spectacular to take place. He's just installed hardware enabling this aircraft to be hacked and flown remotely from the ground.

There are a few more of these scenes happening, at different locations such as Dulles in Virginia and Newark in New Jersey.

*****

Janet had finished her tea over 20 minutes ago. The cabin lights had been dimmed. There's no sign of the cabin crew or their trolley anywhere, so she decided to have a wander around. Maybe she might spot Jared. He could not have gone very far as there are only 200 seats in this aircraft with no way out.

A lavatory door shut, and a tall, slender male caught Janet's eye, dressed very casually. It was Jared. Janet heads for him. She must have walked past twenty aisles by the time she caught up with him, by which time he had already sat in his chair. His was a window seat. It was just as well he was leaving the lavatory as she would have found it difficult to spot him otherwise: right at the end of the section, just two aisles from the last. Janet leant across, resting her waist against the seat adjacent to his.

"Hello there Jared."

He turned up and looked at her.

"Oh, so you found me, finally. I was expecting you; make yourself comfortable as no one's sat here."

Jared moved his book and newspaper off the seat and shoved both into the pocket in front of him, behind the seat in front.

Janet clutches and smooths her dress as she sits down.

"Well then, I think you've got something you wanted to tell me? A bad experience or event in your life? Go on, now is your chance. I'm all ears. Let's see if it's more interesting than this book I'm reading." said Jared.

He took his reading glasses off and put them away in his jacket inside pocket.

Janet starts to shake her head and looks about to get very emotional;

"Well, I don't know where to start. It was a Sunday morning. I'd just got up, and after making myself a coffee and checking in on the baby, I decided to light myself a cigarette. Couple of minutes later, I felt it necessary to open the window, to let some fresh air into the room now, as with the baby thing. I just wanted to get rid of the smoke get it out, away from the baby. So, I went up to open the balcony. After opening the doors, I went over to near the front door where I heard the doorbell ring. I peeped through the spy hole and noticed it was my neighbor from across the other side of the landing, in the adjoining apartment. So, I proceeded to open the door which, just as I did, my cat ran out. I dashed out after the cat. My cat was unable to get any further as there was a further set of doors. However, because my neighbor's door was open, the wind blew across the building through the doors and blew my front door shut. I was in my sleeping gown and pajamas holding the cat. I had nothing, no phone, no keys while my baby was inside. I then panicked. I let go of the cat and asked my neighbor immediately to call for emergency services. By that, I meant the fire engine. Because I tried pushing that door it wasn't going anywhere him being an old man was unable to do anything either. It was no point asking neighbors to smash the door as it would look suspicious. So the first thing that came to my mind was to ring the fire engine. Well, that's just what we did."

By now she is crying... and in an uncontrollable emotional hysteria. With tears across her face which have smudged her make-up, she continues;

"About five minutes later I could smell smoldering, and I couldn't peep through the letterbox because there isn't one. The mail is delivered down in the Fourier in a bank of mailboxes. There was no way to see inside. Then it dawned on me. I'd left the cigarette in the ashtray!" exclaimed Janet.

"Oh man, that's damn awful!" said Jared.

He nodded his head and showed Janet a little comfort.

"Go on Janet. I'm a good listener. I've been told that before. It doesn't cost anything to be a good listener, you know."

Janet stands up and walks to the cabin crew just behind.

"Can I have a tissue, please?"

She sits back down again and blows her nose.

"I've often given much time and had people shed many tears over my shoulder," said Jared.

"Oh, shut up. I'm not finished yet!" exclaimed Janet, crying but smiling.

Jared put his arms up in mock surrender: 'Okay, I'm zipping it. Carry on.'

"By the time the firemen arrived, they smashed the door down. However, before they did that, they drilled a hole through the front door to confirm if there was a fire. There was! A fire in the home! I screamed! I screamed so loud! I'd never screamed like that in my whole life! My baby! My baby!" sobbed Janet.

"The fire service put a hose into the hole they'd created and pumped foamed water into the apartment. Just then, there was a great big bang and the door was broken in using a battering ram and a Halligan bar."

By now, Janet's head is now on Jared's shoulder. Jared has his hand over Janet's hand, trying to comfort her.

"I ran inside. A fireman was trying to grab hold of my wrist. However, his hand slipped, and I managed to break free. I dashed straight towards my baby and picked her up... she wasn't breathing."

A member of cabin crew walked over, giving Janet a tissue and a glass of water. Janet drank the water before wiping her tears away.

"My baby was taken off me by a fireman who then tried to give her first aid. While they were calling for an ambulance, they continued CPR. They continued with CPR. They are pressing her little chest in with two fingers multiple times before blowing into her mouth. It's something I've always been keen on taking time to learn but never dawned on me I'd ever actually need it for real. She never came around. Once the ambulance arrived, they tried their best too, but they drove to the hospital where she was pronounced dead on arrival."

Jared moved his hand to comfort Janet and stayed silent, as there were no words which could describe the horror she had had to go through.

"All that time. I've always blamed myself; it's all down to me. The few events which were crucial in every way, all took hold and led to this. I'm afraid the bullet lies with me," sniffed Janet.

There were a few passengers who began to turn around to look at what the commotion was about.

As the cabin crew station was a mere two aisles back, they could hear and couldn't help but walk over;

"Excuse me, Ma'am, is everything okay?" asked a stewardess.

Janet didn't utter a word but continued sobbing. Jared nodded his head and mouthed "Yes thank you."

The stewardess returned with a hand full of tissues and handed them to Jared. He smiled and nodded his head at her, taking the tissues while still comforting Janet.

"My husband and I were always bickering and arguing after that, as he was never there – never there before it happened, and it only got worse after. I still feel that if he had been there, this wouldn't have happened. He wasn't the best of husbands. Even though I continued with my career, I spent most time with Samantha and did everything for her. Me having a go at him didn't help either. It only made matters worse. Eventually, he felt that he had to move out. I couldn't stand the sight of him – and he couldn't bear to listen to me, telling him how awful he was as a husband. And he blamed me for Samantha's death. Our marriage eventually broke down. It's been almost a year now, and we're already divorced. It's all done and dusted. Just three days ago I visited my baby's grave. I had a feeling that I might not be able to go back for a long while, so I spent an hour there at her side. In my heart, I know that she is somewhere much better than where we are," said Janet.

"Certainly, you know; if I were to tell you the number of amazing things I have seen with my naked eye with the telescopes we have at our disposal, you wouldn't believe me. It's so beautiful up there, and I'm sure she's a beautiful free spirit amongst the heavens," said Jared.

"Excuse me, Ma'am, can I get you a drink?" said a stewardess. Janet turned towards the lady, only to realize her face was level with the stewardess's waist. She looked up into her face.

"Yes, a whiskey and Coke please."

Jared got the stewardess's attention by lifting his right hand.

"Oh, can you get me a drink too, please?"

The stewardess nodded her head profusely while smiling.

"Certainly, Sir, what can I get you?"

"Just a tomato juice, please."

His hand went back onto Janet's hand, clutching it tightly.

Chapter 17
Spectacle

It was early morning with clear blue skies. Overlooking the Manhattan skyline, a flock of birds flew by. Then, peculiarly, a commercial aircraft was seen to be flying rather low over the tops of the skyscrapers. It's 8:40 AM, and most people are already at work. Then, the aircraft struck the north tower of the World Trade Center in New York City.

The resulting impact was so loud that the reverberations could be felt across the whole city, echoing off the buildings around.

The streets surrounding the World Trade Center were gridlocked with traffic as drivers stared up in disbelief at what had just happened. The footpaths were chock-a-block of pedestrians all staring up at the chaos that the resulting spectacular has brought about. And added to the chaos was the migration onto the streets by people leaving other buildings to see what was going on.

During all the commotion, the emergency services were en-route to the scene when, at 9:03 AM, another aircraft struck the south tower of the World Trade Center. This heightened the alert. A coordinated strike of this nature must have been planned and controlled by a hostile foreign nation. The entire of greater Manhattan saw people in their masses vacate all high-rise buildings. People now are terrified to remain in the adjacent towers, as they might be next.

Deputy directors Andrew, Todd and Bob were out taking a walk at the Arlington National Cemetery, which is outside the west end of the Pentagon, about a mile away. Andrew had a 'shield' device in his hand and was following the progress of the aircraft – as could any member of the public using a particular app – while the three of them faced the tomb of the unknown soldier. It was 9:37 AM when a commercial aircraft flies into the side of the Pentagon building.

Conveniently, all good and well, it was going to plan. The three were outside, well away from harm's way.

Sheila McDaniel was on vacation and visiting family in Scotland. That vacation timed rather well.

A total of four scheduled commercial aircraft came down. The two which struck the World Trade Center were American Airlines flight 11 and United Airlines flight 175, both traveling from Boston to Los Angeles. The Pentagon was hit by American Airlines flight 77, going from Dulles, Virginia to Los Angeles. The fourth, United Airlines flight 93, flying from Newark, New Jersey to San Francisco, crashed in a field in Shanksville, Pennsylvania.

"Well, there you go guys, it's not every day you get to see such a spectacle," said Andrew.

"Well, here we go now, full steam ahead with our rapid response, countermeasures and counter strikes," said Todd.

The 'shield' device was displaying an urgent message.

Todd played it on his device.

"This is Sheila McDaniel, Director at the Central Intelligence Agency; I am requesting all authorized personnel to appear before me today at 4 PM at the Pentagon." said Sheila.

Sheila had cut her trip short and decided to charter an Air Force plane to take her back to Virginia. She was in communication with the Department of Air Force, asset management;

"This is the director of the Central Intelligence Agency. I am requesting an immediate evacuation from Kirknewton Air Force Base in Scotland; I need access to any aircraft we have in the vicinity," said Sheila.

"Ma'am, the only plane we have is a C – 17 cargo plane. It is at a German Air Force Base; it's the United States Air Force Base in Ramstein-Miesenbach, Germany. It could be with you in just over one hour. We're getting in touch with them right away," said a logistics officer at asset control.

"Copy that, thank you," said Sheila.

Sheila was traveling to Kirknewton Air Force Base, just over an hour's drive away – she should make it just as the plane lands. She had her security team with her, consisting of three bodyguards as one was driving the vehicle. There was a further two in the next car. Again, they were the bullet-proof black SUVs favored by the CIA.

It was generally raining in Scotland, and even more so during September.

There was a mass evacuation at The Pentagon in case the fires spread. The three deputy directors at the CIA were now amongst the crowd waiting outside The Pentagon. The entire personnel for the emergency services on duty that day had arrived at the scene. That day might have been a bank robber's dream.

As the SUV pulled into the main entrance of the airfield, a sign appeared. A board, white in color with a black border around its perimeter. On it, there was an emblem consisting of a turquoise blue and yellow circle with a yellow crown above. In the center, there are three red diamonds. The airfield is afforded to air cadets Scotland. Below all that, it states '661 V GS RAF Kirknewton' and, even further down 'MoD property – keep out!'

The windscreen wipers rumble as raindrops are squeegeed away from the windshield. It was almost deserted, and no signs of buildings – just an empty field with what seems to be at take-off and landing strip. Only then, in the distance they saw some lights appear, and what looked like a plane heading this way, but it was a good five minutes away as the lights can be quite deceiving. Due to their high power and glare, the aircraft appeared much closer. The SUVs were parked up to the side at the end of the runway, as it would be at least the end of the strip by the time the cargo plane C – 17 finally came to a standstill. However, these aircraft were designed to take off and land in a very short distance, as compared to commercial airlines.

*****

Inside the departures building at Istanbul Atatürk Airport, Janet had decided to make use of the executive lounge for some refreshment. It was a Star Alliance Club lounge. As she pushed the glass door, she noticed that everyone was peering at a news channel that was on all the TV screens. What was unusual was that she could barely get in the door such were the number of people in the room. What had happened that was so important? Just then, while she was watching, she noticed this was live coverage and that smoke was billowing out of the World Trade Center, and one of the towers began to disappear down as though the camera was pulling up. Unless it was the building that was collapsing, she couldn't tell. Until the cloud of dust completely blurred the screen, and there were many screams heard, and people running, which is when the camera cut out.

That was the building collapsing.

"Oh, my God, is this really happening?? Surely not," said Janet to herself.

She looked around. Everybody else looked as shocked as she was.

Jared had made himself comfortable with his feet up on chairs in the departures lounge. He was trying to read his book when he heard a commotion. It was a few people listening to maybe a phone call radio or some online communication, as they have their ears glued to a cell phone device.

Jared decided to walk over as the group was getting emotional and started to scream and shout.

"Hey, what's the issue?" asked Jared.

It was a few Japanese and a German, and none of them could speak good English.

"Airplane crash, into the big building," said one of the Japanese.

"The building brought to the ground has been!" exclaimed the German.

"Zweimal, zweimal." He meant two times or twice.

Jared was a bit confused. He sat back down again, only to then be disturbed by Janet, hurtling across the lounge after abandoning the idea of business class refreshments. She screamed at him from across the lounge, but by this time she wasn't the only one screaming.

"Jared, the fucking buildings in New York have been hit by aircraft! The twin towers, and one's already collapsed. I watched it on live TV just now!"

"Hell, no way!! This country is at war. Or if it's not, it is now!!"

Jared stood up and put his book away and swung his holdall over his shoulder.

"I'd like to go and watch the news. Let's go back to your executive lounge. I'd like to see."

The two of them walked briskly back to the club lounge.

*****

Back at Kirknewton airfield where the cargo plane is almost 30 seconds to touchdown. The landing gear is fully deployed and the sound of the jet engines can be heard. Just as the wind direction briefly changes the sound of the turbines can be heard re-adjusting to the change in air pressure. Only then the rubber tires hit the runway surface.

*****

Inside the office of CNN, Timothy, Janet's boss, is glued to the TV screen, and the phones are all off the hook. They had been inundated with freelance journalists offering to share and sell their news video recordings. However, a helicopter had been chartered by the news organization, so they had their own story.

"I hope Janet is getting on this. Certainly our story of the century. The blue on blue. Or more like goddamn third world war if you ask me," said Timothy.

Timothy took a drink of coffee which had been stood for that long it was now stone cold. Regardless, his eyes were still pinned to the TV screen.

Back at Atatürk Airport, as Janet and Jared approached the Star Alliance Club lounge, there were dozens of people stood in front of the screens, except that the twin towers don't seem to be visible any longer.

"Good God, I hope my involvement and discoveries had no bearing on this, Janet. Did you ever mention to me blue on blue?" said Jared.

Janet turned to him and rolled her eyes.

"Yes, that's right, it was mentioned by you, you mentioned it, you heard it spoken by the CIA as I recollect." Said, Janet.

"Well, this is well above our pay grade. Maybe we're both heading into a firestorm, coming right out from the dragon's mouth!" said Jared.

Chapter 18

Investigative Journalist

"Well, it's something I've signed up to do, and it's part of my job being an investigative journalist," said Janet.

"Well, it's okay for you; I guess with your Samantha passing away, you must be feeling suicidal anyway," said Jared.

"How dare you, you asshole. Well, you've just shown how much of comfort you really are, you bastard," said Janet.

She walked off, pushing through the crowd, towards the Star Alliance lounge.

*****

Back at Kirknewton airfield, the C–17 cargo plane was stationary, and the rear cargo ramp was now retracting. The two SUVs were behind, ready to drive into the aircraft.

"Officer, get us to Washington; we need to be at the Pentagon. Is that what your orders are?" said Sheila.

"Yes Ma'am," said the pilot.

Sheila turned away, nodding her head.

"Well let's get there as quick as possible; we've got an emergency on our hands."

She began to get into one of the seats dotted along the side of the fuselage and prepared to buckle herself up.

Jackson was gazing at the stars just as a shooting star went past. He quickly stood up, only to spill his tea. The sky was completely clear over the Himalayas, and a constellation was visible like it was only touching distance away. He was sat on the rooftop terrace at the Serena Hotel Shigar, enjoying a green tea while admiring the stars, when suddenly;

"That's crazy. Yaar! What the fuck!" exclaimed a fellow guest.

The man walked over to Jackson with a cell phone in his hand.

"Hey, are you an American?" he asked.

"Eh, yes, I am. Why, what's happened?" asked Jackson.

"Hell, have you not heard? You know those two large twin towers in New York City! they've been brought down to the ground by two aircraft flying into them. And I believe a third flew into the side of the Pentagon."

Jackson appeared nonplussed. As always, during this time, there were many things which never made any sense why he was conducting this research into this region in terms of geography. He couldn't share as the findings had to be kept secret. Now, this was adding to the ever more unanswered questions.

"Oh, my – that's so eerie. I'll go and read up on it later in my room. No, actually I'll go now," he said.

As soon as he closed the door behind him, he heard an odd ringtone. He drew his phone out of his pocket. It was his that was ringing. It was a satellite phone, operated by the company Thuraya. He didn't answer it until he was well inside his room with the door shut;

"Elijah Moses, how can I help you?" he said.

"God damn you, Jackson, I have told you not to use your name! Now you're working on a program which is due to have its budget increased exponentially during the next few days. Currently you're just a one-man band, right. But in the coming days, there's going to be hundreds operating in and around the area. So, what you need now is to work on finding suitable accommodation as of immediately, and in the immediate region, as they're going to need accommodating. Now have you been watching the news and heard what's happened with the airline strikes?" said Agent Parker.

"Yes, sir, I have. I've just been looking at it now, and if I can open my damn laptop instead of having you blow down my ear..."

"Well, that's why the damn shit should hit the fan. Early intelligence seems to state the operation has been carried out by a terrorist organization operating from Afghanistan, so we're gonna be showing our presence there in the thousands. So, get your finger out and start sorting accommodation for our lads in the CIA, in terms of being able to accommodate the resources, security, you know... you know what you're doing..." said Agent Parker.

"Message understood. I'll be on it."

Almost 10 AM, and at the restaurant at the Serena Shigar Fort Hotel, it was almost time for Jackson's morning tour. He finished his black coffee and made use of the napkin. As he got up, he gestured a thank you to the waiter and headed off outside. Guest relations manager

Abdul was already waiting there in the sunshine, patiently having a chat with a carpet seller who was running a store within the inside of the hotel perimeter walls.

"Good morning Mr Jackson, did you have a good sleep?" said Abdul.

"Well, yes I certainly did. I think it's one of the quietest places I have ever traveled to in my life. It's so peaceful and tranquil, and there is not much wildlife here of the type that makes a noise in the night," said Jackson.

Upon hearing this Abdul smiled and nodded his head.

"Certainly, Sir, the altitude is so high that there's not many who dare to settle here."

He began to walk in the direction of the big rock that the hotel sat on. It was one of the most prominent features of the whole building.

"Known as Fong-Khar, which in the local language means 'Fort on the Rock' – Serena Shigar encompasses a 450-year-old fort and 17th-century Raja palace," said Abdul. "From the traditional stone and wood architecture to the tranquil sight and sound of the Shiga stream flowing in front of the hotel, the experience here is that of a peaceful home away from home in an ancient and undisturbed wilderness."

"Well, that's exactly what I said earlier," said Jackson.

"The hotel's cherry orchards are quite well known, as is our fresh, homemade cherry ice cream and local balti cuisine. Crafted with fresh, organic fruits and vegetables from our garden."

Jackson stopped and said;

"One question about excursions and trips – Is there anything you can advise on?"

"Yes, the hotel guests can visit five nearby lakes in one day, with three offering boating facilities for charters and cruises," said Abdul.

"Oh, that's nice – I'm here for a good few days, so I'll bear that in mind," said Jackson.

"And also, within driving distance there are many ways to enjoy the captivating beauty of the Shiga Valley. There are stunning natural treasures like the Katpana Desert or Biama Nakpo, which is also known as the Cold Desert and is one of the highest deserts in the world. There is also Concordia Glacier, around which are clustered some of the highest mountains in the world, including K2."

Abdul was now walking up some stairs into a room like a museum.

"You can follow a trekking trail up Shigar Rock; browse the handicrafts of local artisans at Skardu's Puran Bazaar; hike into the Deosai Plains, which is the world's second highest plateau, keeping a watchful eye for Snow Leopards, Himalayan Brown Bears, Golden Marmots and Tibetan Wolves; pay a visit to a 14th-century mosque, or explore the historic villages of Chinpa and Halpapa," he said.

Abdul was about to carry on talking when Jackson intervened.

"Hey, have you heard about what's happening in New York with those aircraft?"

"Well, I don't really watch TV myself, but they were talking about it here, and it sounds very bizarre and a tragic accident. If it has happened, my heart goes out to all those who have lost friends and relatives," said Abdul.

Chapter 19
Goddamn Tora Bora

It was a slightly windy day, and the leaves were blowing across the carriageway. It was the landing strip at Davison Air Force airfield in Newington, Virginia, just outside Washington. It was Sheila McDaniel's flight, just arrived from Scotland. Not long after it touched down the bay doors began to drop, and the black SUVs arrived. It was only a twenty-minute drive to the Pentagon building from here, straight up the interstate highway 395.

As the SUVs were traveling down the highway, Sheila's phone rings.

"Sheila McDaniel speaking, how can I help you?"

Sheila distances her phone from her ear slightly, while the President hits out at her intelligence-gathering. It apparently hasn't gone so well, given the country is under attack.

"Goddammit, Sheila! We've got planes coming in from different directions. God knows what's happening – we don't even know if it's a hostile nation! I need you to get me some answers, and they need to be provided pretty damn quick!"

"Yes, Mrs President. I am heading back to the Pentagon right now where I will brief my entire team. We'll be going through everything with a fine toothcomb, starting with all flight data, also retrieving the Blackbox, passenger lists and so on. I'll be sure to keep you informed."

"Well, I sure as well hope you do, as I'll be waiting," said the President.

As the SUVs approached the Pentagon, they were checked over using the security protocol procedure and waved through. Sheila walked through the corridors at the Pentagon. The section she worked in had not suffered any damage an all personnel had returned to their stations. However, there were still hundreds of emergency service officers in the area working on the clean-up operation, such was the devastation caused. The plane completely demolished the Pentagon's outer core and disappeared into the basement. It was no longer visible from the outside.

There was echoing off the corridors, a clicker-clatter of shoes. Sheila walked down the hallway with her security guards. She recognized many faces who turned to her, and somehow felt that they needed comforting and reassuring that the matter was under control, and the perpetrators would be brought to justice.

It had just turned 4:05 PM and Sheila opened the door to the 100-foot room and walked in.

"Hello to you all. Looks like we've reached that point," she said.

Sat inside are Mac, Gerry, Todd, Andrew, Donald, Bob and Alexandra. Alexandra has been away on Maternity leave.

"Alexandra, nice to see you back; when did you return? "

"Yesterday. A week early but hey, looks like you might need me," said Alexandra.

Sheila dropped her Filofax onto the table;

"Todd, Bob and Andrew, and everyone: I need you all to work together on this, and it's all about making sure that we're seen to have done our jobs with no stone left unturned. For us to do that we must be provided with all passengers who were on those aircraft, and make sure that any talk related to an aircraft strike is recorded, so that we can construct a theory as to why anybody would have a motive to hijack commercial aircraft."

Andrew had his hand up. Sheila wasn't keen to relinquish the stage, but realized to not do worked against her.

"Go ahead Andrew."

"I understand we need to gather together all the evidence we can to incriminate those former detainees with regards hijacking on terrorism charges," he said.

"We've had their voice recordings analyzed by software to regenerate their voice and enable us to produce a recording of them discussing an attack of some kind, nothing too specific but it's enough to show intent, when our law enforcement agencies manage to obtain a recording," said Alexandra.

Sheila began to take notes and place names against each of the records.

"So, guys, I need to draft a speech for the President to give to the leader of Pakistan. It needs to be so profound and resonating, that they end up giving us unrestricted access to the countries involved – obviously under the prefix of fighting jihadism," she said.

"War on Terror," said Todd.

"I've got a brilliant one, we need to imply and sound that we are serious – as serious as a bull in a China shop. How about, 'if you don't give us unrestricted access, then we're going to make a goddamn Tora Bora out of you'?" suggested Donald.

Sheila turned away with a smirk on her face. Mac pulled his pen out of his mouth and points it up;

"Yeah! I like that. I came up with, 'you're either with us or against us!' If you're with us, then expect billions of dollars in aid. If you're against us, then we're going to make a goddamn Tora Bora out of you!" said Mac.

"I will authorize our plan of attack with the President later today, and also approve emergency funds, as it's best to buy out a nation rather than bombing it to submission, especially when we are dealing with a country that could launch a nuclear weapon that could land on Israel within minutes! So, I think the best option would be to offer them billions in terms of aid, and sweet talk should eventually create a division within the country between the haves and the have-nots," said Sheila.

"Yes, I get it, we're going to spoil them rotten; the leadership of Pakistan," said Mac.

Sheila continued making notes. She was preparing for a live telecast with the President, and so needed credible sources, answers, and a strategy of attack.

"So, to recap – what I needed was a draft outline of what the President will address to the leader of Pakistan, as to gain access into Afghanistan, you must have permission to fly over Pakistan. So, 'you're either with us, or you're against us! If you're with us, then you will receive billions of dollars' worth of aid, which I personally couldn't care less how you spend – house in Knightsbridge, whatever. On the other hand, if you're against us... well, we'll make a goddamn Tora Bora out of you!'"

There were giggles around the room.

"So, any more suggestions?" asked Sheila.

Chapter 20

The Shangrila Hotel and Resort

Just then, there was a knock on the door. It was security, who entered the room and handed a note to Sheila.

"Ma'am, you are all requested to stay in the room for a conference call with the President."

"Okay, thank you officer," said Sheila.

Sheila was handed a note and looked at it briefly before putting it down on the table.

"As you all heard, the President would like us to remain in here until the conference call has taken place, which should be short," she said.

The clock on the wall showed only twelve minutes remaining until 5 PM.

*****

Back at the Star Alliance lounge at Istanbul airport, Janet decided to make use of her time by having a look at hotel accommodation for when she lands. As she would arrive at Islamabad International airport and so be in the country's capital, she decided to go onto a hotel booking site to browse options. With her CNN-issued credit budget of $50,000 a month, she wasn't tight on money and could go for a top end hotel. She went on to booking.com and selected five-star accommodation, searching from highest price down to the lowest. She decided to check the reviews out, and opening an adjacent page on her browser she types in 'best hotel chain in Pakistan'. The page took a few seconds to refresh.

At the top Janet saw 'Serena Hotels'. She clicked on the link and noticed there were many pictures which contained scenery from a variety of regions, giving her the impression that this chain may have top hotels in more far-flung areas across the country. She hovered the mouse over until she saw one which was surrounded by mountains, and there was one in Islamabad which she would come back to. The mountainous one was called Shigar Fort Hotel, in Skardu, Pakistan. She clicked on it and lo and behold it was surrounded by what appeared to be the Himalayas. She opened another tab on her browser and it went to a map where she entered Skardu, and it zoomed in such that she could clearly see that the town was almost on the foothills of K2 and others of the world's highest peaks on earth.

"Bingo!" she said to herself, smiling.

She clicked on the hotel website and proceeded to book a room. Prices ranged from $250 to $400 a night. She decided to make the booking from tonight, so that she had a room and bed ready for her on arrival, as her flight would be arriving into Islamabad in the very early morning and check-in for tomorrow would almost definitely be after midday, if not even later in the afternoon. As it was still before midnight she went ahead and made the booking, and she decided to organize herself a transfer as they had chauffeur-driven cars which pick guests up from the airport. So, she went ahead with adding her flight itinerary into additional notes.

*****

Jackson was waiting in the sunshine, as he had arranged an excursion with the hotel. He had been introduced to a local individual who was familiar with the region, who coincidently was another Mr Khan. Salim Khan. This would be more useful for Jackson in terms of navigating roads more easily, as this individual was a retired officer from the Force Command Northern Areas. Today he would go ahead with this local guide and use his vehicle. However, his personal driver, Mr Khan, was due to arrive this morning; he could come along too.

"Mr Jackson, your guide is here," said the concierge.

"Hello, you must be Mr Khan?" said Jackson.

"Yes, many of us have the name Khan here. Call me Salim. If you want to sit in the car, I'm ready to go," said Salim.

"Well, my personal driver, who I've been using since my first day in Pakistan is arriving very shortly, so I'm just going to wait for him to arrive. He's just messaged me and is in Skardu right now. So let's go and have a chai black tea," said Jackson.

The two proceed towards the restaurant. On their way, they passed a small carpet shop – one of the little outlet stores in the hotel – where a few samples of carpet are hung outside. Jackson has a quick feel of one of the carpets, but Salim intervenes;

"Sir, we have many shops here which I will drive you past and show you much better varieties at lower prices."

"Oh no, I'm just looking; I've got too much equipment to start buying anything," said Jackson.

They arrived at the restaurant, Jackson pulling open one of the wooden double doors for Salim and then following in behind, closing the door as he did.

"Thank you, Sir," said Salim.

"As Salaam Alaikum." Then to one of the restaurant staff, "Can you make us two chai, please?" Then, "So, I have a question, Salim."

"Yes, you're welcome to ask," said Salim.

"I want to pick your brains. I'm looking for an ideal hotel complex in this region for some colleagues of mine who are due to arrive – and as you are local, I'd value your opinion."

"You want to poke my brain, I don't understand," Salim frowned.

"Oh, it's just a figure of speech, it means I want to get some information from you. I want your opinion, your ideas," said Jackson.

"Oh!" exclaimed Salim. He laughed. "You Americans have a different way of explaining things. Here in this country, we literally say what we mean. There's no... how do you say, figures of speech, or sarcasm."

The doors to the kitchen are opened and a waiter arrived carrying a tray with tea and sugar lumps in a bowl. He placed it all on the table.

"Sir, is that all for you?" asked the waiter.

"Yes, I am okay... would you like anything else, Salim?" said Jackson.

"No, I'm fine too," said Salim.

Jackson used his fingers to put sugar lumps in his tea before lifting a little teaspoon to stir his drink. While stirring, he gazed at Salim;

"My colleagues want to stay in a hotel in this area, and a grand one, but not necessarily as grand as this one." Jackson looked around at the splendor the hotel had to offer. I mean, this hotel is vintage."

He began to smile.

Chapter 21
Intrusion

"We need one which can provide a reasonable amount of security. Perhaps one that is high up on a peak or ridge and has a good vantage point, so it can easily be surrounded by security personnel. Which hotel would you recommend?" asked Jackson.

"I understand why you ask. My job has meant me visiting many hotels to pick up clients. There is one which is very awkward to get to. It has its own road leading to it. It's in the valley next to a lake. The Shangrila Resort Hotel," said Salim.

Jackson looked up at the ceiling, shaking his head.

"Not really the best place as people can get high above and get a vantage point. You understand what I mean by being able to look down? With binoculars, they can see inside," said Jackson.

"We are going that way today so you can look for yourself. It's surrounded by trees which obscure a lot of the lines of sight. We will go, you will see," said Salim.

*****

The Turkish Airlines flight TK710 had boarded, taken off and was now cruising at thirty thousand feet. An hour into the journey, there was a clatter of the refreshments trolley. Two crew members started to roll the cart down the aisle. Just then, there was an announcement;

"Good evening ladies and gentlemen. We shall shortly be serving light refreshments. And we also have meals for those who would like something more substantial."

Janet was sitting back with her eye mask on, which had been on for a good twenty minutes and one would have almost thought she was fast asleep. Just then;

"Hi, whiskey and Coke for me please, thanks," she said, pulling her eye mask away and sitting up.

*****

The wall had a screen hanging on it, and currently all eyes are on it as it shows the desk at the Oval Office. Sheila was sat at her desk adjusting her earpiece, and an aide attached a microphone to her collar.

"Ma'am, you are good to go. You're on the air," said the aide.

The President then addressed the crowd of directors and deputy directors at the Pentagon.

"This is your President, and I am addressing my most senior personnel who are sitting in front of me. Our nation has not suffered such a big loss since the attack on Pearl Harbor. Sheila, as regards the current situation has there been any update as to why we may have been targeted, and by whom?"

Sheila gulped, and took a deep breath, exhaling slowly.

Just then, there was a knock on the door and in came an administrator carrying a file which was bound and sealed and labeled as confidential. He handed it to Sheila, saluted her and walk straight out. It was as though a great burden had lifted off Sheila's shoulders.

"Hold on, Madam President, I've just been handed vital evidence."

Sheila opened the file, starting with tearing open the sealed envelope, which was made from a cardboard material. She then began to slide out a bunch of A4 sheets bound together with Treasury tags that contained pictures and names of individuals. She turned the pages over until reading something which made her freeze: information that had been highlighted: Al Qaeda, the terrorist organization, and its leader, Osama bin Laden's name; references to his hideout, and that of his living in a remote region in Afghanistan. It also stated that it was believed the operation was conducted and organized and funded by the spiritual leader, Osama bin Laden, who was a Saudi citizen who had been expelled from Saudi Arabia and had been on the run, living in exile in Afghanistan. He was an heir to a corporation which was worth billions of dollars, the bin Laden group.

"Madam President – we have just had handed to us intelligence that the organization behind the attack is the Al Qaeda leader who is in a hideout in Afghanistan. Named as Osama bin Laden. He is a Saudi citizen who, many years ago, was expelled from the country and has been since living in this hideout in Afghanistan. It appears that he was the backer financially and spiritually, as he was once the heir to the multi-billion-dollar corporation, the bin Laden group," said Sheila.

"Well, it seems that information is beginning to move around. So we need to get to the bottom of this all and bring to justice whomever is responsible, wherever the hell they are," said the President.

"Madam President. I would like to take this opportunity to request emergency aid to allow us to deal with the situation. We are now in a war-like situation. All our armed forces have had their readiness moved up to DEFCON 3, as this has far-reaching implications. It requires many of our intelligence staff to relocate and therefore will take a great deal out of our allocated budget. Not to mention the use of military aircraft in the region," said Sheila.

"How much are we looking at right now Sheila?"

"I envisage an initial $5 billion spread over three years, Ma'am," said Sheila.

"I'll get that approved right away. Right now, I am preparing my speech which I will give to the leaders of Pakistan and Afghanistan. I will need your input. Do you have that ready?"

Sheila nods her head while she looks at all her counterparts in the room. She then turns to the screen to face the President.

"Yes Madam President, we have that for you and will send it over right away. Afghanistan is a landlocked country, so accessing it requires us addressing the leader of Pakistan. I do not believe

Pakistan has any reason to object; indeed, the opposite, as the consequences of an objection would be of grave concern to them."

"Right. Thank you, Sheila. I will contact the leader of Pakistan right away."

The bedside table lamp clicked as the light was turned off. It was almost 11 PM in Pakistan's capital, Islamabad. The Pakistani prime minister had just laid down for the night.

The phone began to ring.

"Yeh harami khon ho gah!" said Prime Minister Sadik of Pakistan.

That meant: 'Who can this bastard be calling at this time of the night!'

The President reached his arm out to turn on the lamp while still lying in bed. He then reached for the telephone and pulled the cord towards him under the duvet. All was quiet while he listened.

"Ah! Yes, yes, right, right, Gee. Yes, Gee, I, okay."

He turned around in bed and pulled himself up, rubbing his eyes. The phone got connected and President Hilary Carlton was on the line.

"Good evening Mr. Prime Minister Sadik. I hope I haven't rung at an inconvenient time and woken you. As I'm sure you are already aware, our nation suffered an attack and tragedy yesterday."

"Hello, Madam President Hilary. No, it's not inconvenient. You're welcome."

"Our intelligence services have gathered evidence of a terrorist organization or group, Al Qaeda, the leader of which is Saudi citizen Osama bin Laden, who is in a hideout in Afghanistan. He has been expelled from Saudi Arabia and is in exile in your neighboring country Afghanistan. Forgive me if I sound harsh at this point, but you're either with us, or you're against us on this. If you're with us, we will assist you with billions of dollars' worth of aid. However, if you're against us and fail to cooperate, then we shall have no choice to make a goddamn Tora Bora out of you. Do I make myself clear?"

Prime Minister Sadik rolled his eyes and was silent for a little while. He turned to look at his wife, who was already fast asleep. It seemed he was caught between a rock and a hard place.

"Yes, I understand. Please carry on. What is it specifically, you want?" he said.

President Hilary had a fine silver pen in her left hand, and a list written down on a sheet of paper. She tapped the pen against each item on the list as she proceeded down it.

"Firstly, we require air support, and to be able to pass over Pakistani airspace to enter Afghanistan. Secondly, we require that we can send equipment to Afghanistan via your shipping ports and use your road or rail routes into Afghanistan for our supply convoys. Thirdly, we require 5000 US diplomatic visas issued to our intelligence team, who shall operate across Afghanistan and Pakistan and much of the area where this Al Qaeda group is likely to have fighters and sympathizers. The hideouts come within the borders of the Durand Line." said the Prime Minister.

The Durand Line was an internationally recognized line and stretches across the porous

2,430-kilometer (1,510 mile) international border between Afghanistan and Pakistan.

Prime Minister Sadik's eyes rolled again.

"That's a very contentious subject and region," he said.

"We can start with these three for now," said the President.

Sadik seemed somewhat nervous. He took a deep breath in before giving his reply;

"Madam President – I will contact my ministers and seniors in the agencies who will give you all that is required, and if you have any issues you can contact me, you have my word. Everything will be offered to you, and we can promise you the utmost cooperation at this stage. I just have one question: how many billions in aid are you offering us?"

"Well, at this stage, a $50 billion aid package involving military hardware and loans with, I'm guessing, conditions attached. However, what you do with a lot of that is entirely up to you. If I don't get what I want, heads will roll, I can assure you of that. America has been put on to the highest alert since the attack on Pearl Harbor, and believe me, we could quite easily send you all back to the Stone Age if need be; I'm sure you understand what I'm getting at."

"To be quite frank Madam President, I'm tired of all the skulduggery going on right now!" said Prime Minister Sadik.

"Well we'd better make that a $50 billion aid package then," she said.

Prime Minister Sadik's eyes light right up just then.

*****

The road ahead looked slightly bumpy. Inside the four-wheel-drive Toyota jeep Salim Khan, the local tour guide, is driving Jackson and his assistant Mr. Khan. They just arrived at the Shangrila Resort, which Salim Khan had advised Jackson the best location for his team to stay in. Just as they came to a junction leading into the resort, Jackson leaves the vehicle;

"Hey damn it, this looks fucking amazing. It's just what we really fucking need. A large lake, a private lake surrounded by all those private guest houses, many chalets. they are all afforded a lake view, as well as being part of one complex which we could book out altogether and use as our base camp," said Jackson.

Jackson turned round to look at Salim and smiled lavishly. He was excited.

"Salim, hey guy, my goodness you're a goddamn fucking genius mate. This is exactly what we really need. I can't give too many details, but this is perfect! I'm going to make my way over to the reception... and see what they can do."

He climbed back into Salim's vehicle, and they drive slowly along the narrow road behind the chalets over to the reception.

On first impressions when you were confronted with Shangrila Resort. You couldn't help but notice the waterfront chalets that were of an ancient Chinese architecture all in front of a refined lake-front with a garden and mountain views. Set along Lower Kachura lake with views of the Karakoram mountain range, this elegant resort was 3 km from Upper Kachura lake and 18 km from Skardu.

*****

Janet had passed through airport security at Islamabad International airport. Her flight landing was very pleasant, and she effortlessly gone through security and immigration at the airport. She was now looking for her car driver from the Serena Hotel. She spotted all the hostesses waiting orderly, all with signs for hotels and tour providers so travelers could identify them. She passed a few, such as Marriot, Pearl Continental. Until one caught her eye: JANET DENNIS. Below her name was a professionally printed logo of the hotel chain Serena Hotels. Janet waved at the driver. He relaxed his arms with relief, put his sign away, then rushed over to assist Janet with her luggage. He took the trolley from her hands;

"Hello, a very early good morning, Janet," said the driver.

As he was walking. Zafar began to talk.

"My name is Zafar, and I'm your driver today. The hotel is approximately 20 minutes away." Said Zafar.

His ID badge was clipped on his shirt where you could easily it. It was the airport's procedure. You could also see the hotel emblem and logo. Janet just wanted to get into her hotel room as of right now. She could sleep for a whole week, as she was that exhausted.

Two individuals were walking through the corridors of the Pentagon. We see them from their backs as they're walking away. Those they passed might salute them as they walked by, due to their senior roles. They finally arrived where they were heading, and knocked on Sheila's door. They were Andrew Lopez and Bobby Singleton.

"Welcome, good morning," said Sheila, as they walked into her office.

"Ma'am, we had those diplomatic visas submitted for our field agents and have had them back approved, so we have five hundred processed and good to go," said Andrew.

"Oh, that was quick," said Sheila.

"Also, we have our airbase in the Gulf States ready with all the aircraft necessary to deploy the five hundred into the region right away – we're just waiting on your approval. If you'd like to sign this document, I think we'll be good to rock 'n' roll," said Bobby.

Sheila had never moved a pen so fast. Without as much as a blink of an eye, she lifts her Parker pen, takes off the top and signs. This now signed, shall allow the CIA to send across the fix hundred field agents into the tribal regions and further across the two countries of Afghanistan and Pakistan. It's referred to as PAKAF.

"Thank you, Ma'am. That'll be all for now." said Andrew.

The two men left her office.

Across America, hundreds of families said farewell to their family members in service, as well as the family members of the CIA field agents as they got ready to leave for duty to Afghanistan and Pakistan.

The five hundred CIA field agents were boarding internal flights to Washington to be briefed and receive instructions today, and then leave tomorrow for the Gulf Air Base in Al Udeid, Qatar. It was the largest U.S. military facility in the Middle East.

Civil aviation flights arriving throughout the day at Dulles International Airport in Washington saw many CIA field agents having their passports scanned, and there was a shuttle bus on, organized for the transfer of these agents into the Pentagon. Once briefed they would be heading off to Andrews Air Force Base, just the other side of Washington.

Inside the Pentagon.

The briefing was taking place later that same day. It's given by many high-ranking officials, including Andrew and Bob.

Inside one of the great halls, a few chairs scuffle as they were moved about. It was almost 6 PM before all parties due to receive the briefing finally arrived. The interior of the large hall had a very light wood finish, possibly a natural wood cladding. It had the effect of a school assembly hall, with ceiling lights which are hanging down on wire cables. Just about the only thing missing would be the naughty step.

"Listen, folks, let's get a move on and get cracking. It's already gone ten minutes past six and we need to get you folks out there ASAP, right," said Andrew.

Everyone quietened.

"Right, firstly, as you are all aware you're being assigned as field agents in Afghanistan and Pakistan. You're due to leave first thing tomorrow morning. Except you won't be on a commercial airline as you were when you arrived today, but a military cargo plane such as a C – 17. You'll be parachuted out at certain strategic locations, which are where we believe there are Al Qaeda operatives grounded in and other networks and organizations such as the Haqqani network," said Bob.

"The Haqqani network is an Afghan guerrilla insurgent group using asymmetric warfare," said Andrew.

"Your supplies have already been delivered. They have been parachuted as we speak and you will have transponder locators to gain access to them. They mainly consist at this stage of your food supplies. Once you retrieve those, you shall confirm your location, and a further sortie flies past delivering your high-end technology items specific to your roles, such as night vision goggles, cameras, software, hardware, tablets, you name it, and not forgetting your weaponry. Now before the weapons delivery, it is paramount that the region has a recce carried out," said Andrew.

*****

Inside the USA B-52 aircraft flying at 50,000 feet above the Himalayas, the crew are getting ready to drop their payload when the rear ramp fails to deploy.

"What's wrong with it," said a crew member.

"Oh for God's sake, we're flying past our coordinates," said the co-pilot.

The issue is finally resolved and the gate begins to drop.

"Fucking drop it quick time, damn it... otherwise it'll all end up in China!" said the captain.

Just then, all too suddenly the transponders are all activated, and the pallets begin to roll off the back of the B-52, loaded with those supplies destined for the CIA field operatives.

Chapter 22

Champagne

It's very early morning at the foothills of Chogolisa mountain. The sun is still below the horizon. Chogolisa is a mountain in the Karakoram region of Pakistan. It lies near the Baltoro Glacier in the Concordia region which is home to some of the highest peaks of the world. Chogolisa has several peaks, the highest on the south west face rises to 7,668 meters.

A tent is pitched up along the side of the valley leading to the mountain. The wind is blowing across, and the snow falls. A couple of young backpackers from the United States are trekking here on an adventure and plan on reaching K2 base camp tomorrow. The tent is relentlessly shaking about.

"Hey Michael, we need to be leaving early in the morning to make it to base camp tomorrow. Can't wait to finally get to open this champagne, fucking drained carrying it all this way," said Silvia.

Both youths – boyfriend and girlfriend – have back packed from the USA and had various stopovers including Paris, which is where they picked up the champagne.

"I know – our rations aren't enough to stay here any longer; we need to get back on our feet. We're not opening that champagne until we reach that base camp... making it possibly the highest altitude champagne bottle opened on record. Guinness book of records here we come... but, not before you suck me off a little. So, let's see you get crazy, baby," said Michael slightly breathlessly.

There's a sound of a zip undoing, and the tent's side began to open and Michael stepped outside.

"Oh my God, God it's freezing... I bet my piss will freeze before it hits the ground!" he said.

He walked away from the tent no more than ten meters, and began to undo his multiple layers of clothing, finally drawing out his penis. He began to take a piss, and as he did he leant over and spat as well – maybe trying to land it into the same hole his piss made in the melting snow. Mike stopped for a moment, admiring the very early-morning freezing cold weather amongst the high peaks. He rushed back into the tent and proceeded to zip it back up.

"I said stick it out so I can suck it out," said Silvia.

The two began to pleasure each other, followed by the tent beginning to shake as things evidently became more heated.

Just then the tent zip opened again... and Michael's hand reached out, holding Silvia's bra. He scooped up snow in both cups, drew his hand with the bra back into the tent and zipped the zip.

Next minute, Silvia let out a deafening scream, followed by "You fucking asshole!" – he had put her snow-filled bra back on her breasts.

It seemed he was forgiven though, as the tent soon began to shake again.

"Oh, please, don't stop," Silvia could be heard to say.

As they both were reaching climax, there was suddenly an almighty thud. A pallet landed containing boxes stacked and strapped up with a GPS transponder bleeping away, no more than 15 meters away.

"Michael, what was that!"

A bunch of parachutes came out of the sky and landed silently on and around the pallet.

Michael, lost in the moment of being in his girlfriend, was incapable of any response other than a brief growl.

Registering his indifference to the interruption, Silvia did the same, moaning as he ground against her.

Just then, another pallet landed straight out of the sky together with a set of parachutes – this time a mere 10 meters, if that, from the tent.

And just after that, a final pallet landed directly above their tent, crashing on top of it just as Silvia climaxed. Everything went silent, including the pair.

All that was visible now was a pallet stacked with boxes, strapped down with a transponder bleeping away. Just then parachutes descended softly, landing on top of the pallet and where a tent once stood – which was now a crime scene.

*****

Andrew moved away from center stage and pointed at Bob who acknowledged his turn to speak by nodding his head and walking over to where Andrew had just vacated.

"Good evening folks. Good to see you all here, you made it. I would like to start with making you aware we have at least a dozen field agents who are operating in the region as we speak and are organizing accommodation for you. Apart from tonight, you will have accommodation to check into. Secondly, to repeat what Andrew said, the accommodation is in an area to which supplies can be safely and securely delivered.. I have a message here from my field agent showing the accommodation – the Shangrila resort – from above. The resort surrounds a large lake, which will mean the deliveries dropped from the air on pallets will have floats attached to ensure buoyancy if they land in the water. The resort has been exclusively booked by us for an indefinite period."

The resort had in fact been booked on a six-month rolling over contract, with undoubtedly many disgruntled customers who would find that their bookings had been canceled last minute by the Shangrila. It wasn't the first time this had happened. There had been instances in the past where the US administration had bought out entire hotel buildings so as to temporarily relocate their embassies at short notice.

"So from tomorrow night, you will be based at the Shangrila in the northern territories, not far from K2, the second tallest mountain in the world for those of you who like mountaineering."

*****

The Toyota Jeep was slowly driving across the stony dirt track with a lake on the left and mountain views to the right, surrounded by lush pine trees. Jackson was sat in the front passenger seat while his new guide Salim Khan was in the driver's seat and Jackson's private driver was in the back. As they approached the resort Jackson was looking at the lake and noticed the sunlight shimmering off the water's edge. It reminded him of when his father used to take him fishing in a lake closer to home.

"I wonder how deep the water is in the middle. Judging by the water feature, I'm guessing it's man-made," he said.

"Yes, you're right, the hotel was founded by the late Brigadier Muhammad Aslam Khan, the first commander of the Northern Scouts who liberated the Northern areas in 1948," said Salim.

"So, in the middle... I'm guessing it's much deeper than the edges?" said Jackson.

"Not too sure. There might be some old pictures in the lobby or office which may give us some indication," said Salim.

"Oh well, I'll have the specialist equipment soon which will enable me to measure the depth," said Jackson.

The Toyota finally arrived at a building with a reception sign. Jackson stepped out and headed straight for reception while Salim made his way out and followed behind, and Khan after that.

Before entering reception, Jackson looked up at the building again. It was built using ancient

Chinese methods and architecture. The roof parapet line was painted red. The tips of the eaves curled round, almost spiral, like a sea shell. In Chinese mythical tales, they had dragons that blow fire whose tails curl round like the flame amidst a fire –to give an image of strength and power perhaps. Jackson turned the handle on the door to reception, pushing open the door and stepping in. A clerk sat in a little office at the back of the reception area. He rose to his feet to greet Jackson.

"Good morning Sir, how are you? You're checking in?" he said.

"Well, no, not exactly. I need to speak to your manager regarding a huge block-booking. I need to book the entire resort." said Jackson.

"The whole resort!" exclaimed the clerk.

"Yes, that's correct. I am from the US administration, and I have been given the task of finding suitable accommodation for five hundred individuals who will be arriving tomorrow – which requires me speaking to your manager. The money will be wired across electronically."

The clerk lifted the handset on the phone on the office desk and pressed a button.

"Gee, Sir for Tum ko Milne aya koi shahs. He wants to speak to you. He's from America and wants to book the entire hotel."

It was a full ten minutes before a door the opposite side of reception to that which they had entered on opened, and a rather old-looking man, walking with the aid of a walking stick, entered the room. He approached Jackson, who was standing by the office desk looking annoyed.

"I'm guessing you must be the manager?" said Jackson.

The man extended his hand to shake Jackson's.

"Good morning Sir, how can I be of assistance?"

He spoke perfect English, eloquently if rather slowly.

"I'm from the US administration, representing the central government. Can we go and sit somewhere as I would like to discuss a large booking with you?" said Jackson.

"Certainly Sir, I'll get my aides to bring some tea and coffee and light refreshments as well," said the manager, turning to his clerk and speaking in Urdu;

"Please ask the kitchen staff to bring over tea, coffee and light refreshments. We'll be in my office."

"What's your name?" the manager asked Jackson.

"Me, I'm Jackson."

"Mr. Jackson, follow me to my office. You'll like the scenery."

Jackson stepped forward. Salim Khan opened the door, and all four men headed out.

"Salim and Khan, can you please wait here. I need to discuss things with the manager." Then "Mr. Manager, what's your name?"

"I'm Khaled, Khaled Mahmoud."

They walked along a windy footpath lined with cobblestones until they came across a hut almost on the edge of the lake. It even had a pier of sorts which went out across the lakefront, and there was a boat tied to it at the end.

"Come on in," said Khaled, opening the hut door.

They both walked in, and Khaled closed the door as Jackson sat down on a chair.

"So, Mr. Jackson, tell me what you would like." Khaled said.

Khaled picked up a book off his desk and went across his office and placed it neatly onto a bookshelf beside his desk. He turned to Jackson and walked back to his desk, sitting down on his chair behind it.

"Khaled, what I have for you is an offer which I'm sure you can't refuse. I'm working for the US administration as part of the ongoing operation regards the 9/11 attacks in New York and so on. We are conducting operations throughout Afghanistan and Pakistan, and I have been assigned the task to organize accommodation for five hundred personnel who are due to arrive tomorrow. They require accommodation, so it's a case of booking up the entire resort for the foreseeable future: a block-booking which is on a rolling contract, for an indefinite period. I'll make certain all the salaries are paid to all individuals. The buildings will still need to be maintained etc. I have been instructed to search for ideal accommodation and my guide here, whom you saw just now in reception, Salim Khan, made me aware of this facility which I think is ideal and meets our needs. We have it all. And I just want to make sure that I'm speaking to the right person to confirm that we are good to go ahead. We will just need to establish the cost for booking the entire venue for the next six months," said Jackson.

Khaled looked somewhat dazed. He was holding his hands together and spinning his thumbs around. Round and round. He looked at Jackson.

"Mr. Jackson. It's almost $2 million for the six months; not long ago I did a rough estimate. But what am I to do with those guests who have already booked and paid, not to mention the guests already here?"

Jackson smiled.

"Listen, Khaled. I expect you to compensate financially. Those who are already here will be compensated in cash and transported to other accommodation. Those who have bookings in this week will also be compensated. I will make sure that the appropriate amount gets added on to the two million dollars that you require for the six months."

Khaled began to smile and nodded his head.

"Mr. Jackson – maybe somewhere in the deal, you could find something to sweeten me with as well."

He stroked his beard.

"You know, I'm not a very rich man and a little bit of cash could help us a lot. I have a son, Iftihkar. He is in the Armed Forces here with the FCA, and you know, I'm sure he will be able to assist you. He's been in the regiment that deals with... oh, what do you call that department which pushes troops out of planes?... yes... that's it... paratroopers. He is one of those paratroopers. He has children who he would really like to send to private school, which we can't afford, and maybe one day go to an American University... but it all takes money."

Jackson nodded his head and smiles back at the hotel manager.

"Not a problem. Khaled, I'll cast aside contingencies, a balance which will set you up with US$500,000. I can easily lose that here. How's that? I'm guessing it would be enough for an application to a university in the United States and get your grandson a student visa issued. You've got my word."

Khaled smiled again, and extends his hand to shake Jackson's.

"Mr. Jackson. We have a deal. I'll get my booking clerk to cancel all those bookings ahead of tomorrow. For reasons beyond our control. As the resort got flooded, this works well with the kind of weather here. I'll issue them with Rs30,000 compensation for the inconvenience caused – I'm sure that will sweeten them up – and give them transport to any other hotel in the region. So yes, Mr. Jackson. We have a deal. Thank you."

Just then the door behind them opened. It was a neatly smartly dressed young chap with a tray of refreshments: a teapot or two, coffee cups and an assortment of something which resembled biscuits.

"Mr. Jackson, help yourself: what would you like, tea or coffee?" said Khaled as he picked up his telephone's handset. He phoned through to the clerk, asking him to put a hold on any further bookings and to come over to his office for a briefing on what to do next.

Jackson poured himself a black coffee, and guessed by the local custom of black -tea-drinking here that this would be Khaled's choice.

"Sugar, Khaled?" he asked.

"Two, Mr. Jackson. Thank you."

Jackson walked over to the window and looks out.

"Lovely scenery. I'm just gonna go out, over there onto the pier to make a phone call," said Jackson.

He opened the door, stepped out and closed it behind him, leaving Khaled alone. He strolled over to the pier and continued to walk until he reached the end, where he took out his satellite phone from the inner pocket of his jacket. He selected the favorites option, before pressing number two which is saved as Bob. The phone rang as Jackson's gaze began to settle on the shimmer and shine of the sun's rays across the lake's surface.

"Hi Bob, things are working out rather well here. I've located the premises which we're to use as our base camp, and I've agreed with the manager here, so things are moving forward. I'll be emailing you the details regarding the bank account the funds need depositing into, and the amount, shortly. You can make an advance deposit together with our reference which I'll send you. Meanwhile, can you begin to deliver supplies to the following location. It's my location: 35°25'36.0"N 75°27'18.6"E

35.426667, 75.455155."

"Right, lovely, I've got that. I'll organize the basic contingencies right away, such as medical supplies, local clothing, food rations, food supplies, etc. – and once I have confirmation you have the area is secure, the remainder of the supplies including tactical weapons and equipment," said Bobby.

"Oh, just one more thing, make certain that you have the inflatable pallets as the locale is predominantly a lake. The resort consists of chalets which are surrounding a lake, so pallets are very likely to land in water," said Jackson.

"Right, I see. I'll get that organized for all the supplies at this coordinate location. We've just had DARPA manufacture and design raft-type inflatable pallets which, depending on how heavy the load, will inflate to a volume to counteract and disperse and keep everything above water on impact. Thanks, Jackson. Take care, and all the best."

*****

Janet was sitting at a table in the dining room of the Serena Shigar Hotel, where Jackson was already checked in. It was evening. She'd traveled over from Islamabad.

She'd been sat at the table for five minutes, having a look through the menu when the waiter walked over;

"Can I get you anything to drink?" he asks.

"Can I have a whiskey and Coke please," said Janet.

The waiter for a moment was unsure how to respond. He quickly made the decision there wasn't any point in asking for any form of ID, as Janet was clearly an America.

"Yes, Madam, as you wish."

He heads off through the doors into the kitchen and before long returns with a tall glass of Coke and a miniature bottle of whiskey. He places both on the table and leaves.

"Thank you," said Janet.

Janet was reading a book which she'd picked up in the airport at Islamabad, while waiting for her transfer flight to Gilgit and onward journey to Skardu. She'd managed to get a seat on the next available flight. It meant she'd needed to spend most of the day at the capital's Serena Hotel as the next available flight had luckily been that same day, but in the afternoon.

The book was titled *The Hidden Treasures of Pakistan*. She was hoping it would give her some inspiration and unlock some thoughts and ideas in her mind as to what the fuss was all about, or maybe she just needed a geography lesson.

She turned to the first page where she saw a map of the country. She spotted something on the page that caught her eye: a mountain, and right next to it a picture of a lump of rock. It was a Himalayan salt crystal. It was meant to be good for curing certain illnesses.

"I always wondered where Himalayan salt came from," she muttered to herself.

Janet had a Himalayan salt lamp at home in her bedroom. And now she'd learnt something new: where Himalayan salt comes from. The Himalayas region straddles many countries.

Janet finished off her whiskey and Coke as the waiter returns again.

"Madam, do you fancy anything from the food menu?"

Janet had a quick look and spotted the lamb karahi dish. It resonated with her, as it was a dish which she had at an Indian restaurant in her home town. It was the last meal she had with her husband ever at a restaurant. It was called lamb ginger curry there.

"Yes, I'll go for this lamb with ginger. Oh, and get me another Coke and whiskey please."

She continued reading her book and noticed a diagram which showed the Earth's crust. It was the area beneath the Himalayas, displaying the plates of Asia and Europe, amongst others, pushing together which is causing the Himalayas to rise about a centimeter each year. The crust was the thickest at the point of the summits, between 100 to 150km deep from the top of the peaks down to the molten lava.

"Wow, that's remarkable!" muttered Janet.

Again, the doors opened, and the waiter walked in with another Coke and whiskey. He placed it on Janet's table before picking up the glass she had emptied together with the miniature whiskey bottle. It wasn't long before Janet finished off this drink too. The main curry dish hadn't even arrived yet, and her whiskey and Coke was gone. By now Janet felt a little tipsy and her thoughts felt a little looser in her head.

It was colder outside than most of the rest of the country, due to the high altitude. In fact, it's the coldest part of the world Janet had ever visited as she'd never left the USA.

Just then the main door to the restaurant opened. Janet turned her head as a cold wind blew in, against her ankles. Janet was wearing sneakers and never had socks on, so the cold wind brushed against her ankles as though something was stroking her. Making her uncomfortable.

It's Jackson. He walked in and closed the door, stopping the draft. He looked round to see which table he'd like to sit at. But before he has a chance to decide;

"Elijah, is that you? What the fuck! Oh my god, it's you, you've grown a beard, where the hell did you go and what the fuck are you doing here?" exclaimed Janet.

Jackson was an alias for Janet's dead marine husband. In the marines, his name had been Elijah, Elijah Moses. Jackson is completely still, frozen, and lost for words – unable to respond to a disbelieving Janet.

How had Janet come to know of his whereabouts? Was there someone on the inside? He wasn't meant to disclose his mission objective: he can't even be a good ex-husband by civilly explaining things to her – the ex-wife stood staring at him, waiting for an explanation. he slowly bowed and shook his head. He walked across to a table, slid out a chair and sat down.

"After our child died in that fire, I couldn't live with you, and soon after I was offered a new role with the feds. I took up the offer. As for contacting you, you're a page in the book of my life that I tore out. You are the only person I can ever blame for killing our child," said Jackson.

Janet rolled her eyes. After two whiskey-and-Cokes and feeling a little easy at letting out her emotions, she picked up the empty whiskey glass and slung it at Jackson.

"Don't you ever fucking call me a murderer! She was my baby too! I gave birth to her! I know what it felt like grow her inside me!" shouted Janet.

Smash! Glass shattered all over the floor and across the table where Jackson sat, and when it struck his head.

"You psycho bitch!" he growled.

The waiter rushed in, wondering what on earth was going on. He had a tray in his hand, which contained the lamb ginger curry dish. He placed it on a table and rushed over to Jackson;

"Sir! Are you okay Sir?"

"No dammit! What's it look like!" exclaimed Jackson, lifting a serviette and dabbing his forehead which was now bleeding.

"I'll get the first aid box, Sir."

As he went to do so, the other two continue their altercation.

"I mean, what the fucking hell else was I supposed to think... You're at home with our Samantha that day... nothing else to do, and that happened... There is no other possible explanation... I loved that child... I had paternity leave as well... I was heartbroken... dammit Janet!!" said Jackson, sobbing.

The waiter came back with the first-aid box and placed it on the table in front of Jackson. Jackson was quite familiar with putting bandages and plasters on and proceeded to do so.

"I'm with the CNN news agency now. An investigative journalist. I'm now probing into a topic which surrounds the speculation that the USA has an interest in this region due to some space race which is likely to take place or come to fruition over the coming years. Come on now Elijah, you have something you have to tell me, your smell's all over this. Working with the feds, a new alias... come on, the people of America have a right to know, right, journalist?" said Janet.

Jackson, or Elijah, was busy with sticking a plaster on his forehead.

"You're speaking to the wrong person, Janet, as I'm not obliged to say anything. What I would like you to know is, it's all for the best; it's all for the benefit of the people and security of the United States. I know it seems a bit far-fetched, but believe me, if we are not here, then the world as we see and perceive it today will no longer be."

"To hell it is, I've heard someone who's quite senior at NASA referring to a blue on blue. I'm a journalist; I know pretty damn well that's friendly fire, and within days we have a 9/11. Something doesn't seem quite right, and I'm sure you have some connection to it."

"Oh, I can't take this anymore. I'm going to have to check out!" said Jackson/Elijah.

Later that night, Janet approached the hotel reception asking for assistance with finding a local guide. The sky was obviously dark by now, littered with stars and just as Janet turned to look up at the stars;

"Yes, there's Salim Khan. He's a local tour guide and very experienced with the local terrain, and geography. Mr Jackson from America – he has been guided around by Salim." said the hotel clerk.

Just then, a shooting star passed by as Janet was admiring the starlit sky. She immediately had a feeling this Salim Khan was going to be her lucky star to guide her around.

"Oh that's perfect, thank you. Could you call him? Or better, could you give me his contact details?" said Janet.

Just then, an elegant smartly-dressed man stepped forward from behind the clerk. It was the guest relations manager, Abdul.

"Hello, Mrs. Janet, we haven't met. I never had the chance to speak to you. I think you arrived very early in the morning and went to your room. I'm the guest relations manager Abdul."

"Oh, okay." She said.

"Each morning at 10 AM, I take new guests for a tour of the hotel. You'll have noticed it's full of history, hidden treasures and secrets. I'm sure you'd be very intrigued and find it interesting. We also have a few ancient artifacts here."

"I was certainly not aware."

Janet turned her head to look at Abdul's badge as she'd already forgotten his name.

"Thank you for the offer, Abdul, but I'll tell you what you can do for me right now. What I need is this Salim Khan, to take me around on a guided tour."

"Oh, don't you worry then, not a problem. Janet, This Salim is my brother. I will speak to him tonight when I get home. We live together. I'm Abdul Azam and he is Salim Khan Azam. I'll make sure he's here in the morning for you, but not before I get to take you on a guided tour," said Abdul.

Janet's face brightened up and she began to smile.

"Super, that's lovely. I'll be more than happy. After breakfast, I'll come right out, and we can go from there, right. I'll have everything ready, as we say in America, to 'rock and roll'. I'll have everything packed up for tomorrow... is what I mean. I suppose it will be a busy day after being guided by you."

Janet walked to her room.

Later, she called home. She rang Gail at NASA, then Jeff at the LAPD.

"Oh, hello Janet, I saw your name come up on my phone," said Gail. "Hey, is everything okay, why are you ringing so late? It's 10 PM here."

"So I've made some new discoveries... you're not going to believe this... my husband is not dead! He's not dead! I've just seen him!" said Janet.

"What! OMG... that is so fucking creepy! I bet your first thought must have been, you're looking at his ghost!" Said Gail.

"And he's working with the feds! As he tells me... apologetically."

"What a creep! Your husband! So what the hell happened to him?" asked Gail.

"What the hell happened! You know exactly what and how our Samantha died. I ended up throwing a glass of whiskey at him. An empty one... he's not even worth wasting whiskey over... ended up patronizing me, making me feel guilty about my Samantha. It's him all along, working on a destructive path of destroying the world 10 times all over. He is very selfish, and very unaware. I don't know where he is coming from. To be frank, he's not in the right frame of mind! But, I am meeting someone tomorrow who is going to take me on a tour. It's somebody who has been guiding Elijah – my former husband – he's now called Jackson. It'll help me get a better understanding as to what on earth is happening over here. I'd like you to come over and join me... if you can make it? What do you say?"

"Hey Janet, I'd love to, but apparently I'm contracted to work here on my position at NASA. You've got it made... getting paid to travel. You just don't know how much I'd love to come out. Sorry," said Gail.

Janet shrugged her shoulders and takes a gasp of air. Seemingly understanding.

"What about Jeff at the LAPD? Make sure he's aware where you are. And, I'm guessing you'll have some more information to pass us tomorrow. Nice catching up with you, Janet. You take care. I'm getting anxious now," said Gail.

Gail was at the office. She'd been on hands-free talking to Janet her whole way to work. She headed straight to Derek's office.

"Dad, you know, there's a lot of activity going on in North Pakistan. A friend of mine... she's a news reporter... what do you know about what's happening over there?"

"Hello sweetheart, happy to see you're doing well. Well..., you know, it's all beyond my control. You know the CIA were listening in on us, and it was something which had been assigned to them. And now, if any scientists are working on that project, they're under the jurisdiction of the CIA and bound by the State Secrets Act. So, I wouldn't be able to tell you anything, even if I knew. Besides, I haven't had a job offer come through, whereas a few here, working in the program, have had offers come through and have been poached. Reassigned." said Derek.

"Right, I'm off. Just to let you know, I know what's happening, and I'm keeping in contact with Janet," said Gail.

Gail left the office with not the slightest hint of an idea as to what her dad might know.

Just then, she had a thought, why doesn't she get something off Jeff, so she can place a bug in her dad's office. That might be an idea to mention it to Jeff when she saw him next.

Chapter 23
Terminal
Velocity

The US C–17 had just left the US airbase in the Middle East. The Gulf State of Qatar. It was not the only one; there was another six behind it, and today the entire 500 CIA field agents were due to arrive in Pakistan. They expected to be arriving just in time for breakfast at the Shangrila resort in Skardu. The last of the seven C-17's was still just visible on the horizon...

The 500 agents were due to land at the resort using the HALO method. High-altitude military parachuting is a method of delivering military personnel, military equipment and other military supplies from a transport aircraft via freefall parachute insertion. HALO jumps were developed by the military for covert operations over enemy territory – the objective being to prevent detection of the aircraft as well as the jumpers. In a HALO jump the parachutist leaves the plane at altitudes of up to 30,000 feet, opening their parachutes at the last possible moment to avoid being detected by enemy troops. As such, jumping from that height, the parachutists will reach speeds of 126 mph for about two minutes. Because of these high altitudes, they need to wear oxygen masks and carry oxygen tanks. Hypoxemia, a grave condition caused by lack of oxygen in the blood, is one of the risks linked with HALO jumps.

The agents were checking their equipment once again. No valve is loose; everything required to be tight is tight. All the 'T's are crossed in the 'I's dotted.

It was almost 6 AM. Seven C-17 planes were flying over north Pakistan when the alarms begin to go off: the first set of bells alerting them that they've reached their destination and the first aircraft's interior lighting was turned off. The back tailgate began to drop, and an air force officer began a final brief. The entire team was required to listen to the safety protocol for a final time.

"Listen! Folks! It's your time to jump now," said the officer.

The officer was stood in the middle of the C-17 half speaking, half shouting.

"You've all gone through numerous training procedures. You'll get your 2-minute warning and then your 30 seconds soon after. Just remember to repeat them all in the back in your head. I'm afraid if you shit your pants, there are no toilets until you land! So, make sure you get down there, damnit!" exclaimed the officer.

Looking out through the back of the ramp, which they were due to all jump out shortly, the sky was beginning to look lighter. However, it would seem much darker below as the aircraft was flying so high up. Even though the huge doors were open in the back of the plane, somehow it wasn't causing a whirlwind in the aircraft. Everybody was by now wearing their masks with oxygen supplies. The pressure had dropped completely to equal that on the outside the plane. They all gave their oxygen bottle, flight suits and parachutes over their shoulder one last check before beginning to run out the rear of the aircraft. It was a sequence

almost akin to a team of football players running
onto the football pitch before kick-off, except this
was in three-dimensional space. Once in the air,
it then seemed all too real. It was almost like they
were in a computer game simulation. Some being a
little more confident than others. Some beginning
to outwit others while some just froze like starfish
with their arms and legs opened. Occasionally
some dotted around and moved about two different
locations, but all were pretty much near enough
that terminal velocity somewhere in the region
approaching 126 mph.

Later, the parachutes begin to open one at a
time, surely until the entire 500 had opened.

Slowly but surely their training was kicking in.
Eventually, the planned altitude of 2500 ft above
ground level (AGL), was reached. One by one the
parachutes began to be deployed. Not automatically
but by the field agents pulling on a tether. Their
oxygen tanks by now were almost empty.

*****

It was almost 'Salah' time. That's the Muslim
prayer. 'Fajr' is the morning prayer, Muslims must
perform at sunrise. Khaled was a devout Muslim.
He performed his prayers five times a day. He was
already up performing his ablution, thus cleansing
the body using water. And getting ready for 'Fajr'.
Khaled decided to do his prayer and just as he was

about to lay his prayer mat down something caught his eye. It was the moon, something caused the light coming from the moon to flicker as though something flew past it. He turned to look and what he saw completely baffled him. It was somebody falling out of the sky and straight into the lake. It was the parachute which came down after that briefly screened the light travelling off the moon.

Just then Khaled realized that there were guests arriving today. Before he decided to apprehend this suspect or intruder he needed to make sure that it was not one of those guests. Then, others began to land in the lake.

Just then, Khaled spotted an inflatable dinghy which began to speed across the water. It was powered by an engine and went around making sure everyone in the water could get lifted out if they weren't able to swim. It was Jackson.

"That was unlucky, I'm chuffing soaked! Shit! My diving gear would have come handy," said Pete McKinley as he was pulled out.

Pete Axe was one of the field agents, an English man currently working for the Americans. He was an experienced diver, except in this case without his gear.

"So, you made it for breakfast, well done; at least you're on time," said Jackson.

Numerous others were landing around the chalets, in the gardens and occasionally on top of the roofs.

The ones who hadn't landed in the water were now sat in the restaurants waiting for breakfast, while the ones who had fallen in the water were promptly checked in and making use of the facilities to get ready. At 7 AM at the start of breakfast, Jackson did a roster count, and there was one person unaccounted for.

"Hey, good to finally see you, Agent Jackson. It's good to put a face to a name," said Agent Harrison.

"Yeah, it sure is. Listen, I know we've been talking a lot over the phone, but this is where the real work begins now. I'm feeling positive."

"Excellent, that's the spirit. It's what we need," said Agent Parker.

The two agents Harrison and Parker were pulling off their skydive suits while talking to Jackson in the restaurant.

"As for your work Jackson, you've done us well, but just to mention that I'll be taking control of everything on the ground as of now, and you can continue on your work as a local guide and assistant," said Agent Harrison.

Jackson was aware this day was inevitable.

There was nearly 500 in the restaurant, mainly stood, as there weren't even the chairs to seat them all. The entire restaurant was jammed with personnel. So, to get everyone at the table for breakfast, the group had to be split into three separate groups.

"Okay guys, that's enough. Listen up, there's far too many of us here. Breakfast will be split up into three seatings: for all those with a surname with a first letter between A and G, please remain in the restaurant; for all of you between H and

P, please come back in half an hour, at 7:30; the remaining folks with a name from Q to Z, I'm afraid it's 8 o'clock, sorry folks. Oh, and by the way, I'm glad you've made it. Welcome. We are at 500 –1, so unfortunately there is one missing. We'll wait till after breakfast and if there's no sign of him, it looks like we're going out on a hunt," said Agent Harrison.

"So, enjoy your breakfast. By the way, there's no bacon on the menu. We did try our best, but no-go," said Agent Parker.

*****

Janet placed the knife and fork, side by side on the plate and lifted her napkin to wipe her mouth. She'd just finished her breakfast at the hotel. She picked up her handbag and walked out into the sunshine. It was already 10:05 and Abdul was already stood with the carpet seller chatting away. Janet walked over to him, and she can't help herself but walk to the carpet stall when she realized she'd got the CNN credit card, and she won't leave here without first buying a carpet. Although Abdul was itching to take her on the tour.

"Oh, dammit, that's so gorgeous! Very art deco."

It seemed turquoise at first, except up close one realized it isn't, rather an array of greens and blues. It was the one her heart was now set on and she reached her hand out and gave it a rub. It would be fantastic to have such a fabulous handmade rug in a home. She lost attention briefly when she realized her house is not so very homely as it once was, but... oh whatever. She hands her credit card to the shop owner;

"It's okay, I'll take just this one, so lovely, you charge this card."

"Janet, don't worry – I'll arrange for this to be delivered to your room so you don't need to carry it; we can just carry on," said Abdul.

"Oh excellent, that is handy," said Janet.

It was almost 10:40 am, and Janet had already gone around the hotel with Abdul and was already excited to meet up with Salim Khan, who was outside the hotel, sat in his car.

"Janet, please meet Mr. Salim, and Mr. Salim, you make sure you take good care of our Janet. She's our golden girl, you know," said Abdul.

Janet proceeded to throw her handbag into the car. It was a rather old Toyota Jeep, but nevertheless fully functional and versatile to serve their need. She braced herself and sat down before swinging her legs around and inside, as it was rather high off the ground.

"Cheerio, Abdul; thanks ever so much for your help. I'll be seeing you soon, we'll discuss later. Over dinner perhaps, goodbye for now," she said.

Abdul blushed then.

Janet reached out with her right hand to shake Salim's hand, but was met with a disapproving reaction.

"Thank you Janet, but here we don't shake women's hands. It's a religious thing, you know," said Salim.

Janet rummaged through her bag and found her sunglasses, put them on and turned her gaze to him.

"Okay, I'm fine with that," said Janet.

"On the other hand, what I would like to ask you, Janet, is where would you like to go first?"

A cheeky smile appeared on Janet's face.

"Oh, I know just the place. You know the resort that you've taken Jackson to. That's where I want to go; I need to see what he's up to. He's my ex-husband!"

"Oh, I see, in that case we better start our journey as it's at least an hour's drive. We've got to drive through the town of Skardu first. If you need anything from the town, let me know as I can stop. You'll see that we'll be passing the airline ticket shop, in case you have a last-minute change of heart." Salim turned to look at Janet with a smile as he drove.

Just then Janet's phone started to ring. She pulled it out and saw it was her boss at the news organization, Timothy.

"Hello Timothy. I've managed to weed out some more information, but first, I'd like you to know I've met my former husband. Yes, my ex-husband, the supposedly dead husband. He's bloody staying at the same hotel as me! When I saw him, lost for words is an understatement!"

"What the hell! You met your dead husband Elijah while in the remote mountains of Pakistan? What a small world!!" said Timothy.

"Yep! The slimy ball bag is here, and now with a bandage around his head, as I flung a whiskey glass at him. He was patronizing me! How fucking dare he! Anyway, I've managed to find his driver and convince him to come and work for me."

Janet turned to look at Salim Khan to see his reaction to her wanting him to work for her on a full-time basis; and she was waiting for approval from Timothy.

"Okay, well, if you must. I'm guessing Salim is a local guide and so knowledgeable with local culture, history, cuisine, etc. Fair enough. After all, I know you're able to look after yourself, you've been in plenty of sticky situations, but it's good to have someone around you," said Timothy.

"My man's rate is Rs40,000 per month," said Janet.

Salim concentrated on his driving and looking ahead just as he should, but occasionally peeped over to Janet.

"OK, we're good to go! Timothy, I've just had my man agree to this job offer. That's about what $400 per month but I won't let you down and will do us proud," said Janet.

"Well, I better let you get on then. I'll give you a call later today. See how things are getting on, see who on earth else you've bumped into."

The two continued driving around the mountainous region, while in the distance, the high summits were ever more present and visible, snow-covered as though it was a backdrop at the theatre. Occasionally Salim stops to take a pause and give Janet the opportunity to step outside and take pictures.

*****

Back in the restaurant, the third group was now sat having breakfast and a briefing. The whole entourage team had audio contact with each other. The team had been made aware that the weapons delivery shall take place first thing in the morning. They are due to cover the area by securing as much ground as possible. Delivery shall only take place once they were in their positions and good to go, and had confirmed as such.

Meanwhile, nearly a hundred had already gone off in search for the missing agent. There was a chance he might not be alive, due to the parachute or oxygen or his suit failing.

"Listen folks, you're the final group to have had your briefing. You are to join the others on the search for our missing colleague; you will make your way over to the south-east side as it's the only area which is still to be covered.

*****

Inside the huge hanger building at 1535 Command Dr # D211, Joint Base Andrews, MD 20762, there waited with its engine running, spewing out toxic carbon monoxide, a black CIA SUV vehicle. Waiting inside was Sheila McDaniels. Right now it would not bother her one little bit if the gases leaving the tailpipe were funneled into the car, slowly killing her, her feelings of guilt just then being so all-engulfing. She had just been briefed about her daughter Silvia's death, informed on how a stray palette loaded with supplies fell onto her when she was inside her tent. Sheila hadn't even known her daughter was traveling in the Himalayas.

She continued to flick through the report outlining the events which led to her daughter's death. All which she authorized.

In about an hour, a C-17 will be arriving with her daughter.

"Ma'am, can I get you a hot drink?" asked the driver, an agent with the CIA.

Sheila nodded her head silently.

The agent said no more – it didn't seem to be a good time to disturb the CIA's director.

Almost an hour went by until they heard the C-17 touch down.

Sheila was already outside the hanger.

As the rear ramp began to deploy, Sheila composed herself as she walked across the tarmac to the aircraft. She was wearing a long black wool coat. It was pouring down and her umbrella was losing its battle against the waterfall, not helped by gusting wind. The darkest day of her life compounded by the gloomiest of weather – the metaphor weighed heavily on her heart.

When the ramp finally touched down against the concrete, a coffin was rolled on a trolley down the ramp. There's no USA flag draped over as Silvia did not die in combat.

Sheila walked over to the coffin, with each step more troubled, taking more strength. Tears leaked from her eyes.

On the top of the coffin, at its top, there was a window covered by a hatch. Sheila opened the hatch, and on seeing her daughter completely lost her composure, bursting into tears as her body lay helplessly across the coffin. Anybody present couldn't have been in any doubt of her heartbreak. And it did not help that she was bound by the Secret Service Act not to mention or disclose anything.

*****

It was almost midday and Janet and Salim Khan were not now far from the Shangrila Resort.

Just then, they heard a strange, fluttering-like noise coming from the sky. As the two looked up, they saw parachutes. Hundreds of parachutes. They were dropping what looked like pallets with drones attached. Janet stared hard, trying to make out the details. They were pallets which had a steering mechanism –devices which consisted of propellers. As the pallets came down, the propellers spun, guiding the pallets to a predetermined location – creating propulsion to ensure they landed at the target site – which it would seem, was the Shangrila Resort.

Salim hit the brakes of his Jeep. He had to stop and look. He quickly got out of the vehicle, and Janet followed suit. What on earth was going on? The two made out the tiniest of vapor trails as if an aircraft had flown by at an immensely high altitude, as the plane wasn't even visible. In another direction much lower in the sky, there was a pallet with much larger parachutes. It looked to be loaded with some sort of supplies. They were approximately 1 km from the resort. They got back into the vehicle and continued their journey, until at the next junction – the one for the resort – there was a roadblock;

"Janet, this is very strange. I've never had this happen before!" said Salim.

The road closure signage wasn't something the local police used. It seemed foreign.

"The police here don't set up roadblocks like this. This is really odd," said Salim.

There were people in dark clothing, like combat gear, guarding the roadblock. They seemed to have guns. Salim climbed out of the car and walked towards them. Janet followed, except this time she wore a body camera on her coat. They walked past a roadblock sign and approached the men. They looked foreign, or at least not local. On the left stood a black man of Afro-Caribbean descent and on the right was a tall white male in shades. Both were wearing microphones and earpieces, and gear around their necks such as vision goggles and binoculars. They both pulled guns which they had had concealed;

"Excuse me, you need to stop right there! Sir, Madam, this is a restricted area; you need to step away and return to your vehicle immediately," said Pete, one of the field agents.

Stood in front of Janet were two of the 500 field agents, including Pete, who had arrived that morning. They had had their weapons delivery. A further three men then appeared behind these two. Janet had her body camera recording. She started to walk backwards. A speaker began to play local language instructions: 'Yeh Ilaka Tum Or Sabeh Keh Leye Bandh Ho Chukha.'

"Come on Salim, let's get back to the vehicle. I've got what I need, for now," said Janet.

Salim turned to look at her. What was she talking about?! They hadn't got anything yet, and Salim had been looking forward to the complimentary refreshments which are provided to all tour guides, especially ones who bring in business. They'd been on the road for over an hour, and he was exhausted.

"Stupid sods, bloody idiot... I'm still owed a tip from my previous trip," muttered Salim, following Janet back to the Jeep.

"Janet, what do you mean you have everything? We haven't done anything yet and who the hell are they? They seem like Americans. What the hell are they doing here? It's like the President of goddamn America is due to arrive! Who could possibly be so important that they have to secure the area so well?" said Salim.

"Salim, look, I'm wearing a body camera, right. I'm sending this to Timothy right away."

Salim looked up at the sky and began to nod. He understood.

Janet pulled her tablet out, which has a data Sim card installed for a local telecom's operator in Pakistan, PAKTEL. She installed the SD into the tablet after taking it out of the body of the camera. She opened her email and addressed a new message to Timothy before clicking on 'select file' and adding. One touch and she attached her latest video.

"There you go, Timothy. I'm sure he'll really like this. It's the first categorical evidence showing that we have an interest in the area. I'm sure of that, and I'm sure Timothy will air it on TV tonight," said Janet.

Just as Salim was about to start the car. He'd only got as far as turning the ignition, when another tourist turned up. He got out of his minivan and took off his sunglasses, then approached the Secret Service field agents. Pete stepped forward to the tourist.

"Hey, I'm Clive. I come here every year. What's the issue? I received my email about a flood! Listen mate, there's no damn flood here – I've already checked with the neighboring hotels. Now let me get through."

"Sir, I'm going to have to ask you to leave. This is a restricted area, government property, under the United States of America. So, if you turn back to your vehicle and make your way, I'm sure everything will be well and good," said Pete.

Clive unsurprisingly looked confused. He turned his head towards the minivan, and then looked back at Pete.

"Listen to me, you, I'm not taking no for an answer. I come here every year to this same hotel, and I want to stay here. Same as if I'd booked myself a villa, and I wanna stay in that villa. I'm not asking for much, so just move out of my way and let me through," said Clive.

The field agent looked a little more serious. Just then, a few more appeared behind him.

"Sir, if you don't step aside and get back in the vehicle, we're going to have to detain you as being in contravention of a Secret Service act which prohibits all unlawful entry onto restricted government property. So, can you please get back in the vehicle and leave immediately!" said Pete.

"Listen, fuck you!" said Clive.

Clive threw a punch at Pete and knocked him to the ground. Clive was a big lad in his 50s. He'd spend many months welding, earning good money, and liked his holidays. He wasn't in a mood to be played around with. He'd had a few to drink earlier during the flight and then a few more at the duty-free during the stopover in the Middle East. Also, just now during the road trip. He was well over his limits. He had a weakness for alcohol, but it and he could sometimes both be his own worst enemies. He was married with two boys, but occasionally he liked to travel solo, to clear his mind.

"You son of a bitch! Oh boy! It's your unlucky day today, Man; you're getting detained and incarcerated!!" said Pete as he clambered up.

Just then, two other agents came rushing over and grabbed hold of Clive and bungled him into a van. They pinned him to the floor while they handcuffed his hands behind his back.

"Yeah, you see, you fuckers! I said I wasn't taking no for an answer! I want the holiday I've paid for!" shouted Clive.

It was evident that he was intoxicated.

While Clive was driven away into the resort, a blacked-out vehicle came through the check post and a window had to be opened to reveal its occupants. It was the doctor of hypnotherapy, Dr Ishmael and his psychiatrist counterpart Dr Jacob.

The doctors were visiting in order for Dr Ishmael to implant memories into the locally arrested detainees – detained as a result of their links to extremist organizations – to enable them to carry out suicide bombings across the region.

*****

Timothy was sat at his computer when he opened Janet's email. As he watched the video, which continued onto the arrest and detention of Clive, Timothy had already decided that after a minimal amount of editing he'll air it on the next hourly news bulletin;

"Now, ironic as it may seem, US forces, special forces and the Secret Service have been spotted by our CNN reporter Janet at a remote outpost in Pakistan – at a resort known as Shangrila. Shangrila is a hotel resort. What could our servicemen be possibly doing at a resort? This raises even more questions which we shall endeavor to bring you answers to very soon. Thank you for listening, and feel free to post any comments on our Twitter page. We'll leave it there for now. This is your 6 o'clock news," said the news presenter of CNN.

*****

It was early morning, and the agent Pete was required to visit his detainee to sign paperwork, as he was the detaining officer in this instance.

"Is your stay comfortable, Clive?"

"Listen! You! If I had my burning gear, I would have burned my way through all these bars. These metal bars right here. Like a butter knife flowing through butter. My welding skills would have come in handy."

Pete pointed at the microphone he was wearing;

"Well, that's interesting, thanks for letting me know. Everything you say is being recorded by an AI computer, which analyzes your voice and geotags it. Any alarming messages, threatening

words or an underlying threatening message...
you're digging yourself into a big hole. Carry on
talking," he said.

One night, a contingent from within the Secret
Service entourage organized a dawn raid. They
broke some doors in and carried out a series
of arrests during their mission to locate an
individual who had sympathies with and links to
terrorist organizations, as well as assets such as
ammunition. The team brought him straight to the
resort to gain further intelligence.

A few days later, the individual was released.
There were no bail papers. He was just driven
outside the resort and let go out the back of a Suzuki
Jimmy, a small 4 x 4.

As anticipated, within days there was a suicide
bombing with three Pakistani troops and half a
dozen bystanders killed when a bomber detonated
an improvised device in the Pakistani city of
Peshawar. The bomber happened to be the very
same man who was detained by special forces at
the Shangrila resort.

The phone was ringing. Dr Ishmael while
enjoying his Shangrila Kosher full continental
breakfast. He picked up his freshly squeezed
orange juice and drained the glass. He then
wiped his mouth on his napkin. Then he answered
the call.

"Dr Ishmael speaking."

"Hello, Dr Ishmael. Judging by the time, you're
probably enjoying your breakfast. I just wanted you
to know, excellent work!" Said Andrew Lopez.

"Sir, I still haven't received my reference code for the Swiss bank account you promised. I'll need that for payments made. Otherwise, I'm going to lose interest in this whole topic... for me to use my initiative and be one step ahead of the game, I suggest you carry through with your side of our deal. I understand my work here is paramount to your efforts gaining ground. You understand me?" Said Dr Ishmael.

"Doctor, you just leave it with me, everything will be set in motion. Your work here is paramount, and I fully agree, so you just stay put and rest assured we are in full control. In fact, a delegation is flying over to see your team next week," said Andrew.

"Okay, I will be in touch soon. Thanks for letting me know," the doctor replied.

He put his phone back on the table and finished his specially imported smoked salmon with locally sourced scrambled eggs.

Chapter 24

Hypnotism

The sound of a key entering a keyhole. Then noise of a bunch of keys brushing against metal as the one key was turned. Clive's cell door opened. He turned his head to see who it was.

"You have a visitor, Clive," said Pete.

There were two other agents beside Pete, both armed with automatic rifles.

Clive was taken into a room... someone was in there already but they were facing away from him. He was confused.

The visitor turned around. It was Dr Ishmael wearing a mask which looked like Clive's wife.

Before Clive could say a word, the two agents grab hold of his arm while Pete prepared an injection. A dose of a hallucinogenic drug.

"What the fuck is this, I'm fucking alright, get away from me!" shouted Clive.

He tried to resist, but hadn't a chance.

Pete tapped the syringe, and injected the liquid contents into Clive's arm.

Pete and the agents vacated the room, leaving Clive and Dr Ishmael alone.

*****

It was the following morning. The blade of the 'Black Hawk' helicopter was turning faster and faster.

Pete and the other agents escorted Clive into the helicopter, but there was one thing different:

Clive was wearing an ugly body vest. Ugly for two reasons. It wasn't a bulletproof vest, far from it – it was a vest containing multiple pockets, all containing explosives wired to a trigger, which Clive held in his hand.

The intent was to land near a market in a bazaar, where Clive would head off to the market, where he would press the trigger and kill as many people as possible.

Maybe in his drugged-up mind he believed his wife and children were in danger and he had to carry out this task to save them. Whatever happened in that room between Dr Ishmael and Clive was anyone's guess.

As the 'Black Hawk' began to gather enough speed to produce the thrust required to take off and eased off the ground, gradually gaining height, Clive started to look slightly confused as opposed to a minute ago when he had been entirely focused and eager. He looked down at his hand and started to roll his eyes. His fist tightened, and his thumb squeezed down on the trigger.

"BOOOM" went the 'Back Hawk'.

There was another 'boom' as the fuel exploded.

The aircraft was a ball of flames and came crashing to the ground. It wasn't even 50 feet in the air.

All that was left was burning wreckage in the grounds of the Shangrila resort.

*****

The nation of Pakistan suffered many such attacks over the coming years, multiple suicide bombings in crowded public gatherings right across to market bazaars and military check posts. Eventually, the public didn't have the stomach any more, and things began to change. Society began to fragment. There was a hunger for a change of regime, with every single member of the public and every level of organization, regardless of their caste or creed, culture or religion. Thousands of people had died across the country in such attacks.

All this bloodshed and violence led to a civil war. There are many factions within the nation which fought against central government competing for local control. Eventually, things escalated to the point where the issue was addressed at the United Nations General assembly in New York. A resolution was ratified and endorsed by many countries in the world, mainly NATO nations such as the European Union and the United States of America, Australia and New Zealand —mostly Western governments. They agreed to the notion that what had gone before be dissolved, and independent nations were formed, to promote each of the individual states, traditions, languages and customs, such as Sindh, Punjab, Gilgit and Baltistan, Baluchistan etc.,

Furthermore, eventually, at least half a dozen orders were recognized, and, on September 11th 2013 the nation of Pakistan no longer existed. Instead, the region now consisted of six separate countries straddling from the Arabian Sea in the south right the way up to Punjab and into Gilgit and Baltistan in the northern areas bordering China. Many years of bloodshed had led to the independence from the central Punjabi government, which mainly controlled, ran and influenced the bulk of all decision-making and operations within the former nation of Pakistan, primarily due to a more significant population.

As for all the nuclear assets, they were dismantled and decommissioned under the scrutiny of the International Atomic Energy Agency, IAEA.

Most of the former leaders were now living in exile across the Gulf states. This all came as a big relief to its old neighbor and nuclear rival, India which had been at war with Pakistan three times – knowing that its former enemy no longer posed a threat as it was now a cluster of smaller nations with reduced military budgets. It could never challenge India, especially militarily.

No more than a year after September 11th 2013, when the nation of Pakistan was remade, the neighboring Chinese state, Xinjiang province had a People's Movement. There was a mass uprising, which was at first mainly galvanized by a local few who harnessed the power and efforts of the many to produce one massive march against the army. This involved tens of thousands of deaths in just one day. However, it also led to an international movement by aid agencies and governmental organizations right the way to freelance media organizations, bringing awareness to the plight of ethnic Uyghur people who were native to the province, and only to that province: it forms their identity. It highlighted the need for the Xinjiang province to have its people's beliefs, cultures and religion at the heart of any agreement which may be brought about at the United Nations assembly in New York.

A case was lodged against a certain few in the military establishment at The International Criminal Court (ICC), which is an intergovernmental organization and international tribunal that sits in The Hague in the Netherlands. The case was against individuals who authorized violence against unarmed civilians, which led to the deaths of tens of thousands on that one horrific day.

It was the first time the phrase 'break-away Chinese state Xinjiang' was mentioned in the United Nations assembly. All this eventually led, three years on, to a unanimous agreement being ratified, which led to the resolution 911 being implemented at the United Nations. The Xinjiang province should become an independent nation free from all constraints and laws of, and obligations and responsibilities to the People's Republic of China. And another year on – September 11th 2018 – the Xinjiang province became an entirely separate nation.

At this point, the entire area surrounding K2 was no longer territory of either of the countries which once stood proud in this region, be it Pakistan (now no longer one country), or China. A border no longer existed between them.

The region became a marvel of growth and opportunity. The territories of Gilgit-Baltistan (GB) and Xinjiang both became an immense investment opportunity for America and a cavern for the world's wealth. As the United States plowed so much money into it, it eventually became addicted to the region's dollar possibilities. There was an agreement signed which included a clause: upon any failure of payment or default on credit, the region surrounding the Himalayas, such as K2 would be handed over to the United States for 100 years.

There came a time when the inevitable did become a reality. The country of Xinjiang, and GB, both failed to make payment on a tunnel project which was the first of its kind in the world. It was the world's highest tunnel and motorway, covering the K2 region. It was dubbed the White Elephant and was initially regarded as unnecessary, but ground-breaking in technicality. This was also the world's longest border crossing, with the ends in separate territories and the tunnel going through the mountains.

Even though the United States now controlled the area surrounding K2 as per the clause in the contract, a report was handed into the parliaments of Xinjiang and GB stating that a referendum should be carried out to determine if the two nations would like to become states of America. And that is what happened. The referendum was carried out by the people of GB and the people of Xinjiang, who overwhelmingly voted to join the US. It was 52% for and 48% against. On September 11, 2019, America no longer had 52 states, but instead 54 states.

Local politics, culture and socioeconomics were left almost unchanged. As is already the case with all present states within in the USA, their laws to some degree remain based on local customs. However, part of what was agreed was the date the two countries were to become incorporated into United States.

A decade on from where we left off, certain individuals within the previous circle of the CIA and Secret Service were retired, if not deceased. A decade brought a lot of change. Janet no longer worked as a CNN reporter. She was detained and incarcerated due to attempting to infiltrate restricted sensitive areas multiple times. She had to sign an agreement which stipulated that she was prohibited from returning to any US sensitive sites, and therefore couldn't work any longer as a science correspondent.

However, she decided to remain in the region, at least before it became an American state, as it was now. She could stay unhindered due to her citizenship. She particularly liked Skardu and had grown fond of the region. She was in her late 40s now and worked at the local bookstore in Skardu.

Janet's former editor at the CNN, Timothy, was no longer around. The agents Harrison and Parker were retired.

Due to the massive investment from central government. The region was transformed during the last five years, making it now one of the most highly developed areas in terms of infrastructure in the world, let alone the USA.

Khaled, the owner of the Shangrila resort, was in town today. He was visiting with his son, Iftihkar, who had five years ago graduated from Massachusetts Institute of Technology (MIT). Iftihkar was also an opponent of the new order, the Washington government. He was a patriot of the former nation, Pakistan. Before leaving for his studies abroad, Iftihkar had spent a year in the FCA paratroopers' commandos. His father was apparently a very, very wealthy man. Indeed, as the whole resort now was bought over by the US central government for $15 million, and Iftihkar, an only son and only child, was in line for the inheritance.

It was the season of Polo. Polo was a game which was played in this part of the world using certain local horses that were specific to the region and had evolved to adapt to the high altitude. Polo matches were held at the highest altitude, at grounds in the lush valleys surrounded by snow-capped ranges.

Janet had heard of these matches and decided to pay a visit as she was looking for a topic to write on. This literally would start with the perfect backdrop scene.

The winter season was almost finished, and a match was scheduled. Janet was sat amongst the female crowd in the viewing stand. She was aware that many of the local bachelor men were arriving with horses and on horses. One man was cut out slightly differently. He was not only driving but had arrived in a 1970s vintage red Mercedes-Benz SLC convertible. This evoked some old memories. She remembered that very red Mercedes-Benz from a US soap drama called Hart to Hart. It was the exact same red Mercedes out of the Hart to Hart drama.

A drama about a self-made millionaire Jonathan and freelance writer Jennifer, who are the Harts. A globetrotting married couple that had a talent for finding mysteries wherever they went. Even when they were uncovering thefts, espionage and various skulduggery, they still found time for romance.

Given the surrounding scenery which consisting of soft, natural warm colors, and three tones of rock, stone, sand and the green, the car struck a contrast against the backdrop.

Janet had the strangest feeling – a tickling sensation all over her body, like clusters of feathers stroking and caressing her, edging her over in the direction of the car and its driver. She could resist the lure no longer and decided to walk across to Iftihkar.

Iftihkar had the door open with the bonnet up. The bonnet was up to allow him to make some adjustments with the fuel and air intake as the air is very light up here.

"What a gorgeous car! It's bringing back memories from when I used to watch it on the TV drama Hart to Hart," said Janet.

Iftihkar turned to her. He was a rather handsome looking man, she thought.

"Ah! Well, have I got a surprise for you, Madam. It so happens that this is that very same car. My father's been annoyed with me ever since, as would any father be, actually, as I spent $500,000 from his inheritance on a car, and a silly car at that," he said.

"Well, yes, I'm not surprised as that's an awful lot of money. But, I'm sure it's well worth it. And I'm sure you take good care of it. As I'm sure you take good care of the lucky women in your life as well," said Janet.

Iftihkar burst out laughing.

He looked into Janet's eyes.

"You really make me chuckle. You're an amusing lady."

She returned his gaze, and felt the tickling sensation again. Suddenly she felt shy under the intensity of his attention.

"Oh, okay I'm writing a book about the region, on people's lives. So, what was it your father was involved in which resulted in him leaving you with so much?" she asked.

Janet leaned against the car, her fingers stroking the paintwork as she continued looking at Iftihkar. Her nail varnish and lipstick were the same red color as that very red Mercedes-Benz.

"Well, it was something on which I disagreed with my dad, but I guess he had no choice on the matter. That was a compulsory purchase order which instructed him to sell the Shangrila to the US government Department of Defense due to its significant location in the district. They required an outpost in the region and this was the location they apparently needed," said Iftihkar.

As he spoke, he couldn't help noticing that Janet's fingers were rubbing over his car. It could be interpreted as very arousing.

"The whole $13 million," he said.

Janet's eyebrows shot up, and her eyes lit up. It was a stark variation to her menial salary which she got from the bookshop, which was substantially smaller than the salary she used to receive while at the CNN News Corporation.

"Oh wow! That's certainly a life-changing figure, isn't it? Compared to what the average member of society must live on. I guess it generally comes down to being responsible people, unlike my spending habits; I was dubbed the Chanel lady when I worked for the CNN news organization as a journalist in a previous lifetime," she said.

"Well, I'm going to head back towards Skardu. I live not far from the former Shangrila resort," said Iftihkar. "If you are heading that way, I could drive you back?"

Janet smiled, a sparkle in her eye appeared.

"That would be fantastic!"

The public transport which Janet arrived in was obviously much better than what it was like here over a decade ago. The flying taxi service was doing wonders, as it cut out the winding and twisting passes that the roads follow. It had gone from one of the poorest regions of the world to being one of the wealthiest.

Janet could have returned home quicker via the flying taxi service, but they both knew she wanted to be in Iftihkar's company – her own private bubble with him, without the distraction of others. The journey back could be just as slow as it wanted to be.

Chapter 25
The Affair

The red Mercedes was driving through the great modern highways on tarmac as smooth as a billiard table. Iftihkar was behind the steering wheel with Janet beside him. The roof was down.

Just then, as they were turning a corner, a gust of wind lifted Janet's dress, blowing it right up into her face and revealing her legs. Even though she had leggings on, which were golden, shiny, soft and silky to touch, nevertheless the moment did an excellent job in revealing her posture and her tightly toned physique. Iftihkar lost his concentration on the road for a moment as his gaze drifted across to her. It wasn't the best time for one to lose sight of the highway.

As Janet pulled her dress down over the top of her legs, she looked ahead and screamed;

"Oh my God, look out!!"

Iftihkar had had his eyes pinned on Janet's amazing legs, but at her scream he snapped back to look at the road.

"Oh, shit!"

He hit the brakes while steering the car out of the path of oncoming traffic and back onto the correct side of the road.

They both took a deep breath.

"So, Janet, what brings you to the state of GB?" Iftihkar asked.

Janet turned to look at him, keeping her dress tightly tucked under her tightly closed legs now.

"Well, I was a CNN reporter 20 years ago, I got assigned to work across here. You understand it was the old order here back then. I was keen on being assigned here because I had a hypothesis. I'd discovered there was an intent to orchestrate an event. I don't know if you've ever heard, but many people believe that our own US government orchestrated the 9/11 attacks to get a foothold in this region," said Janet.

Iftihkar's jaw dropped and his eyebrows lifted. His gaze did not move but remained pinned to the road ahead.

"Well, that's terrifying to know there are actually people, people out there that believe this. Why so?"

"Well, remember I'm an investigative journalist... it's my job to know. But as for my sources... well, due to me having contacts at the National American Space Association, who presented me with some information, and there was also an LAPD officer who used his clearance and access to listen to conversations. In fact, I heard certain individuals mention that there was due to take place a 'blue on blue': a spectacular event which would allow the United States to get to this region due to massive public support. It was the only option they had, you know. How else would they have turned up without reason on China's doorstep?" said Janet.

Iftihkar nodded his head.

"I understand, I'm certainly not one for this new formation; I can't stand Washington. I was a true patriot of the former nation Pakistan, you know, I was even a paratrooper in the army. It was something I did before I went to the United States for four years to do my Bachelor's in science. I went to MIT in Massachusetts where I got my first," he said.

"Oh yeah, well my granddad was known to have sympathies with the IRA in Northern Ireland. He even made donations... I know how it feels," said Janet.

It put a smile on Janet's face, knowing that Iftikhar had traveled to the other states.

"So maybe you've been to California?

"Yes, certainly. I have traveled to at least a dozen states across America. Now California was obviously first on my list. Obviously, one's gotta do that one, given it's where the film industry is based, mainly. And those twelve states also were ones which I traveled through when I did a fly-drive holiday. I drove across in a Winnebago, ending up in California, which is where I flew back from," said Iftikhar, smiling.

"Oh wow, that's fantastic! So, you're a well-traveled man and not just a well-groomed man, Mr. Iftikhar. I wonder what other facets in your life you excel in? Maybe someday you'll show me? Or even tonight, perhaps, when maybe you can take me out to dinner?" said Janet.

She moved closer to him, and turned to look at him.

Iftikhar could no longer resist but peek; he felt he had a right to and a duty to. The road ahead was clear and was now straight. He made an assessment and his eyes slid across to look at Janet. Her eyelashes fluttered at him with her gaze locked on him, no more than a foot away from his face.

Iftihkar almost blushed as he turned his attention back to the road.

He nodded his head while he smiled and began to chuckle.

"Yes Janet, you are a witty lady. Unfortunately, it won't be my dad's former Shangrila resort restaurant, but there's another lovely restaurant in the region, which is part of the Aga Khan chain of hotels. It's called the Serena Shigar Fort. They've got excellent cuisine there. How are you for curries?"

Janet knew too well the Shigar Fort, as it was where she had stayed when she first arrived in the region. She'd ordered the ginger lamb, which had almost ended up in her ex-husband's face. Janet looked up into the sky and imagined herself smelling that curry, as she draws in the cold fresh Himalayan air.

"Oh, I am fond of the curries, my favorite being lamb ginger. I love it, it's scrumptious. I'm guessing you might like it as well?" she said.

They were approaching the town of Skardu now, and Iftihkar began to slow down as they were approaching a junction.

"Yes, Janet, that makes two of us, lovely aren't they. Now, which way are we going? You must guide me from here. I may be sophisticated, but I sadly am not a mind reader. I would be delighted to take you out tonight. How about I pick you up from yours at 6 PM. There's nothing I've got in my calendar which can't be rearranged."

"So just carry on a little further down... just to the right there... second right...and it's on the right... yes, fine, I'll be ready for you for 6 o'clock. I'm looking forward to learning more about the mysterious, rather handsome local bachelor Iftihkar," said Janet.

Iftihkar pulled up outside Janet's home. He then pulled over across the road, where he does a quick U-turn before grinding to a halt and pulling up his handbrake. He turned towards Janet and smiled at her, wondering whether to kiss her. But no, not yet – he's wrong, that's a little wishful. She smiled and got out of the car, smiling back at him – maybe just playing hard to get for now. She waved, tapping her watch;

"6 o'clock."

Iftihkar sped away, the rear tires spinning in the dirt track.

*****

Across the rest of the United States of America, huge protests erupted, people were raging over what seemed to be totally unnecessary spending cuts in welfare and local amenities. Galvanized by social media, public sentiment had been fermenting for a while, against these spending cuts which had affected the entire country.

Chapter 26
Missing Trillions

Now, for the third day running people were out on the streets protesting the trillions of dollars which had been earmarked for a new revolutionary propulsion system to put a starship into space.

It wasn't even a full year on from the year the newly formed states had become part of America. It was still the year 2020. Not even a year had passed from September 11th 2019. When the central government announced the plans, it meant massive budget cuts across all other departments, and across states, affecting other states in terms of infrastructure and development.

The only justification for money to be earmarked and sidelined to the two states GB and Xinjiang was that it was only this region which had the geographic location suitable for such a monumental project, a project which would make sure for centuries to come that the USA remained a dominant world nation.

Many scientific departments across America relocated to this region. When it came to manufacturing, robotics engineering, science, space organizations such as NASA, etc. the states of GB and Xinjiang were doing very well indeed.

Back at NASA, Jared, who was more senior now, was coming towards his retirement. However, at this moment he was responsible for overseeing the entire project. This was his baby dubbed the 'Spaceport Himalaya'. He was due to manage it from conception to completion.

Jared had many specialists working for him, ranging from specialisms in robotics to magnetism, from electronics to mechanics and meteorology to geology. One such individual was a Dr David Steadman, who wouldn't stop telling people how he'd lost his wedding ring?

At the earliest stage, during the conception, private corporations were gathered to generate cash. This in terms of private sponsorships for individual rights, such as catering facilities, hotels, entertainment onboard the starship as and when it was complete, even a golf course. The likes of McDonald's restaurants, Frank and Benny's and Pepsi-Cola plowed in millions. However, it was a drop in the ocean against the entire budget, which could amount to $100 trillion.

There was also the idea to generate funds by floating a part of it on the stock exchange. However, that notion didn't see the light of day.

Artificial intelligence was used once again for the design and development of the spaceport drive shaft, for launching by accelerating the shuttles, right down to specific details. Details which, an Auto CAD – computer-aided design software –drafted to millimeter accuracy a technical drawing – which in turn got fed to robotics to form the physical model in real space, as well as the excavation works – all this passing seamlessly across the different mediums.

This all settled the initial theoretical findings that Jared discovered with his software, although be it version 2.0 now. The exact location of Spaceport Planet Earth was literally the summit of the K2 Mountain and penetrating down through the crust to a depth of almost 150km. At this depth, however, the rock was still solid but the heat was obviously unbearable for any human to work in.

However, this brought about a huge advantage and a future saving to eventually launching those shuttles. Geothermal energy. This was an untapped resource which could be utilized, and only due to the depth achieved – which in this case was a part of the very nature of the beast itself. The heat at the bottom of the excavation would be used to generate the energy required for the entire delivery and deployment phase: the entire energy that was required for the magnets to generate magnetism to push shuttles vertically up the shaft.

Geothermal energy was the heat from the center of the Earth. It was clean and sustainable. Sources of geothermal energy range from the shallow ground to hot water and hot rock found a few miles beneath the Earth's surface, and down even lower to the extremely high temperatures of molten rock called magma.

Geothermal energy in this context referred to the free source of energy, where the water was heated via the geothermal heat in the ground to spin round turbines that duly generated electric power.

Geothermal energy was thermal energy created and stored in the Earth. Thermal energy is the energy that governs the temperature of substance. The geothermal energy of the Earth's crust originates from the original creation of the planet and from radioactive deterioration of materials.

Now, geothermal power is power generated by this energy. Other technologies derived in use comprise dry steam power stations, flash steam power stations and binary cycle power stations. Geothermal electricity generation was currently used in more than two dozen countries, while geothermal heating was used in many more.

But all this was well and good, but not at all going to be made use of until its completion as the construction of the entire 'Spaceport' was to be carried out using machinery and robotics that would be powered with electricity generated via a purpose-built electrofusion reactor, built right up in the Himalayas.

The Baltoro Muztagh Mountains rested to the north and east of the Baltoro glacier, while the Masherbrum Mountains lay to the south. At 8,611 m (28,251 ft), K2 was the highest mountain in the array, also three others being at a height over 8,000 m within the 20 km. The glacier gave rise to the Shigar River, which was a tributary of the Indus River.

Chapter 27
Glaciers

The rivers in the region, such as the Indus, were fed by the glaciers. These were a source of drinking water to over a billion people in the area. The glaciers produced water which fed rivers that traveled across many smaller countries in the region including China on the other side. As such, further along the glaciers one came across rivers which flowed into India. This fusion reactor was drawing water from the glaciers away from these very rivers.

However, on this one stretch, the glaciers had affected the flow of water further down, not only in GB but also in the neighboring country of Punjab and Baluchistan.

There were mass protests at this epic project and a lot of public sentiment and anger at the whole notion.

Media organizations were all too good at turning the heat up by disseminating material by digital means – portraying the belief that all was well and in the public interest. This 'Spaceport Himalaya' was under construction by the United States government up in the Himalayas, and the lack of water was affecting people's everyday life, affecting their crops, farming, agriculture, not to mention general drinking water.

Hence why there was now a campaign, a movement which was unavoidably going to turn militant. This was something which Iftikhar Azam was inevitably to become intrinsically entwined and linked with.

*****

Iftihkar sat patiently waiting in the red convertible. It was getting a little chilly, but he is well dressed, wearing a local woolen Jacket. The sun is now lower in the sky and shining right at him through the windshield.

Just then, as the wind blew across some rusty leaves, Iftihkar just about makes out a silhouette of a slim figure appearing, striking in front of the glaring sun. It emphasized all those tiny hairlines scratches in the glass, all there due to years of abrasion. A charming smile appeared across Iftihkar's face as he realized the silhouette was of Janet, whom he so desired to share company with.

Getting closer to his car, all those colors of her clothing and her make-up coordination were getting ever sharper, brighter and more in contrast against the glare of the sun as it distorts the very essence of serenity. She looked to be wearing khaki which is quite common in this region, except as she came closer it was obvious it wasn't the case. She was dressed in a red silk dress. However, she was wearing a long woolen tunic jacket. Covering her head was a scarf, akin to a Persian rug in patterns. The influence of Persian rugs in fashion stemmed as far back as, well centuries.

"Oh my, it's getting a little chilly now," she said as she pulled the handle to open to car door.

"Agreed, I think I'll put the hood up," said Iftihkar.

Janet sat in the passenger seat, careful not to get her dress caught anywhere against the clumsy chrome work, as these old vehicles seemed to have knobbly bits hanging out. A stark difference to streamlined modern ergonomic vehicles. And far-fetched compared to the autonomous flying taxi which was operational this year.

She shrugged her shoulders and puts her arms around herself, rubbing herself warmer.

"Yes! I think that's a good idea!"

Iftihkar's arms reached over to the back to pull the roof over the top. Janet was quick to take advantage of the opportunity to admire Iftihkar's waistline. Maybe she can catch a quick glimpse of his six-pack if any, as he certainly didn't seem the type who would let his figure fall out of shape.

A cheeky smile appeared on her face as she did manage to catch a glimpse of flesh beneath his shirt.

There is a clunk followed by another clunk, as Iftihkar pushed the clasps tight against the body of the car just above the windshield. Now the car is an enclosed setting. The two of them share the little bubble, a small personal enclosure, with only the two of them. The heating is already running, and the interior begins to heat up instantly.

"Janet, you're looking so fashionable, and I must add your perfume certainly smells exquisite. So elegant, you look as sweet as you are," said Iftihkar.

"Thank you, Chanel number five, to be precise," said Janet, smiling.

Iftihkar was driving now, not in any rush to get anywhere. Taking it gently around the slow bends and along the highway which was set against great cliff edges, with drops of hundreds of meters to the bottom.

As they were driving a drone passes overhead carrying two passengers. It was its own kind of quiet-loud in its own distinctive sound – completely separate from anything else, sounding a little like four sets of electric whisks or maybe electric toothbrushes running in synchronization.

It was all well planned as by the time they'd arrived at the Shigar Fort Hotel the sun had just dropped beneath the mountains, which in turn called for much of the lighting in the hotel to be turned on.

Iftihkar parked the vehicle, and as soon as he did, he rushed out of the car to the other side to open the door for Janet, who swung her body over, and her legs out, one at a time. A smile appeared on Iftihkar's face, a cheeky grin as he enjoyed Janet's legs as she climbed out.

He shut the door before rushing across to the other side and closing the driver's side. He then joined Janet who was stood waiting.

Iftihkar considered himself the ideal gentleman character that a lady of Janet's statue would yearn, right now. Kind of like they used to have in the year 1970, the year his car was manufactured. He reached his arm out;

"May I?"

Janet linked her arm around his arm, and the two walked into the hotel.

"Certainly," she said.

As the two of them walked arm in arm into the hotel, it was obvious that they were expected. They were both greeted, eye contact mainly at Iftihkar, and were walked over to the restaurant.

Iftihkar walked to the restaurant door, opening it for Janet. As she entered the restaurant, Janet couldn't help but notice a well-arranged table displaying flowers and candlelight.

"Oh, that's so sweet... so sweet, Iftihkar... so thoughtful... it's just wonderful to give me such attention," she said.

Iftihkar pulled a seat out for her to sit down. She was careful of her dress, making sure not to fold, catch or pull it; she held it firmly against her legs as she sat down.

"Well, Janet, you know what I like most about this restaurant... it's the fact that after a meal, we can go out and admire the stars right above us. As you noticed, it's kind of isolated... few neighborhoods around... hence its name, very appropriate to its presence and location... isolated and nested within the mountain scene."

Janet helplessly smiles and picks up the drinks menu.

"Well, Iftihkar, I've been on many dinners due to my reporting career, but they tended to be very formal, no frills. This is the icing on the cake," she said.

Janet notices pomegranate juice on the menu as the waiter turns up;

"What can I get you to drink? Sir, Madam?"

"Janet... let's try the pomegranate. I'm sure you'll like it. At least it's going to remind you of your red wine. On that note, I don't drink as I'm teatotal, don't consume alcohol, don't know if it's due to common sense or religion, just chose not to,"

Janet nodded her head to the waiter.

"Me too, yes, I'll try the pomegranate. Thank you."

The waiter takes away the drinks menu. He then walked off leaving the pair in close company. It's a quiet corner in the restaurant.

"Actually waiter, can you get me a small shot of vodka as well," said Janet rather loudly.

The waiter just manages to catch that and returns to the table.

"I'd like a shot of vodka as well, please," said Janet.

"Certainly Madam." The waiter nodded and made a note.

Janet got up and put her hand on Iftihkar's hand;

Just off to the bathroom, I'll be right back."

She picked up her handbag and headed off towards the door, except there's no bathroom sign, so she stood looking around.

"It's outside; you'll see it to your left as you leave," said Iftihkar.

She left the restaurant, closing the door behind her.

When Janet returned, she found a glass containing her vodka beside a glass of pomegranate juice. She sat and began to pour the vodka into the juice. As she did, she looked at Iftihkar."

What she was thinking was anyone's guess... maybe she hopes the alcohol will help her relax and fall in love with this elusive and rather charming Iftihkar.

"Makes me more at ease and comfortable, you probably won't understand, not being a drinker," she said, wanting to explain.

"Janet, somebody once said that a man tends to go for a woman in his life, who mirrors his mother. Well, you're far from that, you're completely not like my mother. Had my mother still been around, she would be... well, shocked to say the least. She'd certainly frown upon this, dining with a non-believer who also drinks," said Iftihkar.

Janet took a sip of her drink and placed it back on the table. She puts a hand on Iftihkar's arm. She seemed to be very touchy;

"Well, Iftihkar, in life we often make decisions which we do because we want to move on and make certain changes from the past. I'm one for believing that everything happens for the best. And if we are sat here at this table beneath the stars, well, it's no accident; it's because you want it to happen."

Iftihkar began to chuckle and smiled at her.

"Ha, ha, ha, ha, ha, you're an inquisitive and witty lady Janet. I told you so, earlier. And very well put – I must say you're good with your words. The fact that you were once a journalist certainly radiates through. Maybe you have been doing your homework about me too."

Janet smiled, taking her hand off his arm and picking up the menu. She brought it up to her eyes;

"you mentioned that ginger dish, well... as it so happens, I am starving, so let's order shall we."

"Yes, certainly, that's it. The lamb ginger it is. Let's get one lamb ginger and one chicken ginger."

The waiter caught Iftihkar's attention and came over. Iftihkar placed the order and the waiter left the pair once more.

This time it was Iftihkar's whose hand found Janet's.

"Janet, you know what I like about you? You seem like a sophisticated woman, am I wrong?" he said.

Janet's blue eyes opened wide, and her mouth opened and she began to shake her head as she smiled. Her eyes pierced into his, like the stars.

"Well, that's nice, but I hope that's not all you see me as." She replied.

"Oh, there certainly is more, much more. You're so exquisitely beautiful, and you're oozing with glamour. The beauty shines out of you as it does across the night sky, littered with those stars, completely devoid of flaws. Every facet of you is as beautiful as the next, and I feel thrilled being able to sit here and tell you that," said Iftihkar.

Janet really did blush just then. Her cheeks began to glow, all too visible from within that pale white skin as she looked up and smiled, A streak of blonde hair falls forward into her face. She looked down and pulled the strand back to where it should be.

By now the pair had voiced their feelings and made one another aware that they were mutually attracted. Janet was a beautiful lady, and Iftihkar was helpless at feeling attracted to her. However, Iftihkar was a well-educated bachelor who was well traveled and talented, not to mention wealthy and undoubtedly with interests in current affairs, politics and science which the pair could talk over for hours on end.

Once they'd eaten, Iftihkar walked Janet outside.

"Janet, I'd like to show you something now. Something which would help me to explain what I see in you," he said.

The pair walked up the ancient cobblestone steps to the rooftop above the restaurant. As they both investigated the night sky, the stars were now all visible as their eyes adjusted to allow more light in. It is almost as though the pair are cloaked with a black sheath of gleaming twinkling lights and sparkley glitter which they can practically reach up and touch. The clarity was breathtaking, and a far cry from what one would be able to see while looking up above from within a light-polluted city. Being perched amongst the mountains in an idyllic location, devoid of any form of light pollution gave them an awe-inspiring view.

Coupled with their romantic evening meal, it went hand in hand, like a treat. A perfect backdrop.

"Janet, you mean to me what these stars signify and mean to the night sky. They are meant to be together; their contrasts work together: one goes with the other. It was meant to be. We might be different in some ways, but I feel happy being with you, just as much as these stars will be within the night sky." said Iftihkar.

In the sky, just when the pair were observing its tranquility, so well defined by Iftihkar, miraculously a shooting star passed by.

Janet moved closer to Iftihkar, and suddenly felt herself being huddled towards him. She did not resist. Her lips touched his. They stood together, alone on the dark rooftop terrace under the dark night sky, enjoying each other with no one to watch or disturb them. With Iftihkar's arms around Janet, her silky dress felt warm in touch, and the softest thing he'd ever put his hands on. Also, the scent of Chanel 5 was effectively complementing his sense of smell while his sense of touch was being satisfied by the feel of silk against his skin.

As Janet's body might have felt the cold, Iftihkar can feel the warmth from her body through the touch of her silk dress, the dimples due to cold chill in her pale white skin can be felt behind the silk fabric, ever more as the cold night air got even colder. Janet now must keep closer and embrace Iftihkar if she was to stay warm.

Chapter 28
Tendering

The shower was turned on in the en-suite and the noise of water could be heard. Iftihkar was still in bed and had his duvet enveloping him. He turned to look towards the bathroom and sees the vanity mirror on the bathroom wall all steamed up. The door wasn't completely closed shut, leaving a slight aperture. He noticed something distinct, it was a heart drawn out on the steamed mirror. He smiled.

Iftihkar throws his head back into the soft goose feathers filled pillow. It had been a rather pleasant and entertaining night, being able to share the company of someone who was as sophisticated and well informed as him. As it came to light, both Iftihkar and Janet had a keen interest in current world affairs and circumstances which brought about new economic conditions.

Which was the topic of discussion the night before, after they'd had their romantic evening meal, and then enjoyed being beneath the stars? But sure, of it. Once the stargazing had come to an end, whatever concluded after that happened in this magnificently comfortable, lovely bed, they'd both shared.

Janet had just stepped out of the shower. As she walked over to the vanity mirror, she could see the reflection of Iftihkar in bed, gazing at her, looking at her through the mirror before her – through the mirror that hadn't been wholly steamed over, as a result of her cleaning away a heart shape over it, wiping away the steam to reveal a heart shape silhouette.

As she turned the hot water mixer tap on in the basin, she noticed the label 'Grohe', its German label engraved on the mixer tap, which is a rather fancy brand and a trusted and well-established brand of sanitary hardware, which is a fact she was aware of due to her staying in many hotels during her reporting career. There was a knock on the door which Janet didn't hear as she was busy brushing her teeth. Iftihkar clambered out of bed, quite well was aware it was the breakfast in bed he'd ordered the night before. Even so, he looked through the peep hole in the door to check, and yes, it was room service with his breakfast. Iftihkar turned the latch and opened the door. A suitably attired gentleman stood with a tray with a host of dishes covered with matching stainless-steel luxury dome dish covers of high-grade silver.

"Good morning, Sir,"

"Thank you, splendid. Just on the table please," said Iftihkar.

Just as room service left the room, Iftihkar was quick to close the door right after.

He began to lift the dish covers to reveal the dishes, to take a peek. The smell of scrambled eggs became intense just then. The toast was correctly placed neatly in the toast rack, half brown bread and half white bread just as he'd ordered. The juice was also correct: one glass of orange and one grapefruit. Just in case. He wasn't sure how fussy Janet might be. Then Iftihkar felt his shoulders being gently squeezed. Janet was behind him. He found that very comforting, and his eyes closed.

"Oh my, Iftihkar, you sure do know how to spoil a lady. I am so impressed," said Janet.

Janet kissed his left cheek just to the underside, and then his neck while squeezing his body tightly while she stands behind him. She was still in her bathrobe. Now, since breakfast had arrived it would be pointless keeping it standing; she might as well tuck into it now.

"Janet, make yourself comfortable. Let's get eating. I'd hate to spoil the breakfast by letting it go cold. After all, it's not every day we get to order breakfast in bed, is it?"

He smiled at her.

"Absolutely, let me grab a chair," she said.

Janet certainly understood Iftihkar's point. But she couldn't help, while dragging a chair over to Iftihkar, squeezing his left leg while kissing him on the lips.

"Thank you, again, Dear," she said with a cheeky smile.

"Oh, wow! I almost forgot. I ordered newspapers!" exclaimed Iftihkar.

He looked beneath the tray and pulled out some newspapers, as he'd ordered, 'The New York Times' and 'USA Today'. Iftihkar put one on the bed as he began to read the other one.

"What do we have here, 'The New York Times' and 'USA Today'.

Janet picked up the 'USA Today' newspaper and started to flick through it. Lo and behold, both the papers are splattered with the same headline, 'The USA to begin on its biggest ever infrastructure project to date': 'Today, the USA federal government is to undertake its largest ever procurement, $1 trillion of machinery and equipment. Tenders have gone out to various manufacturing organizations, ranging from robotics to manufacturing, from machinery to tunneling.'

"Well, it looks like the cavalry will soon be here," said Iftihkar.

*****

The jet engines were beginning to turn until the screaming sound is profound. Jared had been assigned his own private jet, an executive aircraft manufactured by Agusta Westland AW609 TiltRotor, described as tilt-rotor which enabled it to take off, almost vertically, such as a helicopter except in mid-air. The blades rotated at 90° around its axes until they're forward facing, when it then resembled an airplane. As he was quite senior, in fact, head of the entire operation of the spaceport, he was afforded this indulgence, which some would describe as an executive toy. It assisted him in getting to places promptly, as even with excellent infrastructure and spending, it could be no match when it came to being able to deliver a practical transport method. The region undoubtedly was still a place that required executives to travel in helicopters, just as the highways were still by far the slowest means of getting around.

"David, I've got to get going. I'm off to the 'Manufacturing Hub' to check off certain equipment, make sure it's all arrived and fit for purpose. I'm not having any hiccups again," said Jared.

"Rightly so, especially when expecting 2000 tons of copper core, and 500 segments of the quadrant magnets. It'll be a disaster if it doesn't match our grade and spec," said David.

"Yes, I'm quite aware of that David, you continue with your theory. Let's hope you finally find that wedding ring of yours you've lost."

Jared walked away from David while still talking to him. The jet was waiting for him. The 'Operation Headquarters' for this endeavor was newly built in the foothills of the K2 mountain range.

It was once home to K2's basecamp, where all mountaineers set off from to conquer K2. Now, due to the project, all this area was a no-go zone, cleared of any form of tourism or mountaineering. The 'Operation Headquarters' consisted of at least a hundred or so separate pods bolted together to form a building resembling a space colony due to the physical extremities here.

The shafts and tunnels would, however, be connected to this point in the range, together with an underground network consisting of mainly the vertical axis, which signifies the central launch pit and further arteries for the purposes of pumped heated water.

"Vrooosh," the jet took off, heading off into the clear blue sky, leaving David stood still with his ID badge flapping around from the turbulence of whirlwind produced by the propellers. He's left behind to do his homework.

*****

"Well, my ultrasonic is giving me the right result. This will be my benchmark. Our set standard for the rest of the segments." Said Jared.

He was nodding his head. He had just inspected the first magnet, which in ovality terms comprises of a tiny fraction of a full circle, half a quadrant, thus eight will make a complete full circle. Also, he continued over to inspect the copper quality, taking a sample for analyzing it later in his laboratory. He got some bolt croppers and snips at some cabling. Tomorrow was a big day. He was due to be presented by a host of manufacturers who would be demonstrating their machinery and equipment and present on how each would plan on mining and burrowing. Extract the rock through K2 to depths of up to 150km. With their method statement and design details they're due to showcase, It would be a chance to exhibit and demonstrate their methods on how each of them would achieve this. Jared would have the opportunity to decide which one to go for. Many factors would determine which corporation gets the awarding contract. Factors such as timescale, costs, safety, which were all paramount. There were three companies giving presentations. It was a day Jared had been looking forward to most of his life, or at least his working life.

So far, what he had seen today, he was happy with. His jet took off from right in the middle of the 'Manufacturing Hub'. The resources required to produce many of the components expected to form the future 'Star Ship' were extracted from Afghanistan. This was a much cheaper option as it was all locally sourced, saving a logistical conundrum.

Another Uber flying drone taxi landed. It was Janet's ride home. It landed in the beautiful picturesque courtyard of the Shigar Fort hotel where they had stayed the night. Iftihkar gave her a hug and kiss on the lips;

"Give me a call when you get back home, just so I know all's well and good, Honey," he said.

Janet waved and smiled as she walked to her drone taxi, making sure the blades have stopped before she gets anywhere close. She sat in and closed the glass lid above her. The route was already set via her mobile app on her iPhone, and instantly the blades started to turn. Within a matter of seconds, she was flying above the Shigar Fort and out of the grounds.

Just then, as Iftihkar was looking up into the sky watching Janet fly away, his heartbeat began to slow. He'd already started to feel that parting company with Janet was leading to some form of sickness and unhappiness. It was the longing of being close to her. This was now giving Iftihkar the motivation to continue to remain happy. As not having Janet around now was making him unhappy, he realized that he had become rather fond of this beautiful lady and had gotten very attached to her. In truth, if he admitted to himself, the fact was he was in love with a woman he had only known for a couple of days. He felt it would hurt his ego, his image, and make him seem soft. He needed to 'man up'. Except, falling in love is something which can happen to anyone, and is something which has no timescale to compare against.

Chapter 29
Venice

Jared observed the time on his watch. Except it was no longer referred to as a watch. It might be strapped around his left wrist, but it does much more than a watch. One could do whatever he or she needed to via their wrist, communicating by projecting apps. He was just listening to the concluding part of one of the method statements which is a demonstration on how a company planned to carry out the fabricating and excavating of the spaceport. This organization was expecting to quarry out the vertical axis using explosives, and this isn't something which Jared was too impressed with. It doesn't leave much in the way of imagination into the thought that things might go seriously wrong.

The region around the venue at 'The Manufacturing Hub' has had its highest ever level of security. There were a dozen or so F35s in use, at least half invariably in the air. This due to the US Federal government and lobbyists, who were there to make decisions and make a comment on the liabilities of the schemes. They arrived after touching down at Skardu Airport, in US Airforce Bell Boeing V-22 Ospreys, An American multi-mission, tilt-rotor military aircraft that encompassed both the vertical take-off and landing (VTOL) and the short take-off and landing (STOL) capabilities.

"As you know we have a long-established history of quarrying using drilling methods and setting explosives off in the deep pockets, which are formed via drilling. We expect to blast our way down and consequently the now loosened stone, rock and whatever else we might come across being dug out and removed before continuing once again. So, as you might imagine, we continue with this, repeating ourselves until we reach the desired depth," said the chief engineer and Head of Scientific Research and Development at 'Tech Tonka Corporation'.

The CEO was happy cheering away, clapping away well impressed with his display, be it rather soon.

Jared was anxious to get up to the stage and introduce the next presentation.

"So, ladies and gentlemen, I would like to welcome our next delegation, representing 'Rock Technologies and Innovations Corporation'."

Jared began to clap his hands. A small splash of bubbly left his glass due to the shaking of his wrist. He'd kind of almost forgotten what he was holding in his hand. It splashed across on to his right-hand wrist, and a drop settled on his cufflinks. He threw back what was left in his glass so he could continue cheering with the rest of the crowd.

"Good afternoon, I'm Omer Copeland, CEO at Rock Technologies and Innovations Corporation. Let me first put up a visual of what we are all about. For the last 20 years, we have pioneered the technology in robotics engineering for the use of space exploration. Now, when we begin to expand that and multiply that in scale and in size, that's the mechanics of what I'm talking about. The technology in the past has proved successful, so why not build a much larger device, a device that is able to break up a lot more rock and furthermore be able to withstand the harsh extremities that are above and beneath us. So, we aim to use pretty much what we have already pioneered but manufacture it on a colossal size. For example, this device, the robot." The CEO pointed to the overhead display behind him.

It showed a mechanical rover with multiple arms, which can maneuver around rough terrain and walk over and across crevasses.

"This weighed 500 kg when we sent it to Mars. Well, imagine it as now weighing 500 tons, and 100 times in scale, powered by electrics via a power lead which is supplied off the fusion reactor. Also, we would deploy a tunneling boring machine sent down with this rover to whichever section we worked with first. In this case, it would be the summit."

The crowd was mainly comprised of representatives from the US Federal government and lobbyists, who were there to make decisions and make a comment on the viability and feasibility of the plan that each of the delegations was exhibiting today. However, there wasn't much surprise at any of these techniques, just yet anyway. Nothing new was being suggested. Something revolutionary and ground-breaking was what they'd set their sights on, as they'd be approving an initial package worth $1 trillion dollars, and then more in stages. So, they had high expectations and needed to see something extraordinary.

After another 20 minutes of visual demonstrations on computer modeling and animation, Jared decided to walk across the stage and make himself heard;

"Right, ladies and gentlemen, it's time that we had a break and enjoy some refreshments. There is champagne on ice and caviar. Please feel free to help yourself.

It was Jared's birthday today. He toasted himself as he drank some champagne from his refilled glass. But, as he told himself, the older you get, the less it matters.

He walked over to tables where glasses were laid out, with champagne on ice and caviar. He looked through the transparent screen and saw a massive contraption at the indoor exhibition hall, a variety of apparatus brought in by the delegates.

Jared helped himself to some caviar. A member of the catering services team walked over holding a bottle of champagne. Before Jared can say anything, the catering team member refilled his glass to the top. He nodded his thanks.

Just as he takes another sip of the fizz, he is approached by a CEO of a tech giant, which is the third to showcase, after they've finished with their champagne and caviar break.

"Good afternoon Jared, I'm Samson, CEO. We are next to showcase our scheme. This vintage certainly is my favorite. Chardonnay – I had it specially imported from France." Samson Le Sueur, CEO of the tech giant was clearly keen to engage.

"Yes, it's splendid. Well, I hope our team of federal lawmakers can see the light at the end of the tunnel and I wish you all the best. I'm just a pen pusher. It's Congress who will ultimately draw the last line, passing the budget and so on," said Jared.

"Ha ha, this yes, I understand where you're coming from. I remember when not so long ago we had a president in the White House who was struggling even getting his $5 billion passed through Congress. The budget of $5 billion to have a wall built dividing Mexico from the rest of the United States. Well, that certainly didn't go down very well. Federal workers were left in the lurch, without a paycheck for a whole two months," said Samson.

*****

Lovely slender long fingers, with nail extensions which seemed to be extending to the heavens above, colored with sky blue nail varnish, are seen stretching up, pointing up to a book. Just then the hand pulled it out of the shelf. It was Janet at her bookshop. It was doing quite well in this newly formed GB state of America. She's had thousands of books imported halfway around the world from the mainland of the US, as English was new here and had recently been introduced to replace Urdu as a primary language.

Many people were now keen on reading books in English on various subjects. English language books had not been so accessible here. So as Janet is running her own bookshop, she was doing a lot better than she first anticipated. She was getting this book ready for a customer who placed an order on her website. As she put it in the bag, together with a till receipt and business card, the door opens. It was Iftihkar;

"Excuse me Madam, a certain individual is on the hunt for exceptional elegance, and where else might one look, other than right here at your abode. How is my dear Janet, this fine, lovely afternoon?"

Iftihkar slowly edged towards the counter, which Janet is stood behind preparing this order. Janet looked as beautiful as always, as the first time Iftihkar laid his eyes on her, which was a mere few days ago. She blushed. Her strawberry blonde hair complementing the redness in her cheeks. It was a little cold today, and there was the first-thing-in-the-morning-issue surrounding the heating.

Iftihkar leant over the counter, and Janet, without the need of encouragement, leant over and kissed him. She grabbed hold of his shirt and continued to press Iftihkar's lips against hers, pulling on his sweater while doing so. When she does stand back and compose herself, she pulled her dress down, and shook her hair back;

"Oh my," said Janet.

She looked round, trying to remember where she left off.

"Oh yes, your book, my handsome friend with benefits, there you go."

Janet passed a bag across to Iftihkar containing the book that he'd ordered. He reached his hand out to get hold of the bag and his hand dipped into it and drew out the book, entitled *Michael Palin – Himalaya*.

"Yes, it's a bestseller. I've always wanted this, and I've always wanted a hard copy. Thanks Janet, it was a long wait. I finally got one. My own personal copy. It's not quite the same, trying to read something on a digital screen, glaring at you. Can't beat a hard paper copy. You know, Janet, not so long ago, some would have speculated the bookshop was going to be a dying trade, but I suppose here, it's otherwise, we've had a resurgence thanks to a new language being implemented on us, bestowed upon us," said Iftihkar.

He leant over and gave Janet another kiss.

"So, Janet, what you think, my lovely. After all, how about you – don't you think we should be going away on a little vacation. I love traveling, but do you?"

Janet continued moving a few books around which is what she does most of the day. She smiled and turned to look at him;

"Well, we could fly to Venice? I'd love it, unless you can think of something else?"

"Well, it's funny you mention that because if we fly with Emirates airline, we pass through Dubai, and they've got a miniature Venice. Not quite the same as the real McCoy though, but we could go there?" said Iftihkar.

Janet finished what she was doing, then left the counter and headed across to Iftihkar.

"No, I think it would be worth going to the real Venice. Let's get planning. I'll have somebody cover my bookshop while I'm away… there's a girl in the town I know who can cover for me. She is looking for a job, and I'll get all the accounts up to date and then we can go as early as next week maybe? I'm fine with that."

Iftihkar seemed happy at the news he's to go traveling with the love of his life. She's going to go flying with him. It had all worked out well.

"Janet, that's splendid. I'll book our flights as soon as I get back home. And I'll get the accommodation and everything sorted, you leave that with me, Honey. By which time you'll have your employee trained up."

He grabs hold of Janet's hand;

"It looks like I've got some work to do, so I'd better get busy. What are you like for time now? Shall we get a quick coffee?"

Just across the road from the bookstore was a Starbucks coffee shop. Half a century ago this would have been unheard of, having a business enterprise based here which actively condones the Jewish state of Israel – and corporation which has flagrantly avoided paying its fair share of taxes across the world.

"Well, give me five minutes. I just quickly need to go back into the office and grab my keys and we can go," said Janet.

She rushed into the room at the back of her shop as Iftihkar walked over to the front of the shop, gazing out of the window. The architecture here more resembles Downtown Salt Lake City in Utah USA. It had completely transformed from what it was like here over 20 years ago. Pretty much the entire town had been rebuilt. Many of the buildings here were not even built to the standards and regulations that they needed to be, to comply with the national codes such as the National Fire Protection Code (NFPC) and Life Safety Code (LSC), hence they had to be rebuilt from scratch. Massive government aid was given to the residents to compensate for them having to rebuild business premises and homes.

Straight across from Janet's bookshop was an elaborate array of shops, forming a shopping arcade, within which Starbucks sat. Just then, Janet squeezed Iftihkar's chest by putting her arms around him.

"Oh, that smells lovely, Iftihkar, what are you wearing?"

"Oh, it's something which I've had lying around for years. Joop! By Paco Rabanne. It comes in a red bottle, and it's gorgeous. I'm sure even you could get away with wearing it, Janet."

Iftihkar grabbed hold of Janet's hand and tugged on it. They both walked across the road to the coffee shop.

Chapter 30
Showcase

The delegation had all gathered back in the conference hall. This time, a few more parties got up onto the stage. Jared was already up there.

"Right, ladies and gentlemen, good to see you all back. We shall now conclude with our last showcase of the day. Let's give a warm welcome to 'TEXTEC Industries' who will be exhibiting their plan and demonstrating their strategy of how we are best to get our million tons into space. So I'd like to leave you with the gentleman to my left, who I bumped into earlier over a glass of champagne. Let's give him a round of applause."

As Jared was leaving the makeshift stage in the venue, a few more began to walk onto the stage.

It so happens that they were many from other private corporations that had no relevance with the technologies required to bring about the spaceport, such as robotics, mechanics and engineering and so on. They were heads of corporations such as Pepsi Cola, Frankie and Benny's, a plush hotel developer such as Hilton and Marriott. We had designers such as Emporio Armani. There was also McDonald's and Burger King. There must have been a total of 30 CEOs who had just gone onto the stage.

"Good afternoon ladies and gentlemen. I'm Samson Cooper from 'TEXTEC Industries' and today I'm going to demonstrate to you that we are the market leaders in bringing about the unimaginable. We will be absolutely and indisputably the winners of this contest, and the ones to undertake the procurement of the spaceport. We refer to it as the

'Spaceport Himalaya'. So, as you can see we have at least two dozen CEOs from various corporations, which will bring along their expertise and finances to undertake various tasks that each is particularly suited to fulfill. For instance, we have McDonald's, which will sponsor the funding, and provide a certain section of the food and catering facilities on board. There is also Burger King and Frankie and Benny's, both of whom will be taking a market share as to the future catering on board the starship. Accommodation will be provided by hotel companies, such as we have here. Then for those who wish to live an opulent lifestyle and have pockets to suit, more luxurious accommodation will be furnished by Emporio Armani, whose CEO is to my right. This is a tiny drop in the ocean, but it provides an example that it's all about bringing lots of heads of various organizations together to achieve the unthinkable – being able to procure specialist corporations, and working together to bring this vision to fruition. This is commonly known as Private Finance Initiative, or PFI," said Samson.

The audience began to cheer, and so did Samson.

"With regards to our methodology, we are quite confident it is the best by which to develop the 'Spaceport Himalaya'. We have decided to go for a long vertical steel cylindrical machine, running inside the shaft as it removes rock beneath itself, dropping ever further down into the Himalayan crust. Initially, this will be erected above the summit in segments, and dropping explosives into the bottom, containing the blast to within its confines down below. Once discharged, the loose material will be sucked away using a vacuum extraction system, and repeated as necessary. The entire cylindrical vessel with a large diameter of 20 m will be dropping, getting lower with the aid of gravity. There will be hydraulic pistons around the circumference, pushing out, securing and maintaining a correct horizontal pitch. Due to the verticality being crucial and critical, as it's a long way down and any slight deviation in the verticality would entail the 'Spaceport Himalaya' becoming a failure and jeopardizing the entire operation." said Samson.

There is trepidation and jubilation amongst the audience in the hall, and much clapping amongst the crowd at this point, bringing a smile to Samson's face.

"Hold on folks; the fun's not even begun yet," he said.

Using a remote, he switched on a large visual display. An elaborate video presentation of a carefully choreographed, engineered operation took place in terms of mechanics. A ring was carried to and placed on to the summit via an enormous gas-filled doughnut-like an airship. In turn, there was another one set on top of it and they were coupled together. It was repeated over multiple intervals. The rock was broken up into numerous clusters of smaller stones which can be sent up using a suction, known as jet vacuum extraction, via a jet nozzle, which uses a vacuum upon the multitude of broken clusters of rocks, down at the base at its tip, which in turn are sucked away and led through up the pipe.

"As you can see here, we have a very well thought out visual presentation of the whole operation taking place. This operation continues, and rings are added on, via the airship, which is circular in its presentation, held in the air by a doughnut-like helium-filled balloon. It's the same gas which was used in the past in the earlier airships. However, this is all dangerous and very flammable, but as you can well imagine no humans are working in their vicinity, or even the entire operation, as it is choreographed using robotics, machinery and artificial intelligence. Human involvement is at a minimum. Humans are merely observing from down below, at the operation base camp, using surveillance cameras," said Samson.

Incredible sound effects were coming out of the speakers, giving the audience an immersive audio presentation and further emphasizing the visual graphics of the display, which was about to get even more interesting.

"Ladies and gentlemen, can you now look under your chairs. You will find some glasses there. They're 3D which will help you see what is happening in the next presentation."

Everybody began to look under their chairs. Within a minute, the entire audience had their glasses on. The lights are dimmed and continue getting dimmer until they completely turned off. The room is much darker, especially as the large glass screens have electronic blinds that have rolled down, enveloping the entire exhibition hall in almost pitch blackness. "

"The next presentation reminds me of when I first watched a movie during my childhood years, 'Journey To The Center Of The Earth'. Except this is nothing quite like it when you compare the visual effects and together with a sound scientific basis. The visual performance you're about to see is based on real, scientific fact. Whatever you are about to see is something which we've already built and tested at our testing facilities in Utah," said Samson.

The video presentation commenced, beginning with a massive explosion. It was captivating the audience with excellent graphics and visual effects. The house is captivated.

The cylindrical rings laid down on a flat surface in the plains of the Himalayas look small in contrast to the vast mountains behind in the background. Until a person suddenly began to approach the ring.

Just then, an airship, considerable in size, began to approach the ring and drop from the sky. It had cables which drop and hook onto the rings autonomously. The latches were fastened mechanically with no assistance needed. The person was merely stood there to give a perception of size, which was well thought of, as without something against the ring it would be tough to comprehend the right size and scale.

The audience was silent, transfixed on this fantastic visual display, and entirely immersed in what the director and artist had envisioned.

It continued further until a depth was reached, at almost 150km beneath the sea level. Now the number of rings, which were in the thousands, would not be grouted as would have been done in a conventional tunnel project. Due to this region being prone to plate tectonics, shifts in the ground beneath, they would not be grouted, but instead would be subject to an alternative methodology of being restrained against the rocky surface. Every ring was much more than just a simple ring composition. The rings consisted of hydraulic rams on the external face and an arrangement of metal pipes feeding the pistons with hydraulic oil. The cylinders were pushing against the exterior of the rock face, which had been blasted away, thus anchoring themselves tightly the rings, in their correct position. Keeping the ring in its exact central location was pivotal, otherwise they may not keep their circular formation – and, in the case of the next stage, which was when the rails become deployed, they would not have anything to anchor.

There was now additional machinery arriving, which was showing the next part of the operation unfolding — this involved sending rails down along the inside of the cylindrical structure, down of the shaft. The tracks were slid down to the bottom, and each one at about every 10 degrees, around the circular shape while looking from above,

thus delivering a total number of 36 separate
rails, this was all wonderfully illustrated using
3D animation, and all displayed on the large
screen. The animation produced in conjunction
with a professional animation developer. One
which has worked on many other full feature-
length animation movies, similar to the kind most
commonly known as Avatar and a few others.

'Stage three' heading was displayed. It must
have been 15 minutes into the presentation, which
now consisted of magnets that are semicircle
in shape; each magnet was forming, a half a
quadrant, of the entirety of the full circle, which
is the standard that has been agreed by Jared.
The materials due to be used are designated and
incorporated into the standardization. These were
attached to the rails via a series of anchors which
are on the backs of the magnet segments, and were
rolled down to the bottom using electric motors,
like skids. However, these would remain down
there behind the magnets and become written off,
absorbed into the overall project and as part of the
cost of the project.

Multiple magnets formed together, rolling down
various sides of the shaft combine to create the
interior of the electromagnetic propulsion shaft.
Once these magnets were powered, consecutively
as shown in the display. They would accelerate a
shuttle which was also in that case, surrounded and
lined by such magnets, however in the opposing
polar – accelerate the shuttle up through the
entire stretch of the shaft, almost 150km, starting

from standstill. Accelerating it to such a speed, marvelously portrayed in the animation as shown, that it left the summit and headed off straight into orbit. However, it was showing at a much slower speed as one would never be able to see the vehicle, the shuttle in motion, if it were not slowed down – its actual final speed, being upwards of 20,000 km an hour.

Once the shuttle reached space, the magnets fell away. The shuttle then maneuvered itself to wherever it needed to go to merge with other vehicles and continue going about its business in the zero-gravity environment — in this case, delivering supplies to the starship.

Suddenly, there was cheering and excitement like there had not been in this venue. It pretty much summed up the conclusion which the federal delegation had made together with representation from Congress as they were also cheering. The display now gave them the confidence, confidence of the entire operation, but under one condition, a prerequisite, only if it was to be left in the hands of this consortium of corporations run by Samson at 'TEXTEC Ind.'.

*****

Iftihkar took the tray containing two caffé mochas, each with a dusting of chocolate on the top, and headed over to Janet, who was sat at a table, facing her shop, conveniently. She could watch her shop while comfortable at the coffee shop, enjoying her coffee with her lover.

"There you are, my lovely, I knew you'd like the chocolate. I think the only thing missing here is the Swiss chocolate. Gondolas, Swiss chocolate, champagne, trip to Venice, it seems almost like a romance novel," said Iftihkar.

He placed the tray down on the table, lifted a cup and put it in front of Janet before taking his and carefully sitting down. He inhaled deeply, smelling the aroma, the exquisite unique aroma of Arabic coffee before tucking in to his cup of the frothy liquid. Up until 20 years ago, it was near enough impossible to find a coffee shop here. There were just those unique ramshackle chai shops.

Chapter 31
Red Roses

Suddenly, a bizarre noise could be heard – it sounded like whining, sucking grinding all at the same time, and it was coming from the coffee machine. A red light began to flash and an insistent beeping began as the alarm sounded.

The shop manager, Sabrina, who was on shift that morning came over to look at the display. It showed low pressure, with the gauge warning light flashing, while the bleeping seemed to get louder.

"Well, that's never happened before," she said.

Sabrina was a petite twenty-eight-year-old with jet black hair, who spent much of her minimum wage on coffee, so she'd decided to work in a coffee shop.

She went over to the sink and turned on a tap. The cold fresh water started spluttering out, slowed to an almost drool, stopped, started again, gushing and spitting without any continuous flow.

"Well that's a problem – how the hell am I supposed to sell coffee?" she groaned to herself.

Just then the door opened, and another staff member walked in. It was her colleague Zara.

"Hey, sorry, I might smell a bit rancid today. I haven't managed to shower. No water!" said Zara.

Sabrina turned to Zara. "We have none here either. It's going to be an interesting day at this rate! No water, no coffee. In fact, no nothing!"

"I switched on the shower this morning, and nothing happened. Like, no water at all. Mind you, I am slightly higher up in the mountain than this shop, but hey, what on earth is going on?" said Zara.

That day, more customers walked in, all with similar stories of little or no water – especially further downstream in the agricultural areas, where there was none at all. In the next day's newspaper, headlines were titled 'A water shortage in the newly formed American state.' ... 'An independent committee is to launch an investigation as to why there is a shortage of water.'

*****

'The New York Times' newspaper was pulled off the rack at a newspaper outlet. Janet was at Departures at Skardu International Airport. She and Iftihkar are off on their romantic break to Venice. Janet sat down after seeing the front cover and headed straight for the main article covering the water shortage.

"An independent committee, yeah! As if! There will be a cover-up on that, I'm sure of it! In fact, this is something I would love to get my teeth into and get writing again. I wish," said Janet.

She turned to Iftihkar, who was sat next to her, fiddling about with his watch.

"I'm talking to you. Are you listening, surely these things adjust themselves by now?" she said irritably.

Iftihkar turned to her, unsure what's upset her.

"What was that my darling?"

"What the hell, you weren't paying attention were you? Typical, talk about men not being able to multitask. I'm sat right here next to you, and you ignore me when I'm talking to you!"

She made a rude sound.

Iftihkar leant over to her and rubbed her shoulders reassuringly.

"Now come on Darling, I am not ignoring you intentionally. The problem will sort itself I am sure. That lake at my dad's former hotel resort hasn't completely dried up, see – they'll have to use it for pumping water out to supply the local community. It's either that or they'll have no running water for even basic tasks. These things happen. Or, someone grossly underestimated something and made a real blunder!"

The flight leaving for Milan with Emirates was getting ready for boarding. An announcement was made. Such was the prominence and presence of Skardu throughout the world of today that many of the international carriers were now flying directly to Skardu.

However, in this instance, there was a change in Malpensa Airport, Milan, for Janet and Iftihkar to get to Venice.

"Flight Alitalia AZ320 to Milan ready to board, boarding at Gate 7. That's Alitalia flight AZ320 flying to Milan ready to board at Gate 7." An announcement was heard on the overhead system.

As soon as it was announced, Janet folded her newspaper and put in into her handbag.

"Well, looks like that's us, Dear," she said.

They both stood, and wandered off in the wrong direction firstly, at a cluster of signboards, before realizing they need to be walking in the opposite direction for Gate 7, which is directly behind them.

As they board the plane, 20 minutes later, Janet realized she is sitting in business class. She turns to Iftihkar and smiles;

"Thank you so much Iftihkar. That's a lovely treat; it's been a while since I've flown business class."

She hurriedly put away her hand luggage in the above overhead compartment before quickly and carefully taking the window seat. There was ample legroom, even though neither of them was very big. Having a gap between the seats meant the two were further from each other.

Iftihkar put away his hand luggage directly next to Janet's before sitting in the seat beside her. He wasn't as close to her as he'd like.

"Yes, Honey, I thought it would be a treat. This is how I travel. I like to travel in style. It's something which I've gotten accustomed to and am rather fond of, and I'm sure we'll be doing much more of it, now that we're partners in crime." He chuckled.

Later that same day, after they'd landed in Venice, the pair were exhausted and headed straight for their hotel 'Hotel Rialto'.

The following day, a gondola pole pushed down into the water, just as a duck waddled about in the water right there, splashing away from the blade. The gondolier was gently pushing the boat down one of the canals, as our duo enjoyed a ride in true Venice style.

Janet was looking rather dapper and stylish in a long black and white dress, checkered with a geometric pattern and a hat to match. The hat had a rather large brim, keeping her pale skin shaded from the elements.

"Oh dear, look at that. I'm sure I've seen that in many postcards and magazines. It's a famous bridge but I don't know what it's called," said Janet.

Just up ahead there stood a rather fanciful bridge. It was constructed from an array of types of stone, all intricately carved to create a Venetian masterpiece which straddled right across the Grand Canal.

Iftihkar was busy looking at his tour guide for a place for tonight's romantic dinner for the two. But not before he'd go and visit a tailor first, to get himself a bespoke tailor-made suit.

"Excuse me, Sir, at the gondolier, do you know of any good restaurants where I can go with my wife tonight?" asked Iftihkar.

The gondolier, carefully making sure that he was well away from the edge of the canal, gave it one last push before addressing Iftihkar.

"Sir, yes, I will show you. There will be a beautiful restaurant where we stop, adorned with red roses, right on the canal edge. You will see. They have music and lights. I show you."

*****

Back at the spaceport base camp, 'Spaceport Himalaya' was rapidly advancing. The fusion reactors were running at full blast, as much of the power being supplied to the machinery, mechanics, and rocketry was being powered by the fusion reactors. This, in turn, was causing a water shortage further downstream. It was also not helping that the region was not having its usual quota of rainfall and snowfall like it had been throughout the last century. Therefore, the project was being commissioned and commencing at the worst time ever as it meant even less water for agriculture, farming households and industry.

Chapter 32

The Mystic and Militant

Later that day, Iftihkar had received a message from his peers, family members and acquaintances back at home that most of their livestock had died due to such a shortage of water, and a local Mystic, 'Sufi', at the Shrine had made them all aware that there was more to it than met the eye. Outside forces from far and wide had the work of the devil in hand.

Iftihkar had the phone pinned against his ear as he was emotionally rhapsodizing away in his native tongue.

"I will do my utmost and see what we can do to change this. There are obviously certain events taking place, such as the spaceport being built – maybe all the drilling is created a deep sinkhole, a cavern in the earth, where all the water is collecting. I'll look into it as soon as I get back."

A candle was lit, it was a red, very slim one, rising elegantly against the fine tableware at the table. The restaurant was indeed as the Gondolier had described it. Its front was ornamented with beautiful fresh red roses, picked the day before, and to make things more fun and special, adding spice to it all, Iftihkar and Janet had arrived via the gondola once again.

Their hotel, 'Hotel Rialto' was built on the edge of the canal. In fact, the only thing separating the hotel from the canal was literally a few plant pots, and traveling by gondola meant they were able to leave straight for the front door, as it were, via a short gondola journey, to the restaurant's front door. Iftihkar had booked a package with the restaurant, which included a pick-up and drop-off service courtesy. As the restaurant was well known for its delicious menu and romantic dinners, and the hotel was similarly popular for getaways, and both establishments were on the canal edge, it had made sense for them to collaborate over romantic packages for their customers. Financially it was a success and tourists received a wonderful experience and happy memories.

"May I take your coats?" asked the waiter.

"Oh, of course, thank you," replied Janet.

Iftihkar followed suit and took his off and handed it over to the waiter. He had managed to find a local tailor who would hand stitch him a suit in time for his dinner the following day. It was jet black with white pinstripes and complemented his white shirt underneath. The pair sat facing each other at the table, with the candle in between them, kind of obscuring their vision a little, as it was at face level.

"You know something, I had this awful phone call earlier about somebody I know who has lost pretty much his entire livestock. It's shocking to say the least. This situation really has me worried. It's the worst kind of a nightmare for someone in the livestock business, and it's come to reality," said Iftihkar.

Janet shakes her head and shrugged her shoulders.

"Dear, I understand your concern, but we are after all having a romantic dinner, so let's not talk about it now," said Janet.

Chapter 33

The Russian Link

At that moment, a man walked by and placed a card on their table, kind of like a business card. It read Igor Draskovic, a Russian name, and 'Investigative Journalist' was written clearly below, with a Russian newspaper organization. Janet picked it up to take a better look at it. She frowned as she turned to look at him;

"Excuse me, can I help you? We were having a romantic dinner here. Please leave us alone."

"Certainly, but not before you hear me out. I understand you're Janet, and you previously worked as an investigative journalist. Therefore, I'm sure you will find my proposition very interesting. I'm offering you a job as a journalist, an investigative journalist, to work for our Russian news organization – covering the story surrounding the 'Spaceport Himalaya'. Scientific research and development on our part, using seismic analogy and an array of instruments, including satellites, has had us conclude that the water table in the region has dropped to almost superficial levels. In fact, the area will become uninhabitable in the next six months. Maybe you would like to do some writing, and as you're an American, maybe get inside and have, as they say, a 'mooch around'," said Igor.

He seemed like he knew a lot more than he had on first impression. What was now on Janet's mind was exactly what was on Iftihkar's. Maybe he had links with the Russian secret service, the SVR.

Iftihkar draws his hand up, waving his finger.

"Yes, I had a message today from somebody in my community, who's lost his entire livestock due to lack of water. There is literally no drinking water left for livestock and this pretty much sums up what is happening on earth. I mean, I don't have a PhD, neither am I a doctor of geography or geology, but I do know that something isn't right, and many businesses are struggling. In fact, you, Janet, had a message about the coffee shop across the road from your book shop having to shut down because they can't make coffee when there's no water."

"Oh, yes, absolutely. Listen Mr. Draskovic, I'll be sure to contact you. Yes, I'd love to get my hands into some journalism and do what I enjoy doing most," said Janet.

And to Iftihkar, she said, "I'll be all right, Dear. I'll get the girl in the village to cover my bookshop – not that there's much business there with a coffee shop shut across the road."

"Well, if that's what you enjoy doing, then I'm with you 100% all the way," said Iftihkar.

He took Janet's hand with both of his and holds onto them.

"I'm sure we can work together on this. I've got some tactical knowledge which may be of use."

One of the biggest smiles one can ever imagine appeared on the Russian man, Igor's face. He had papers in his hand. A bundle of documents. For all they knew he could have been concealing a gun in there. The hallmarks of the Russian secret service were all over him. But now Janet was so determined in her quest to able to help unearth what was causing the water outage, she would do whatever it took. To gather information again as she had previously done in her investigative journalism career, as a journalist excited her such that she was blinded from the possibilities of her being involved with the dark forces of the enemies of the state.

"Excellent, I shall look forward to hearing from you Janet, and Iftihkar, you too, and I shall leave you to enjoy your dinner in peace. Give me a call," said Igor.

The Russian man Igor had yellow teeth, and a face to match – his skin was so bumpy it reminded Janet of the Grand Canyon.

He walked off, leaving the two alone.

"Well, that was rather odd, don't you think? How on earth did he know where we were... sure he was waiting there for us. Nevertheless, I literally can't turn his offer down. Those people need our help, our hometown is in turmoil. One of the most basic things, one of the fundamental necessities to nourish human life is at stake," said Janet.

Chapter 34

Commissioning

Janet had her hotel room phone handset pinned against her ear. It was ringing. Just as she gave up and replaced it on its cradle, it answered. She was using the hotel phone as she was reluctant to use her own phone. She was calling the Russian, Igor. As she crossed the room to the wardrobe, the hotel phone began to ring. Although she expected the call, it still strangely took her by surprise. She turned back and picking up the handset;

"Hello, Janet speaking."

Iftihkar had just walked out of the bathroom. He was in his gown after having a shower.

"It's Igor, you called, I hope you've decided to take up my offer as I believed you would."

Janet nodded her head, then realized he was waiting for a reply.

"Yes, I'd like to see you first though..., we can discuss it over a coffee tomorrow... my status and arrangements, a contract of employment and so on. How about we meet tomorrow morning, say 10 o'clock downstairs here at my hotel, Hotel Rialto?"

"Certainly Janet, as you wish. I shall be arriving at your hotel. The details I have as you called me from the hotel. The same hotel I'm assuming?"

She nodded her head again;

"Yes, yes, it is the same hotel, and if you wish, you can travel here by gondola, as it's right on the canal bank."

"Thank you, Janet, we shall be speaking in the morning. I'm sure and confident that you will be taking up the proposal I have for you. Have a good night, and we speak tomorrow, goodbye."

Janet took the phone away from her ear and looked at Iftihkar. She was smiling, and continued to smile at him. Iftihkar had a towel around his head and is busy drying his hair. He looked at her.

"Sometimes Janet, one's gotta be careful what they wish for, you know. You might be opening a can of worms for yourself tomorrow. Have a good understanding of what you're getting involved in. I'll be there with you. That's, if you need me? I don't disagree with what you're doing, but caution is important."

Iftihkar and Janet were both traveling on USA passports, and everyone in the newly formed states had acquired US citizenship and US passports too.

However, certain aspects were beginning to ring bells, such as the scarcity of water resources. It had always predicted by prominent, well-known thinkers that a future third world war would be fought over water resources, and the USA building 'Spaceport Himalaya' in a region which was the drinking water fountain for over a billion people in the world wasn't going down well. There was a report outlining what other viable ways there could be of providing water, including collection of any produced as a result of geothermal energy extraction. Due to the power generation via heated water and steam which was eating up this precious resource.

"Yes, Iftihkar, I'm a mature adult, I know what I'm getting myself into. You knew about me before you got involved with me, and it's not like we're even married yet is it?" said Janet.

"Yes, yes, yes, I know you do as you please. However, this trip is turning out to be less of a romantic getaway and more a conspiracy trip."

Janet stood up and came round to where Iftihkar was sitting, and embraced him, kissing with parting lips.

"Oh, Honey. This is me – it's in my blood to be an investigative journalist, but I want you to be happy too. I'm sure we soon will see everything come to fruition, and I'm confident we have a future together," she said.

Iftihkar walked over to his closet where he investigates his holdall baggage for a catalogue he has hidden. He pulled it out while his back is turned to Janet. It was a jeweler's catalogue with pages of diamond rings, as there was one which caught his eye. He had drawn a circle around it. it's got a circle around it. Priced at $25,000, he smiled at it, and put the catalogue away. It must be a surprise for Janet. It would be obvious what a man like him would be doing with a catalogue with an encircled image of a diamond ring in it. Iftihkar had ambitions when it came to Janet. He was making plans of buying this ring as an engagement ring for her. He had seen it in a jewelery shop here in Venice, and he planned to buy it while Janet was meeting with Igor about the job opportunity tomorrow.

"Honey, when you have the meeting with your Russian counterpart Igor, tomorrow... Well, I'd like to pop out and visit a few shops. If that's all right with you, I don't think it's viable for me to be listening to what's going on," he said.

"That's splendid Iftihkar, yes, certainly. I'll be fine in the hotel," said Janet.

*****

At the 'Spaceport Himalaya' the construction using future advanced robotics which was fully fledged and running smoothly and the whole project had transformed the region. The millions of tons of materials had all been quarried from the mountainous regions surrounding it. The shaft had millions of tons of steel lining it, then copper ring magnets and electronics had been put down in its place. The 'Spaceport' was running ahead of target, and was due to be commissioned the following month. It was that time which would see many skilled professionals and commissioning engineers carrying out tests using parts and shuttle pods which would be laden with ballast just for a trial launch. The grand opening, which would be held 11th September: referred to as 911.

While the commissioning was taking place and the trial runs going ahead, many professionals would be entering and leaving the region, and security would be placed on highest alert.

*****

It was the following day, and the aroma of Italian coffee percolated the atmosphere. Janet was not at her hotel café, but had decided to take a gondola ride over to a well-known prominent location, the Canal Bar.

Janet had decided she didn't feel comfortable meeting at her hotel, so had sent Igor a message last night changing their meeting place. She was looking out onto a breath-taking view of the Grand Canal with the church of Santa Maria Della Salute in the background... She was wearing her Chanel Number Five perfume and 'Chanel' sunglasses – those distinctive, pear-shaped black lenses with black frames encrusted with diamonds forming the Chanel logo.

There was the sound of geese as they flew in the air in formation. Just then a gondola touched the side of the wall of the Canal Bar, BAUER Venice. Janet put down her cup of espresso. The waiter walked over to her. He was holding a white napkin and was wearing a white apron over a white shirt, with a dicky bow.

"Madam, may I get you anything?"

Janet finished the last sip of coffee and shook her head;

"I'm okay for now, thank you."

Igor appeared next to her, and had someone with him. Maybe a minder, or perhaps he was part of a Secret Service network.

As Janet turned to look at him, she took off her sunglasses, revealing her piercing blue eyes.

"Good morning Janet, I see you've taken liberty and ordered yourself coffee without me. Maybe I can get you another?" said Igor.

He took a seat while his companion or minder continued to stand at the water's edge, out of immediate sight, but not out of range of hearing, possibly. Igor extended his hand to Janet. She shook it.

They both looked down across the Grand Canal, noticing the ripples in the water as a gentle breeze passed by. Igor smelled the coffee and he signaled to a waiter, who approached holding a silver tray and a napkin around his arm.

"Sir?"

"Would like two espressos and get me a bottle of sparkling water, please."

Just then, Janet's phone vibrated on the table with a message from Iftihkar.

"Hello, my lovely, how's your meetup going?"

Janet picked the phone up and replied;

"going well, X X X"

"So, let's talk business, Janet. We at the Russian newspaper, 'The Gazette' have a department which requires an investigative journalist like you. However, as you're in the United States of America, it's only best if we hire you. You'll be freelance. I am convinced you have extensive previous experience. Here in my pocket I have all the necessary ID cards and security passes which will get you through all the security protocol they have at the 'Spaceport Himalaya'. You will be able to pass around freely in all the restricted areas. As well, we have gathered whatever is required for you to be able to accomplish that. So, you leave that with me. As for your salary package, well, you should email me your bank account details and we'll start off with US$150,000 each per year, plus an initial upfront cash advance. There on the table in that envelope I have $30,000 in cash – it's for you today. That's just to reassure you that I'm serious and committed, and the rest I leave with you. You well know what your draft brief is, what is to be your scope – that is to gather information which purports to the shortfall of drinking water in the region by gaining inside information into what's the exact cause, take some pictures and feed me all the information – which, together, we will use for publishing via the news agency and use the social media to generate momentum which will inevitably lead to halting of the development of the 'Spaceport Himalaya'. It's something which needs to be stopped, for the greater good for the region, and please excuse me my English is not so good."

Janet nodded her head, putting her glasses back on.

"Yes, certainly. That's absolutely my niche market. May I add something... I would like to get involved in all you've just mentioned. However, I've got to actually believe in the angle you present and not just report on it, as a piece of information, based on speculation – it needs to be something which we all need to, I need to, have an understanding of. Something which in fact is damaging the environment. I'm not just going to be bought out by $150,000, but I absolutely 100% am with you on the fact that it's something which needs to be addressed, that it is indeed damaging the environment, without a doubt... causing global warming and the shortage of drinking water... well yes...good reason... but if it is simply a case of having 'an issue' with the 'Spaceport'... not a reason good enough for my liking."

The waiter turned up with two espresso cups and sparkling water in a bottle and crystal glasses on his tray. He placed the glasses and two cups of espresso on the table, and lastly he picked up the bottle before putting his tray under his armpit and using the napkin to hold the bottle and twist its top. He poured water into each of the glasses, then replaced the top on the bottle and carefully put it on their table. He nodded his head and walked away.

Igor picked up the glass of sparkling mineral water and took a few sips whilst looking at Janet.

"Janet, I'm delighted. Yes, delighted to have you on board. You will not find yourself in a position where you're ever expected to report on anything incorrect. Something which foreign agencies will have you do, but not me, not us. They do it because, you know, the Americans have all been tight-lipped and have been silenced. Which is why we hear Russia feel that it's something which our adversary is keen to exploit, and something which we are duty-bound to make sure that the world gets to hear about, and you will be our mouthpiece."

Janet lifted her glass of sparkling water. She noticed all the bubbles are rising. She imagined herself rising just like all the bubbles, to the top – it would do wonders for her career in terms of global recognition. It was the most profound discovery of the century, and Janet was about to make it known to the world at large. It was the very essence of what she was holding in her hand which was the primary factor of her making this career-changing decision. The clean, fresh, precious resource of water. And just as she was looking into it, she looked right through it across the canal, the church of Santa Maria Della Salute in the background. She took the glass and drew the water into her mouth.

"Absolutely Igor, so do you have any documents with you now for me to sign?"

"I have here for you. This envelope. It contains all that you need. My assistant at the head office will also be emailing you everything you need, and you just reply by filling in the boxes on the document online. It will be a link to our website, which all employees use to complete documents in electronic format."

Igor took out the envelope from the inside pocket of his coat and handed it to Janet. It's a brown envelope. Janet tore open the flap and looked inside. Cash in US dollars and an ID badge, together with a few other cards to get her past various scanners and security doors.

"That's $30,000 there," said Igor.

Igor reached his hand out once more and Janet shook it.

"Right, indeed you're our right-hand girl, Janet. Very pleased to have you on board with us."

He drained his espresso cup, clearly enjoying it. He was sure of one thing – he'll be making his seniors happy, successfully recruiting their right-hand lady, and having her successfully on board.

Igor again signaled for the waiter.

"Get me the bill please."

*****

Later in the hotel bedroom, Janet was sat thinking about her meeting with Igor when the door opened. Iftihkar, and he had a smile on his face.

"Oh, someone looks happy?" said Janet. She was sat by the Juliet balcony with the doors wide open and the curtains blowing in, admiring the million-dollar view acorss the Grand Canal, surrounded by Venetian architecture.

Iftihkar walked over to her and put his arm around her as he knelt down, giving her a kiss on the cheek. She turned to look directly at him and kissed him on his mouth. Iftihkar squeezed her shoulders, comforting and reassuring her, while deep inside he was happy that she was well, as he still felt uncomfortable with her meeting some random Russian bloke. But it was part of her re-found career.

Janet read his gaze. "It went really well, Darling. I have been given an advance cash sum, and it's a fine salary package of $150,000, which reinstates me as an independent woman striving to change the world, making it a better place, and living the high life. That will be enough to pay for business class flights. I think I will start off by going shopping tonight. Maybe it's time I treated you, Dear."

Iftihkar gave her an astonished look.

"Oh, someone is doing well, I'm delighted for you. Well done, you deserve it," he said.

He had made himself useful, and the time they had been apart too – he'd bought that diamond ring. That engagement ring for Janet. As he was embarking on the challenge of mustering the courage to find the right time to make that proposal... Iftihkar reached into his pocket and put his hand around the box containing the ring... when...

"Also, I've been given all the necessary IDs, equipment and security cards to get me into the actual 'Spaceport Himalaya', including the area which is out of bounds and top secret. So there's one thing which I've learnt... commissioning day and the grand opening, when the first of many shuttle pods will get launched into space, is 11th September. It's a date which I hope we will be able to be a part of. I wanted to witness the entire sequence and launch event. I'm sure there'll be many dignitaries there, but more importantly, see what on earth is happening. It's the scarcity of water here which is the real underlying factor, of our mission... what is causing it?" said Janet.

Iftihkar took his hand out of his pocket, away from the diamond he's just bought.

"Did you say 'we'? 'Us'? Well, Janet, if I'm there I'll be sure to bring along my scuba diving equipment, ha, ha, as I'm a specialist at anything to do with water... "

"Come to think of it, Igor did say I am able to bring in one person with me. It's part of the protocol, as every reporter has a cameraman. So Iftihkar, let's make sure you've got at least a camera with you, please."

Iftihkar smiled. Perhaps, he thinks, it'll be a good time to propose as well. It's all up in the air right now. So long as it doesn't get launched into space, the beautiful diamond ring he just bought that is, all will be well and good.

"Sure, Darling, I'm sure I'll make an excellent cameraman. Come to think of it, we're both going to be very similar to the pair out of 'Hart to Hart'. If you remember... I mentioned it... partners in crime?"

Janet began to chuckle... followed by bursting out laughing. Iftihkar knew how to make her laugh.

Chapter 35

Vacuum Extraction

It was the morning of September 11th and today was that day when the spaceport was due to have dignitaries and high-ranking officials visit. Iftihkar and Janet were well prepared for this day and getting ready that morning. They were up early and had already taken an autonomous drone taxi and landed in the station entrance ready to board the service vehicle to the spaceport. There was an immense gathering of media and VIPs. Also, dignitaries. Many autonomous drones were taking off and landing. The station building was like no other. It was like a fraction of the tip of an iceberg. This was purely the part where passengers were to gain access via the entry point.

"Please hold your ID card to the scanner while your ID is processed. Keep holding it until you're cleared to go," said the security personnel.

Iftihkar was right behind Janet, and the pair in turns got into a large cubicle. Janet got herself in front of the gate before holding her ID card face down on the glass screen which was mounted on a display. Some lights flashed and she was able to move forward as the gate opened. But not before the one behind her had closed.

This left Iftihkar to follow suit. It all worked fine.

"Well, there's only one place to go, and that's forward – it's nearly impossible to get lost here," he said.

Janet nodded. The system was like those service vehicles at airports, taking passengers from one terminal to the next. There was one platform. However, trains were arriving every five minutes.

And there was a display showing time remaining, which was now at 41 seconds. Everybody was waiting patiently, keeping behind the yellow line. However, there was a glass screen separating them from the arriving train. Doors would not open on the glass screen until the train was locked, docked and with its doors against the doors of the glass screen on the platform edge.

The scenery out of the window was barely recognizable as the train was traveling past at such an immense speed. Janet could barely make out an occasional cluster of trees. In the distance, however, the mountains were still recognizable. This train delivered them into the heart of the Operational hub. A magnetic levitation metro was the next stage, which carried passengers to the 'Spaceport Himalaya'. It was September 11th 2020, and today was the day when the initial test sequence was to be initiated, amidst great press coverage. A prototype test vehicle, resembling a pod, would be sent into space. A prototype shuttle vehicle.

Iftihkar and Janet were sat facing each other in the rapid metro link (RMT), linking the Hub to the civilian infrastructure. The RMT had left its station and was en-route to the Hub deep beneath the ground. The train was now under the ground as was remaining 10 minutes of the journey. As the RMT was traveling pretty much horizontally and the terrain altered the further north you traveled towards the Himalayas, soon after leaving its civilian infrastructure hub (CIH), it penetrated the earth. It needed to hit rock face, from where it would travel horizontally through the mountainous strata, maintaining the same horizontal vector.

"There goes the scenery," said Janet.

Iftihkar was already peering out of the window. All that was visible now were streaks of lights flickering past – service lights which were lighting up the tunnel.

"Wow, dazzling, the array of lights going past. Just imagine what the view must be like out of a shuttle accelerating upwards," said Iftihkar.

Just then, there was an announcement through the speakers above their heads.

"Good morning. We'd just like to remind you that we shall be arriving at the 'Spaceport Himalaya' at its Hub terminal, in approximately 10 minutes."

This was not an everyday train and rail journey. It was a vehicle which moved people from one end of the site access to another, due to the complexity surrounding the location. Moving passengers between the 'CIH' and Spaceport HUB Terminal 'SPHT' wasn't viable via anything which didn't run on tracks, as any collision here would result in a total shutdown, hence the need for a metro link.

However, what became increasingly visible when the metro slowed down was the multitude of tracks, as the adjacent tracks began to merge to form one big shaft tunnel. Only this train that Iftihkar and Janet were traveling on was dedicated to passenger transit. The remaining dozen or so were purely for cargo.

Finally, when the train began to slow down, Janet and Iftihkar looked out of the window to see dozens and dozens of various tracks merging into one large enclosed area which resembled a cross between a road-rail terminus and an airport departures hall. However, their section was segregated as the rest of it was covered with machinery and cargo moving about autonomously.

Janet and Iftihkar both stood up and reached for their hand luggage which consisted of a day bag each. Iftihkar made sure he had his camera around his neck, to make his cover for the day more plausible.

Once the service vehicle had stopped, there was an alarm-like sound before the doors opened, and everybody started to disembark. Janet was eager to get out and edged forward as close as she was able to behind the person in front of her.

It was plain sailing from here, as they had already passed through security and they now made their way over to the Great Hall, where many parties were waiting. They were all stood behind the large glass screen which separated them in the passenger departures section from the cargo section.

There were refreshments laid out, such as schnapps, champagne, canapé, no doubt paid for by the commercial enterprises with a going concern.

Further along, on a stage, there seemed to be a few VIPs, including the president of the United States of America. And adjacent to them were governors, senators, lawmakers and military heads, such as chief of staff and generals. Also, by now, the security protocol here involved the Secret

Service, as well as the in-house, private security company which were all armed guards.

Iftihkar walked over to Janet holding a plate laden with cheese on sticks and olives.

"I must say, Dear, this cheese is exquisite. Don't about the champagne, though; can't be very halal."

Janet chuckled.

"You could have got me a glass," she said. "The origin of that cheese is the least of my worries. We've got work to get to. Let's get over to that shuttle vehicle over there. I'm sure that will be passing through the huge bay doors pretty soon, and I want to get to the other side," she said.

"We sure do," muttered Iftihkar.

They began slowly walking over to the shuttle vehicle which was being held in place by a suspended robotic arm which was anchored from overhead rails, holding it on from above, like a grab.

Just then, there was an announcement made over the public address system.

"Good afternoon ladies and gentlemen, it's set to be a wonderful day today. Today is the day when we get to test out our efforts in mankind's biggest transportation development to date. This will enable us to boldly go and do what humanity has never done before. Today we are going to commission and test the very first shuttle vehicle to be launched into the upper atmosphere, using only the energy extracted from the ground. Geothermal energy... from which we produce electricity that shall drive this magnetic vehicle," said Samson Cooper from TEXTEC Industries.

"Traveling through the earth before being ejected from the summit, right above us, at an altitude of approximately 30,000 ft. We're at 1,770 ft right now. I'd now like to pass you over to our states governor, Imran Khan. Let's give a warm welcome." Samson continued.

There was a round of applause as Imran Khan, a former sports celebrity star, made his way to the stage.

"Good afternoon ladies and gentlemen, it's an honor and indeed a privilege to be on the stage today to be able to cut this ribbon and pave the way for mankind to drive forward its greatest ingenuity. I'm sure, for many years to come, we will witness that the endeavors that have led to this accomplishment of building the 'Spaceport Himalaya' will have paid off many times over. So today, on this occasion, I now pronounce the 'Spaceport Himalaya' being inaugurated by myself, Governor Imran Khan on 11th September 2020."

The president cut the silky purple ribbon which was draped around the control panel – a tiny section of the entire apparatus, but for the ceremony of the occasion, it was unimportant.

Iftihkar and Janet were the other side of the control panel and directly opposite some doors. They waited, hoping the doors might open, allow them to get inside the restricted area. The doors had 'DO NOT ENTER' written above them.

It was left now for the ground control to take control and run through the launch sequence, when just then a series of alarms began to sound, and lights started to flash.

Multiple lights were flashing, particularly around the cargo area and the doors, when a huge cargo door began to open and the shuttle began to move into the cargo area. Janet and Iftihkar couldn't believe their gamble had paid off, and didn't waste a second – this was their chance to get inside the restricted area, and they were sure to remain behind the shuttle vehicle as it passed into the restricted area.

Once in, the pair kept themselves hidden which wasn't difficult as the area was astronomical in size – breadth and depth. The doors behind began to close when another announcement was heard through the speakers.

"Launch sequence initiated, preparing to commence atmosphere extraction."

Huge fans could be heard start up. They seemed to draw out the air but without any gusts, or breeze or change in atmosphere being felt. It was eerie.

"Second part of the launch sequence initiated: atmosphere extraction taking place: atmosphere extraction taking air pressure to 4.36 psi," said the humanoid female voice.

Iftihkar looked at Janet.

"I think there's a perfect reason why we're not meant to be here," he said.

The pair walked across the vast expanse, trying to find and see as much of what was in this out-of-bounds area. There was a vast labyrinth full of cocoons, that are shuttle pods, for as far as they could see. It was obvious that there was hundreds of these shuttle vehicles, all inevitably to be launched someday. They came across a hatch which has written on it 'WATER UNIT'.

Iftihkar realized that this was the moment he needed to put his scuba-diving equipment on. He took his day bag off his shoulders, taking out the rubber suit. He undressed quickly and puts on the suit. He put his mask on and opened the oxygen regulator, taking it to the green color display on the pressure gauge, before putting it onto his back. He'd come complete with his oxygen tank too, albeit a very small one, as practicalities of weight and what could be fitted in his bag had ruled anything bigger.

"Oh you, look who came prepared," said Janet.

"Listen, I'm gonna go head down there, and if things hot up I'm going to have to press the emergency distress button... which no doubt will lead to the whole of today's operation closed down, the whole launch sequence that is... see you in a bit," said Iftihkar.

Iftihkar gave Janet one last kiss, his lips huddled around hers for a moment in time, which on that occasion seemed like a lifetime. He then put his mouthpiece into his mouth and opened the hatch. There's water right there. He dived in. It was rather cold to say the least, freshwater melted and progressed down from the glaciers. At this stage, it had not yet been channeled and fed past the molten lava.

Chapter 36
ABC: Airway, Breathing, Circulation

Right now, Iftihkar was underwater, and Janet was heading off into an area where the air pressure was being sucked out to a barely survivable level. Janet finally got near to a trolley vehicle, which resembles an electric airport baggage carrier train, which she took a seat on and began to drive herself into the abyss past all those cocooned shuttle vehicles. She traveled almost 1km.

Iftihkar got to an area which seemed to be even cooler. It was a vast vertical shaft full of water. He drew out his remote measurement device, which he brought along for just this very reason, to get an idea of the distance to the bottom of the shaft – something any good diver would have to know, to be able to calculate whether one had enough oxygen in the tank to survive the distance. He pointed it down and pushed the button, shining a laser down into the abyss. It read at 150 meters. He moved it slightly and pointed it down again, repeating the process. It read at 300 meters.

"Hang on! This is getting deeper," he muttered to himself.

He pressed it once more, and nothing was displayed. It seemed as if it had no finite bottom to it. Well, he wasn't going to try to make it to the bottom if he couldn't get a reading. By now he realized he won't have enough oxygen to make it back if he continued here much longer. It was pure glacier water, and he was beginning to realize just how cold it really was. His camera was set to capture time-lapse images, continuously, one every second, and by now it was at shot no. 3500.

He began to make his way back as his oxygen was almost on empty and he couldn't afford to be taking any more side tracks. He made his way back to the hatch, but not before he drew out a plastic bottle, filling it up with the water.

Janet had reached the end and saw up in front of her the most frightening spectacle she had ever set eyes on. It seemed as if she had the heavens right above her head, and Hell beneath her feet. The vertical shaft was breathtakingly immense, seemingly without a beginning or an end – nothing to aid even the beginnings of a comprehension of its depth and breadth. And that of it which she could make out was surrounded by an array of mechanics, characteristic of a spinal cord. Looking up, she felt as if she was looking through a giant alien fossilized backbone. And she could barely walk. It was a strange feeling as the atmosphere around her was slowly depleted of oxygen, as it was drawn out to create low pressure so the shuttle would travel effortlessly upwards at high velocity. She made her way over to what appeared to be an emergency stop button, but she's even struggling to walk in a straight line now, and half sat down, half collapsed. Due to her brain being starved of oxygen, she began to make irrational decisions. She started to giggle and become delusional. She imagined she had her baby daughter on her lap, and she was going to put her to bed, and everything was well. Although she was sat right under what was indeed an emergency stop button, she was unable to coordinate reaching a hand far enough up to push it. It was this stage, the stage of asphyxiation when being deprived of oxygen, which could result in unconsciousness and even death, due to suffocation – when the human brain began to fail to make rational decisions. And Janet has almost reached that stage.

"My dear baby, it's okay. Everything is okay. I love you. Mummy loves you, Samantha," she said.

Iftihkar had just made it to the hatch, the same one he had used to gain entry earlier – except now he struggled to open it, battling fiercely as his oxygen ran out, the display needle on empty.

The pair of them were in a quandary, both moments from death.

Iftihkar's grip on the hatch began to loosen until there was no strength left, and he fell back, just as Janet's head fell back against the wall she was leaning against.

Blah! Blah! Blah! Suddenly an alarm bellows, echoing through the labyrinth of caverns.

About the Author

Born in Birmingham, in the United Kingdom, I am the son of an economic migrant from the Pakistani side of Kashmir. My parents arrived in Birmingham in the 1960s.

I am one of 9 siblings who had a very troubled childhood and spent 4 years with white English foster parents.

I am well travelled and have visited many countries throughout the world – some typically 'bucket list' destinations; others less so.

In my spare time, I have always tended to pay attention to current domestic affairs and to world news and events, and I have always without fail watched the evening Channel 4 News from the United Kingdom.

I have always been intrigued as to what the future may entail and so have tended to use the news to gain an idea of what might happen. Watching the news has allowed me to establish a perception of the future and an understanding of world and the direction in which it's heading. I worked in the construction and rail industries for 20 years and I have a passion for architecture and an appreciation of the finer aspects associated with building design. However, recently, my emerging enjoyment of and talent for writing has had me begin to realise that investigative journalism might be an undiscovered forte. So, I have decided to concentrate on writing, and be a writer who, I hope, can make investigative journalism entertaining for the reader.

IFTIHKAR AZAM